Her Dying Day

Her Dying Day

A Novel

MINDY CARLSON

**CROOKED
LANE**

NEW YORK

Copyright © 2022 by Malinda Carlson

Published in the United States by Crooked Lane Books, an imprint of The Quick Brown Fox & Company LLC.

Crooked Lane Books and its logo are trademarks of The Quick Brown Fox & Company LLC.

Library of Congress Catalog-in-Publication data available upon request.

ISBN (hardcover): 978-1-63910-012-5
ISBN (ebook): 978-1-63910-013-2

Cover design by Kara Klontz

Printed in the United States.

www.crookedlanebooks.com

Crooked Lane Books
34 West 27th St., 10th Floor
New York, NY 10001

First Edition: June 2022

10 9 8 7 6 5 4 3 2 1

To my parents
Jack and Virginia Ruzicka
You did your best.

Chapter One

~

If you've never been stuck under the bed while your lover has sex with his wife, I suggest you skip it. It's no trip to Disneyland.

And how did I end up staring at his wife's navy blue pumps while their king-sized bed squeaked rhythmically above me? Sheer stupidity.

Rule Number One when you're sleeping with your married advisor is to never sleep with said advisor at his actual house. Keep it in the office, your place, or a cheap motel that takes cash and fake names. Rule Number Two: Never believe him when he says his wife will be gone for the entire weekend. Wives are never gone for the whole weekend. Overnight at most—so you'd better be out of there by ten-a-m-sharp the next day.

There is no Rule Number Three, and, really, I should have been smart enough to stick to Rule Number One, so that Rule Number Two wouldn't have to exist. But I'm not. Clearly.

So here I am, sticking it out in silence while she calls out his name in raptured passion.

"Paul! Oh, yes, Paul! Paul!"

Awkward.

I can't be mad at Martha's shouts of euphoria. I'd done the same thing two hours ago.

I should probably feel something like shame rather than resigned impatience while counting the squeaks of the mattress springs. My mother would have been ashamed of me, carrying on with a married man for the last year. *You weren't raised that way*, she'd say.

Well, I wasn't raised to do a lot of things—like live my own life, have hair shorter than my shoulders, and reside within six miles of my nearest neighbor—but look at me now. I'm in New York City, in my own tiny apartment, and about to become the biggest documentary filmmaker since Michael Moore.

201. 202. 203.

Squeak. Squeak. Squeak.

Okay, so there was one other thing that kept me not so patiently silent under that bed with those luxurious high-count Egyptian cotton sheets—the knowledge that Paul didn't really love her. His marriage to Martha was one of necessity. She was emotionally fragile. Depressed. She depended on Paul's presence to keep her from being swallowed by her own darkness. She might even kill herself if he left, he said.

Not that I was urging him to leave. I was happy with the freedom we'd found with each other. He was free to live his life and, more importantly, I was free to live my own, without rules, regulations, or tethers. The opposite of how I'd grown up.

Or as opposite as I could make it.

Paul calls me Pear Blossom, and I don't even have the urge to smack him for it, like I would anyone else who dared call me the horrible name my hippie-dippy parents christened me. Actually, my full name is Pear Blossom Jubilee Masterson. Awful, right? Doesn't it just scream, "My parents smoked their brains out on dope and started a commune"?

Lord. How do I even begin to explain my parents? It's tempting to tell everyone they'd died. No one wants to hear about dead parents.

They're not dead. They're very much alive and a pain in the neck.

Right after I was born, my parents decided they'd had enough of capitalistic, corporate America. They walked away from everything—family, money, careers—to set up a commune in the middle of the Adirondack Mountains. Well, they hadn't walked away from their entire family. They'd convinced Mom's little sister, Bev, and her husband to join them in the pure, piney air of upper New York State.

No, we—they—aren't a cult, though my parents do exude a level of energy about keeping isolated that would make religious fanatics look lazy. They *never* leave the commune. Ever. Instead, Aunt Bev and Uncle Chuck do all the shopping and sell the yarn we made from our Angora goats at the farmers market.

And then there were our names. I got the worst of it with Pear Blossom Jubilee. My cousins got saddled with Meadow Rowan Nokomis and Tecumseh Sage Archer, but they can actually use part of their names and still fit into the "normal" world, so it's not so bad for them.

I prefer to go by June. It's true that June is also the month I was born, but when the elderly secretary in the registrar's office got confused by my long, hippie name and called me June during my college orientation, I didn't correct her. June. Such a nice, normal, *short* name. Almost everyone calls me June now.

Except Paul. He's called me Pear Blossom ever since he became my advisor last year in the documentary film program at the New York Film School. He told me he liked how exotic it sounded. How it was irresistible to him.

There was something irresistible about him to me too.

He gave me shivers every time I thought about him. Sure, I knew having an affair with a married man was at the very top of the list of Bad Ideas. But he was so . . . *Paul*. Funny, warm, witty, cosmopolitan, well-educated. And if I had to put up with his wife, so be it. It's not like I was in a rush to be married.

Squeak. Squeak. Squeak.

"Paul! Yes! Paul!"

I rolled my eyes. Would this never end?

Moments earlier, he'd given me permission to change my thesis topic. Again. No one ever gets to change their topic more than once and I had just changed mine for an unheard-of third time. But I finally had a topic I could feel passionate about!

He'd sighed as I traced out hearts on his chest. "What's your idea now?" he'd asked, a bemused twist to his lips.

"The disappearance of Greer Larkin," I'd said, breathlessly anticipating his response.

"The mystery writer?" He'd risen up onto his elbows to get a better look at my face.

"Yes," I'd said, bouncing onto him and grinning down into his wonderfully warm blue eyes. "She won five Edgar awards and had seven novels on the *Times* bestseller list before she was twenty-four. She was a prodigy! She'd just released her best book to date, was engaged—about to be married even—and then she disappeared without a trace. Poof! No one has found a body. And," I'd gone on, the excitement mounting, "this will be the twenty-year anniversary of her disappearance. The timing is perfect."

This was the topic I was born to research.

I'm not normally a true crime kind of girl. I don't read the books. Don't watch the movies or listen to the podcasts. No one would confuse me with a Murderino. But this was different. This was *Greer Larkin*. She's my generation's Agatha Christie. I mean, the woman single-handedly saved me from abject loneliness when I was trapped in my family's commune as a child.

I owed her.

Frankly, I couldn't believe I hadn't picked this topic right off the bat. It was like I'd been choosing topics a Good Girl would work on, and waiting for permission to take on a topic as dark as an unsolved murder.

"Fine," he'd finally said. "You can change your topic to Greer Larkin, but Pear Blossom," he'd warned, growing uncharacteristically serious, "this is the last time. We are five months from graduation and, as your advisor, I cannot let you switch your topic again."

"I promise," I'd vowed, crossing my naked breast, trying not to squeal with delight. "Think of it as a second Christmas present."

I'd been about to give him another belated Christmas gift when we'd heard the front door slam, announcing Martha's early arrival home.

Which is why I ended up under the bed, planning my first interviews, waiting for the squeaking to stop, and for Paul to suggest to Martha they go out to Chez Marc for a late dinner.

It was eight by the time they left and I could ease myself out from under the bed, get dressed, and leave. My apartment was dark and the fridge was empty. Paul and I had intended to get Thai food.

New Rule Number Three: Always eat first.

I punched in the number for Tina's Thai and ordered a curry before sitting down at my laptop to outline my to-do list for my newest topic.

"What Happened to Greer Larkin?"

*   *   *

"I cannot believe you were under the bed the whole time." Meadow's voice was full of disbelief and horror.

"It's not like I could just walk out. She was *above me*."

"You know that sleeping with your advisor is wrong, right? I mean, like, wrong-wrong."

I shrugged. "In theory. It's not like I want to break up their marriage. This is fun for right now." *Plus, I like him. For real.*

"And I can't believe you're changing your topic. Again," she said.

Meadow liked order and routine. She hadn't minded getting up at five in the morning every day for goat chores. It was a comfortable routine to her. I, on the other hand, now made it my mission to never be out of bed before nine if I could help it. So I could see why my flightiness around my thesis topic worried and frustrated her. Plus, she's never understood my obsession with Greer Larkin. Which is fine, because I never understood why she didn't want to find out what happened. I didn't hold it against her.

"I love Greer Larkin's books! The crazy mystery around her disappearance will make a perfect topic. This one I'm sticking with. For sure."

Meadow's brow puckered in the way that always made guilt bubble up inside me. She was concerned I was never going to graduate and find a real job. She was dismayed that I couldn't ever seem to stick with anything—majors, boyfriends, favorite ice cream flavors. (Did you know there are more flavors than vanilla, chocolate, and strawberry?) Her concern was sweet, but exasperating.

I couldn't blame her. Even I worried sometimes about my mercurial habits. Only sometimes, though. I liked choice. Liked being able to change my mind whenever I felt like it. I'd had little chance to experience either in the commune. Instead, I'd found that choice and freedom in Greer Larkin's books.

So how could I not leap at my chance to investigate what happened to Greer? I'd been obsessed since I was fourteen.

This case had everything you would need for a dynamite movie—a famous person who'd vanished into thin air, a fiancé people didn't like, a domineering mother, and a feuding best friend. And money. Lots and lots of money.

Meadow liked to take me out for dinner once a month. It was her version of a wellness check, but in more tasteful surroundings. I didn't mind. I was living on student loans, a scholarship, a bit of Paul's charity, and several credit cards, so I wasn't about to turn down a free meal.

Meadow was the responsible one of us kids. Always had been. As a teenager, I'd sneak out of the house at night to head into town with her next to me telling me how dangerous and risky we were being, like my own personal Jiminy Cricket.

Her brother Sage was a blend of the two of us. Whereas I was a rebellious free spirit and Meadow was the steady, responsible one, Sage was the crusader. Currently, he was in Sudan, working in a refugee camp for Doctors Without Borders. A responsible guy who couldn't wait to see the leeward side of the mountain.

When I escaped to New York, I'd vowed I would never speak to my family again. Our parents had a very strict policy about mixing with outside society: Don't. We were barely let off the property. We'd been homeschooled, and I'd never even seen a dentist or doctor until I went to college. Can you say "neglect"? Our parents told us the world was a dangerous place, that we could only be protected and safe if we never left the commune. I'd hated it. No. I'd *loathed* it.

I'd been a prisoner—and Meadow had been the one to unlock the door. *She* talked to me about college. *She* helped me get my admissions tests taken and applications completed. *She* gathered my documents and mailed them out to colleges.

While I kept the rest of my family out of my life, I couldn't cut Meadow out. She was more than a cousin—she was a sister, and my best and only friend. Plus, sometimes you needed to talk to someone who knew what it was like to have been raised in a commune in the middle of the Adirondack Mountains with your parents and an aunt and uncle. Turns out not many people can identify with that lifestyle.

There wasn't much I wouldn't do for Meadow.

"You always promise and you never do," Meadow said.

I gave her a cheeky grin. "Sure, I do," I said. "I promised never to get caught when we would sneak into town, and we never did."

"So," Meadow said and sighed. "Why Greer Larkin, of all people?"

"Oh, please," I said, rolling my eyes. "She's just, like, one of the best mystery writers of all time. Right up there with Agatha Christie."

"Agatha Christie wrote a hundred books. Greer wrote, what? Six?"

"Agatha wrote seventy-four novels, but still. Greer wasn't around as long as Dame Agatha. Just think of what she could have done! She started when she was fourteen. Do you remember how old I was when I made my first film?"

"Was it fourteen?" Meadow said, but of course she knew—she'd heard this story before. She was trying to be polite instead of snarky, and was mostly succeeding.

"Yes. And Greer was fourteen when she got her first novel published. Then at sixteen it was turned into a movie. Just think of where I could be right now if I'd been given the same kind of free rein. I could've been a wunderkind," I said.

"'I coulda been a contender,'" Meadow quipped.

Now it was my turn to sigh. I hoped it sounded grouchy enough that she got that her humor was unappreciated. Steven Spielberg's mom helped him make films when he was twelve years old. You know what my mom did when she discovered my first film on a battered old camera I'd found in the attic? She burned them both in the yard. What kind of mother does that?

I stabbed into my lamb korma with a fury that would have cracked the plate if I'd missed. And then I smiled with the grim satisfaction of knowing how horrified my parents would be that I was eating meat.

Suck it, Mom and Dad.

I noticed Meadow only picking at her food, a sure sign she had her own issues. Maybe that's why she was taking it easy on my flakiness? Girl trouble?

Meadow was in a semiserious relationship with a graphic designer named Faye. From our dinner last month, I got the feeling that Meadow would like this to be more "serious" and less "semi." Maybe that didn't go so well. *Shoot.* I really liked Faye.

I was about to ask how Faye was doing when Meadow broke the silence first. "Your parents would like you to call," she said.

"Ah," I said, in as neutral a voice as I could manage.

"What does that mean?" she asked, defensive.

It means there's no fucking way I'm going to call them. Ever.

But what I said was, "It means I hear they want to talk, but there is no way I'm calling them."

"They love you. They just want to see that you're okay."

"I am not calling them," I repeated. "Just report back to them as usual that I am still a fuck-up, I have one new tattoo, and am still sleeping with my advisor."

Meadow's eyes grew wide and an indignant sneer twisted her mouth. "I would never tell them that. I'll tell them that you're fine and still mad."

"That's almost the truth," I said.

"So you're not mad anymore?" Meadow said, the question tinged with hope.

"I'm almost fine."

Meadow sighed again. She does a lot of sighing when I'm around. I like to think of myself as her excuse for deep breathing exercises.

"You know," she said, her lawyer voice revving up like she was about to address a jury. "You can't just cut your family off for the rest of your life. Are they wacko? Yes. But they are your parents, your aunt and uncle. Family is too important to shut the door on them forever. What they did was in *your* best interest."

HA!

"How's Faye?" I asked, making a deliberate left turn in the conversation.

"Well, that was blunter than normal," she said. I shrugged, not at all sorry, and she shook her head. "She's fine. We have a date tomorrow. Dinner with friends. Next week she's showing some of her art at a gallery in Brooklyn."

Impressive. Meadow had mentioned Faye wanted to break out of her graphic design mold to show off some of her more personal art, but I always thought Faye lacked the egotistical confidence of a true artist. It made her shy about her work. "That sounds amazing," I said. "Tell her good luck."

"I was hoping you'd come. It's next Friday. It's going to be a lot of Faye's artsy friends. I don't really know them. Plus, she's going to be schmoozing. I want to know at least one other person there."

Her eyes were wide and a little scared. Meadow is never scared. Not really. Not even when she was whispering all the horrible things our parents would do to us when they caught us sneaking back into our houses. I really didn't want to go to Faye's gallery opening, but I could never say no to Meadow.

"Sure. Do you care if I bring Paul?"

A fleeting look of disappointment crossed Meadow's face, but she recovered and said brightly, "Sure! But even if he can't come, I really need you to be there. Okay, Pear?"

"Okay," I said. "I promise."

Chapter Two

⁓

Back in my apartment, I kicked my yellow plaid Chuck Taylors into the rainbow pile of shoes by the front door and threw my mail onto the growing stack on my kitchen island. The pile was mostly junk with a few bills hidden in there like land mines. I noticed I'd gotten another letter for some chick named Maya Davenport. This made letter number ten. Some guy William was pretty desperate to get hold of her, and I was starting to feel bad. I mean, ten letters. That's not just a mix-up. I was tempted to read it, thinking maybe I could figure out who she was or where she went, but then I remembered the cardinal rule of living in New York City—Mind Your Own Business. I wrote "return to sender" on the envelope and stuck it in my purse. William should know that his letters weren't getting to his . . . daughter? Sister? Whatever. I had more important things to worry about.

I started slapping notebook paper up on the wall, building a disappearance timeline. My landlord was going to shit a brick when the tape inevitably pulled the paint off the walls, but fuck it. I need visual aids.

Each sheet featured a significant date in Greer's life. From the publication date of her first book (May 9, 1989), to the day she got engaged (December 24, 1996—the ring was a five-carat oval cut from Tiffany's), to the day she vanished (August 24, 1999). On the site we called it "GD-Day." "Greer's Disappearance Day" was too cumbersome to write out, much less read, especially since ninety percent of all posts included a reference to the day Greer went missing.

My fingertips tingled with adrenaline. I'd been preparing for this moment for ten years. I had all Greer's books piled up the couch, ready to reread. Some authors pulled things from their real lives into their books. Maybe Greer was one of them. I knew Greer Larkin's personal story front to back, thanks to GreersGone.com. She'd had a mother who kept her virtually invisible until she'd moved out at eighteen to be with Jonathan Vanderpoole, the love of her life (date: May 22, 1993—also the day she turned eighteen). The affair had been messily splashed in the tabloids—the reclusive teen star had suddenly entered the spotlight. Reporters clamored for photos of Greer at nightclubs and on red carpets, clinging to Jonathan's arm. Then, only six years later, she was just . . . gone.

She and Jonathan went for dinner at a restaurant, then the next day there was no trace of her—except a bit of blood in her car at the Kilmarnock Lighthouse. A tantalizing, taunting clue.

No one knew much about the blood other than that it had come from Greer. There hadn't been any signs of a weapon in the car. But I imagine a murderer would have taken a gun or knife away with him. Had she fought her attacker as he pulled her from the car?

I gave my head a shake. No theorizing. Not now, anyway. I had to focus on the *facts*. And I needed to get my hustle on. Five months isn't a long time in the world of filmmaking.

It's shockingly short, actually. No way would Paul have let me switch topics if I hadn't been sleeping with him.

It was a relief to finally be able to immerse myself in a subject I wanted to investigate more than anything. *Needed* to investigate. Greer and I had so much in common, it felt like we were practically the same person. Okay, maybe not—I'm not a creep—but I felt a kinship to Greer that I didn't feel with anyone else, not even Meadow.

Greer and I both loved mysteries, obviously. We'd also endured suffocating childhoods. Like Greer, my own parents had kept me invisible and sequestered until I moved out to start my real life, also at eighteen. Plus, we kind of looked alike. Both of us had dark hair, were a petite five foot three inches tall, had fair skin, and a mouth that curved up in the corners like a satisfied cat.

I wish we could have met. She would have understood what it had been like to be raised by my crazy, controlling family.

GreersGone had been my only social life as a teen. Completely lame, now that I was twenty-four, but a lifeline when I'd needed it. I'd visited GreersGone at least once a day, making it to the top "sleuth" status after only five years. Consequently, I knew the facts of her disappearance the way Catholics know the Apostle's Creed.

I slapped another piece of paper up on the wall and checked my phone. I couldn't help it. Paul should have texted me by now. But according to the calendar on my phone, he was at the symphony with his wife until ten. I was going to have to wait until at least eleven to text him. We usually texted at this time of night, and I was jonesing for a hit like some sweaty, shaking meth addict.

Rule Number Four of dating a married man is never have a regular time when you text. It makes the moments when he can't get free feel unreasonably unbearable, creating impatience—which is what caused every mistress in Greer's books to make their fatal mistake. I wasn't about to make a mistake.

Not so secretly, I believed that Paul's wife planned these late nights out just to keep Paul too busy to text. But, of course, that would mean she knew about him and me, and that was something none of us could afford to be true.

I thought of Paul stuck in a suit, surrounded by shrieking flutes and screeching violins, and felt annoyed on his behalf. Paul hates the symphony. He'd rather go to a jazz club and sip vodka gimlets.

I wonder if Martha knows that about him.

Actually, a vodka gimlet sounded pretty good. No one drank alcohol on the commune. Our bodies were temples. These days, I kept a hefty supply of vodka and lime syrup on hand for when Paul dropped by. I decided to pour myself one in his honor. I turned my TV to the hockey game too, just like I would have if he were here. I only got to watch TV once a week on the commune, so now I have the TV on to whatever—game shows, cooking programs, reality shows—all the time. I liked the noise. It kept me company when Paul wasn't around.

Ugh. I was feeling shockingly sentimental.

The deadlines for filming were going to bite me in the ass if I allowed myself to get too distracted. My fellow students—or "competitors" as I liked to think of them—were already filming and editing. I was back at the drawing board, laying out timelines and interview schedules.

I fired up my computer and started typing out a timeline for the day Greer disappeared.

Fact #1: Greer disappeared in the early morning hours of August 24, 1999. There were no witnesses, so no one knows the exact time. According to the statement released by the police, Jonathan Vanderpoole, her fiancé, was in the house with her that night, but he was sleeping off the two bottles of wine he single-handedly downed over and after dinner and heard nothing. When he awoke in the morning, her car had already been found by the police. He claimed he didn't even know she wasn't in the house.

Fact #2: A red 1980 Fiat 2000 Spider registered to Greer Larkin was found sitting in the parking lot at the Kilmarnock Lighthouse and State Park. The driver's side door was open and Greer's purse was on the ground, the contents strewn around. From the grainy footage on YouTube, it looked like someone had turned it over and dumped everything onto the ground. I'd always thought someone was looking for something. I mean, that's how I look for something lost in the bottom of my bag. The police never released a list of those contents, saying they were evidence in an open investigation, which has led the members of the fan site to believe that something was missing from or added to the contents of that purse that would help identify the killer/kidnapper.

Fact #3: The night before she disappeared, Greer and Jonathan had entertained the diners and staff of Battaglia's Italian restaurant by having a full-on screaming match in the middle of the restaurant at the height of the dinner rush. This was before camera phones had become the norm, so what really happened has been distorted by multiple retellings. The maître d' told some newspapers they'd been arguing about money, but other diners claimed they'd been arguing about the wedding. Regardless of what the argument had been about, it ended when the maître d' saw Jonathan slap Greer, and Greer storm off, driving away in her 1980 red Fiat 2000 Spider.

Fact #4: Blood was found on the seat of the car and smeared on the inside of the door. DNA tests completed in 2014 confirmed it was Greer's blood. Jonathan's DNA was also found in the car, but as he lived with her, and drove her car occasionally, the police can't say it didn't belong there naturally. An additional hair was found in the car, but was never identified; however, forensics proved it didn't belong to Greer and it was far too long to belong to Jonathan.

Fact #5: A week after Greer's disappearance, investigators learned there was a secret account in the Caymans with eighteen million dollars in it, in the name of Jonathan Vanderpoole. It had been opened eighteen months prior to Greer's disappearance. There were instructions for one million dollars to be automatically withdrawn from Greer's trust fund account—the one her mother, Blanche, controlled—every month and deposited into this account.

Fact #6: A body has never been found. Not in the woods. Not washed up on a beach. Not anywhere.

The money had always been considered the key piece of proof against Jonathan. He'd been stealing her money for a year and a half! The argument at the restaurant could have been Greer telling Jonathan she'd found out he was stealing from her and she was going to leave him. He would have been forced to kill her and dispose of the body. Open and shut.

However, if money was the major motive in the case, Blanche had just as much motive as Jonathan. She was the one in control of Greer's multi-million-dollar trust. And would be until Greer was twenty-five, which she was about to become when she vanished. While I had a hard time believing a parent could murder their child over money, I only had to look at my own history to be reminded that people did awful things to the ones they loved.

*　*　*

Whether or not I thought he was responsible for Greer's disappearance, Jonathan sat smack in the center of the mystery. That meant he was at the top of my list of people I needed to interview on camera. I mean, come on! He was the fiancé *and* the prime suspect. If I couldn't get him, my project was sunk, and I'd be back to an in-depth look at waiting tables as a cliché side hustle in New York. No one needed an in-depth documentary on restaurant waitstaff in New York.

I couldn't believe I'd ever thought it was a great topic to begin with. I'd picked it after a dinner out with Meadow where she had regaled me with a story about a waiter who turned out to be a concert pianist from the 1980s. The filming had gone exactly nowhere. As soon as a camera had appeared, my documentary had become one long audition tape as people seized their big break.

The second person who was, therefore, a "must get" was Greer's mom, Blanche Larkin. Greer's mother was, by all accounts, a battle-ax. She was also my second favorite suspect.

My own mother had done horrible things to me, like burning the movies I made, making me spin yarn until my fingers bled, and forcing me to wear shoes until the soles were mostly holes—but she'd never come close to killing me. She'd even gotten me a puppy when I was ten. I'd named him Wilfred. Had Greer been allowed pets?

Blanche had never married, and I couldn't find a single mention of who Greer's dad might be. Perhaps she'd had her heart broken by some jerk and decided to burn her wedding dreams to the ground. I'd seen jilted brides do a lot worse on those reality shows. Maybe that jerk had been Greer's father. I'd even gone into the online catalogue of public records and found no father was listed on Greer's birth certificate. A major dead end. It seems Blanche had a scorched earth policy.

Blanche was from Old Money. Capital O. Capital M. Her parents used to party with the Vanderbilts and summer with the Rockefellers. She'd never had to work a day in her life. I was shocked to find out she'd been a ballerina. She'd even toured. I found a photo of her in the chorus of *Giselle*, looking smoking hot in her tutu and sleek bun. I figured she, of all people, would want to get Greer's story out there. Maybe even make a plea for the murderer to call and tell her where the body was. Isn't that what mothers were supposed to do?

She'd never made a public plea, though. She hadn't even issued a reward for information on Greer's whereabouts. Perhaps the scorched earth policy extended to her daughter. How did Blanche do punishment?

The truth was, the likelihood that she would sit for an interview was slim. Plus, people like her didn't talk to people like me. I added her to the list anyway.

Next was Bethany Allen, Greer's agent. She'd provide an interesting outsider's view into the family dynamics between Greer, her mom, and her fiancé. She also had the benefit of being on the inside. Authors have a special relationship with their agents. Her insights on Greer's personality will be key.

Last on my initial interview list was Greer's best friend, Rachel Baumgartner. Rachel and Greer had met when they were thirteen at the offices of Greer's agent, where Rachel often visited her father, who was another agent. They became inseparable.

However, the word on the GreersGone site was that they had had a major falling out two years before Greer disappeared. Their friendship had become more turbulent as Jonathan took over Greer's focus, if the tabloids could be believed. Which was pretty much fifty-fifty. I mean, the *National Enquirer* exposed evidence in the O.J. Simpson trial, so you never know.

The Star had published a photo of Greer slapping Rachel at a club sometime in 1998—about a year before she disappeared. Pictures were worth a thousand words, but *The Star* wasn't going to cut it as a primary source. That was Lesson Number One in documentary school—have unimpeachable sources. I did some digging in the public records (all online now—thank you, New York), and found a restraining order issued by Greer against Rachel on September 7, 1998. After Greer disappeared, Jonathan had immediately pointed all his fingers at Rachel, saying that Rachel had been threatening Greer. No proof was found and Rachel had fired back by threatening a slander and defamation suit. Those two were definitely not going to be comforting each other. And Rachel would absolutely want to tell her side of the story.

I spent the rest of my gimlet typing out introductory letters to Jonathan, Blanche, Bethany, and Rachel, asking them to *please, please, please* sit for an interview for my project. Bethany's and Rachel's emails had been easy to find. They both had professional websites with contact information front and center. Jonathan's and Blanche's emails were a bit harder to find. In the end, I relied on old information from GreersGone. There's a chance they could bounce, but I was running short on two things—time and patience.

My nerves jangled as I hit the send button. I downed what was left of my drink and prayed to whatever universal being was feeling particularly benevolent toward me to intercede on my behalf.

As I sat back, breathing a sigh of relief, I was surprised to see my apartment was dark. Following the motivations of Greer's potential murderers had taken all of my focus. I hadn't eaten. My gimlet was gone. The only light came from my computer screen and the TV, which had gone from showing the hockey game to showing *When She Was Seventeen*, a movie based on Greer's book of the same name. I would've taken it as a sign from above, except there was always a channel showing a Greer Larkin movie. It was the scene where Oberlin Hurst was creeping through the house looking for Mrs. Beauchamp.

My chest instantly tightened as my breathing quickened. Oberlin was sneaking along in the shadows, hoping to find Mrs. Beauchamp in time so she could be warned that her own daughter, who had been kept imprisoned in the house her whole life, was the murderer, and that Mrs. Beauchamp was next. The door was slowly opening. The light from the moon draped across her body. Oberlin crept closer. I clutched a pillow to me. We were about to see Mrs. Beauchamp's mangled face.

A klaxon alarm blared. I screamed. The pillow went flying and my heart attempted to leap out of my chest.

I was getting a message.

That phone alarm had seemed funny at the time I picked it, but one day it was going to give me a heart attack. Clicking off the TV, I pounced on my phone like a cat diving for a mouse, banging my shin against my extra-large coffee table in the process. "Stupid table. I should throw you out," I said. And I kind of meant it too. But I was poor, and this had been free on the curb when I moved in.

It was also the only table-like object I owned. After having been required to be at my parents' dining room table for every single (vegetarian) meal at the prescribed time, I refused to buy a dining room table. I ate as much meat as I could sitting on the couch, my plate perched on that gargantuan coffee table. Ignoring the throb of an impending bruise, I unlocked my phone and scrolled into my messages.

My body was sickeningly Pavlovian as it revved up in anticipation of Paul being on the other side of that ding, ready to talk dirty. I was disappointed to see it was only an email.

But then I saw who it was from.

Chapter Three

～

Rachel Baumgartner had emailed me back.

Dear June ~ Thanks for your email. I'd love to talk about Greer's disappearance. I'm convinced Jonathan is responsible. If you can actually prove it, it would be amazing. I've seen some other unsolved crime documentaries that have resulted in positive outcomes for the families of the victims. Maybe you can help us find justice too.

Holy. Shit.

Greer's BFF was going to let me interview her. On camera.

I leaped off the couch and did a fist-pumping, high-kicking dance of joy.

Then, impossibly, the response got even better.

In case you didn't email her, I've forwarded your message to Bethany Allen, Greer's agent. She'll also be interested in talking to you.

Oh my God. This was happening. I was doing a documentary about the disappearance of Greer Larkin.

"This. Is. Awesome," I yelled out, punctuating each word with a punch to the air. I flopped back down on my couch feeling giddy and full of energy.

I had to share the news with Paul.

Me: I sent out interview request emails and already got a YES! Her best friend wants to talk to me!

A few impatient minutes later Paul responded.

Paul: Wonderful! Questions ready?
Me: Uh . . .
Paul: So that's a no.
Me: They are in my head.
Paul: And getting onto paper when exactly?
Me: Soon?
Paul: Well, I guess that's an answer.
Me: Now?
Paul: A better answer.
Paul: Do you need help?
Me: Possibly . . . Come over?
Paul: On my way.

Ready to call this the best day of my life, I stripped down to my red lace bra and added the matching panties. Paul had my spare key, so there was no need to buzz him in. He flung open the door, threw both the locks, and peeled off his suit jacket as he came toward the bed where I was sprawled in a seductive pose, I hoped.

It had only been a couple of days since I'd seen him, but even that was too long since I'd felt his arms around me. I couldn't help myself. I flung myself at him.

He caught me easily. While other forty-five-year-old men's muscles were melting into potbellies, Paul still had all his delicious Kansas farm boy muscles. Crushing my lips to his, I wrapped my legs around his waist and curled my fingers through his sleek blond hair. I loved the way we fit together like this, my legs braced around his hips, while his muscular arms pressed us together so tightly it was hard to breathe. My nerve endings tingled, and I swear I felt sparks where our bodies connected. His lips left mine, nibbling across my jaw line. His end of the day stubble felt deliciously scratchy as he inched his way to my collarbone.

"Oh God, I missed you," he said. "It was torture being away from you tonight."

"I missed you too," I managed. My brain was being overloaded with the electric zaps each kiss sent through my skin.

"You're so beautiful," Paul said, fanning me out across the bed. His fingertips started a slow journey over the swell of my breast down to the curve of my waist.

I grabbed the collar of his shirt, pulling him down on top of me. "I am going to make you so very happy."

He closed his eyes, breathing out a moan of joyous anticipation. "You always make me happy," he said, his voice husky and tight.

"Very happy," I repeated, giving him a wicked grin as I worked to free him from his shirt.

He growled out a promise of his own and threw his now unbuttoned shirt behind him onto the floor before crushing into me again.

* * *

He didn't stay long. Paul could never stay long.

And there wasn't a lot of foreplay in our lovemaking. That happened via text and imagination in the days before we could snatch time together. It usually goes like this: Paul tells his wife that a student left something in his office and he needs to unlock the door and will be right back. He then tells her that he and this fictitious student got talking about a project. *Sorry for the delay, honey.*

I sometimes wondered if she could smell me on him. I certainly smelled him on me. Traces of cedar and smoky vanilla clung to the sheets. What did I smell like to him? I was careful not to wear perfume.

Rule Number Five: Leave no trace behind. Distinctive cologne was what'd gotten George Freemont's killer caught in Greer's book *The Calling of Oberlin Hurst.*

We couldn't afford for his wife to find out about us. Martha—saying her name made bile rise in my throat—was one of the partners at a chic law office in Manhattan. She defended the innocent and not-so-innocent, along with a bevy of celebrities. She was raking in the bucks that permitted their lavish lifestyle. Film professors didn't make a lot of money. Without Martha, Paul wouldn't be able to follow his dream of making another true crime documentary. Plus, they had a prenup.

I understood. Paul's first film, *Inside the FBI*, had been well received, but wasn't exactly a breakout hit. For his next project he wanted to film the life of a Texas Ranger. He even had his lead picked out: a legend among the already legendary Rangers. Paul had been wooing the guy for about five years, and he was finally starting to come around. In the meantime, Paul advised students like me at the New York Film School.

He was a natural at filmmaking and born to be a teacher. Calm. Knowledgeable. Inspiring. I could listen to him talk all day.

His last words before he crawled out of my bed were instructing me to get the interviews nailed down ASAP.

"Tomorrow, if you can," he said. "You're way behind the other students. This whole week needs to be interviews for you."

"I know," I said and pouted. I didn't like it when he treated me as if it was my first year. I was fully aware of how very, very behind I am. "I'll email Rachel back right now, and then approach the agent."

"You've got this," he said, giving me a peck on the forehead.

"I wish you didn't have to leave so soon," I said. It was an old complaint, so Paul only shrugged as he pulled on his pants.

When he was presentable again, he left me with a deep, lingering kiss. It was meant to tide us over until next time, but as his tongue swept my mouth, my body readied for round two. "Pear Blossom," he whispered, a smile on his lips. I moaned his name as he kissed me again. My hands went back to his buttons, but his own hands caught mine, gently pushing them away. "I have to go. She'll start to suspect."

"I know," I said. Because I did know. That was the Ultimate Rule: Martha must not find out. Not only would she crush Paul, she would grind my hopes of making it to Hollywood into a fine powder. Martha knew people.

Paul left and I continued to pout for a full minute before pulling on sweats and getting back onto my computer. I opened my email and asked Rachel to meet me at one o'clock tomorrow. *Oh, and, by the way, could we film in your office? Thanks!*

Hoping she would say yes, I wrote down some preliminary questions before setting my alarm for six in the morning. Something I never did. On the commune, we had to be up before daylight began every day to feed the goats. Now that

I'd broken free, I tried to sleep in as often as possible. *Welp.* Tomorrow, it wouldn't be possible.

Waking at six only gave me four hours to rest. Not nearly long enough. I lay in bed, willing the energy to leave my limbs and sleep to visit. After tossing and turning for fifteen minutes, I put in my earbuds and turned on a podcast as a kind of lullaby.

I was about to discover whether I could fly when my alarm blared into my ears, shooting me skyward. My head banged into the wall behind my bed, making me see stars for a minute. Clapping my hands over the lump that would surely form, I swore bitterly and inventively. I took deep breaths, hoping to exhale the throbbing pain, only to discover Paul's scent still there, faintly. The pain began to ebb away as I wallowed in the satisfied memories, until my body demanded I make magic happen inside my coffee pot.

In order to have an interview, I needed interview questions. They needed to be insightful, too. I had to provoke responses that'd give the viewer more information about their friendship, along with Rachel's view of what had really been happening in Greer's life.

It took hours. I surfed the fan site, GreersGone, while pulling details from my own encyclopedic knowledge of the case. Finally, I felt like everything was ready. I showered, ate some leftover pizza from a couple of nights before, and pulled on a pair of navy blue slacks and a white tunic top that was in no way a sweater. We'd knitted our own sweaters on the commune and they'd itched horribly. When I left, I vowed to never wear a sweater again. This was a knit fabric constructed out of purely man-made materials. Therefore, not a sweater.

This outfit was as fancy as I got. The rest of my wardrobe was jeans and T-shirts from rock concerts I'd never been allowed to attend. Plus, I kind of wanted the longer sleeves to hide my tattoos. I had a great line drawing of an arrow on my forearm and an infinity symbol on the other, but I wasn't sure how a forty-something professional would feel about body art.

I made a mental note not to push up my sleeves.

Rachel emailed me back sometime between when I'd finished my third cup of coffee and poured my fourth. She was delighted to meet today. "The sooner the better," she'd written. *Woohoo!*

Rachel was an editor for a branch of Tuesday Hill, an independent publishing house that had made a name for itself in edgy women's fiction, and she'd invited me to her offices in Manhattan. It was a bit of a hike from my apartment in Fordham Heights. I fretted the entire subway ride that I was going to be late. Being late for an interview you'd requested was a cardinal sin in my book.

Rachel's offices were crisply white, with enormous framed copies of book jackets hanging in the waiting room. I'm afraid my jaw might have hung open for longer than was cool, and I broke out into a cold sweat. A chipper-looking woman about my age was managing the front desk. Her hair was streaked with blue in the front and her nose was pierced. I guess I hadn't needed to worry about my tattoos.

"Can I help you?" she asked. She had kind eyes and a genuine smile. Rare in New York.

"I'm here to meet with Rachel Baumgartner. I have a one o'clock appointment," I said, trying to keep the nervousness out of my voice. This was my first interview. It would set the tone for my entire project. The pressure made my palms slippery.

"Sure," she said. She looked down and clicked some keys on her computer. "June. You sure do," she confirmed. "You have about, oh, five minutes to wait. You can have a seat over there." She indicated a plush armchair next to a coffee station.

The coffee station was a Nespresso machine with about twenty different kinds of coffee pods to choose from. However, I was already working on about seven cups of coffee. If I had another, I would vibrate the earth off its axis. So I sat, gluing myself to my phone to take my mind off the fact that my entire movie could hinge on what happened in the next hour.

Rachel breezed into the waiting area through double glass doors. She was on the taller side, about five-six. Taller than me, that was for sure. She had long wavy black hair and squarish, black-framed eyeglasses surrounding large, intelligent brown eyes.

"Hello, you must be June," she said, extending her hand. Her voice was smoky and dark, like the inside of a nightclub.

"Yeah. Hi. Thanks for seeing me." My phone dropped out of my lap as I jumped up to shake her hand. My face heated up to about a thousand degrees as I bent over to pick up the phone. *Not a great first impression.* Her grip, however, was firm and friendly.

"My pleasure," she said. "Now, let's see if we can't bring that rat bastard to justice, shall we?"

Chapter Four

∾

Excerpt from
Murder Most Foul
An Oberlin Hurst Mystery by Greer Larkin

*H*e *stank of sweat and onions. The face she'd grown to love and trust twisted into a hideous mask of pain and hatred. Flecks of spittle hit Oberlin's cheek as she shrank away. Her wrists hurt where the wire cut into her flesh. Her ears rang from her knock on the head, so she almost missed his first words, quiet and controlled.*

"She never loved me, your mother." Peter sounded almost reasonable as he continued to connect wires to the horse-shaped lightning rod. "She always said it was her parents that didn't approve, but I knew better. If she'd loved me, she would have come with me. She would have been on that train."

"She does love you, though. I'm sure of it," Oberlin cried. A crack of thunder made her jump. Rain began to splatter onto her face.

"How come she never recognized me? Or acknowledged me? I've been her father's chauffeur for five years. I took a shitty job in this shitty house just so I could see you grow up. So I could see her," he said and spat. *"Even when I left notes for her, presents for her, she never looked at me twice. Well, screw her."*

Chapter Five

Rachel didn't waste any time on small talk. "Get your camera rolling. I've got a lot to say."

I barely had my first question out of my mouth when she took over the interview.

"An eel has less slime." Jonathan was too loud, drank too much, smoked too much, spent too much money, and was a self-centered show-off who made every event about him.

And, apparently, Jonathan snores.

"This sounds annoying, but not like the behavior of a killer," I said. "What is it exactly that makes you believe Jonathan would kill the woman he intended to marry?"

"Jonathan's a controlling bastard! He didn't like that Greer was famous, yet he loved the lifestyle that Greer's fame provided. It made him . . . insecure. Jealous. So he clamped down on Greer and pushed her mom and me out of her life. If he thought Greer was going to leave, he would have definitely killed her."

Would Greer have actually left Jonathan? Other than that one fight in the restaurant, I'd never heard that their relationship had been anywhere near rocky. Although my own rebellions had been quiet, subtle, sneaky. My parents hadn't known

I was leaving until I came down the stairs with my suitcases packed. Safer that way.

"And did she threaten to leave?"

"There was that fight in Battaglia's. I think she must have threatened to that night."

"But she never told you, her best friend, that she was planning on leaving Jonathan?"

Meadow had known I was leaving my parents. She'd been my safe haven while I'd waited for my first term at college to start. I couldn't imagine Greer taking off without her oldest friend helping her. It was one of the major reasons why people—why I—believed Greer had been murdered. I just didn't know who'd done it.

"Noooo," she said slowly. "Jonathan kept her away from me and her mom. But their fight in the restaurant is proof enough for me. She was leaving and he killed her because of it."

"But she never reached out to you for help."

"Jonathan made sure of that."

"How do you know that Jonathan was the reason you two didn't talk anymore? You and Greer could've simply been growing apart. Friends often drift when a serious boyfriend enters the picture."

Her eyes flashed. "This was more than *drifting*. He was purposely isolating her from the people that loved her. He demanded her attention, acting like a petulant baby when he didn't get what he wanted. Then she'd have to buy some insanely expensive present to make up for it. Look. I don't think you get what's happening here. I'm out to nail this piece of shit to the wall, so you can either help me or get the fuck out of my way. And if you can't do either, I will be forced to eliminate you from my path."

I blinked at her. Was that a *threat*? Rachel's face was hard and her eyes had the same quality I'd seen in some of *The Real Housewives* women. We were moments away from having a table flipped. My body tensed, getting ready to bolt. If shit went down, I was not going to be around to be collateral damage.

She shut her eyes and took a deep breath, reining her anger back in. She looked down at her manicured hands, studying them. Sighing, Rachel said, "I think Greer was being abused by Jonathan. We never saw any bruising, so I don't think the abuse was physical. I think it was mostly psychological. Greer was never able to stand up for herself. I don't think she'd ever uttered the word *no* in her life. Jonathan took advantage of that. He told her she was being silly if she was uncomfortable. He insisted that he needed the money more than she did. Her accolades were thanks to him. She would never be a superstar without him. She would never write another book if he wasn't there." Rachel looked up at me, tears in her eyes. "He broke her. He made her think she was nothing, that she was *worthless*. He's a vile son of a bitch, and if I could get away with it I'd kill him with my bare hands."

An aching grew in my chest. Imagine one of the best authors of our time being told they were worthless. *Believing* they were worthless. If this was true, Greer had suffered. A lot. But it didn't mean Jonathan had killed her. Rachel hadn't handed me any proof of a murder.

But it also didn't mean he was innocent.

I was still shaken by Rachel's threat to eliminate me if I stood in her way. For my own sanity, I wanted to chalk this session up as one big bitch fest. But what if her carefully controlled anger had spiraled out of control? And what if Greer had happened to be there? Rachel was a strong, powerful woman. The kind of woman it's dangerous to underestimate.

Rachel could slam Jonathan all she wanted. But talk is cheap. When would someone have any damn *proof*?

My face must have been painted with my impatience, because she'd called me on it in the middle of the interview. Narrowing her eyes, she said, "I can see you don't believe me."

I shrugged. "I didn't say that. Though, if you had some proof—like a letter or email—that would be great."

I caught the glint of a tear in the corner of Rachel's eye. All her hardness had been a thin veneer covering a wounded core. For her, Greer's death might have happened last week instead of twenty years ago. Taking a deep breath, she slid the veneer back in place, asking, "Have you ever been in love?"

Surprised, I answered, "Yes."

"Did love ever make you do stupid things?"

Every day. "Yes."

"But love is supposed to make you better, right?"

"I suppose so," I said. I wasn't sure where this was going, but I kept the camera rolling and my voice neutral. I could always edit it out later.

"Let me tell you, Greer never missed a day of writing. From the time she was twelve, she wrote every day. Every. Single. Day. She'd wake up at six and write for three, maybe four hours straight. Then she'd eat lunch, and start editing her writing. When she met Jonathan, Greer's writing routine went to hell. She started sleeping in. A week would go by and she wouldn't open her laptop. She wouldn't return calls from Bethany, her agent. No author does that. Your agent is your lifeline to getting your books published. And when we'd ask what was going on, her excuses were always flimsy. She was tired. She was sick. She'd gone out of town unexpectedly. Her writing was suffering.

"Her fifth book? *The Girl Who Sang a Tune?* It showed how much her craft had slipped. She was lucky it got published. So if this was love, why did it make Greer fall completely apart? Why did it destroy what she had?"

I didn't have an answer for her.

* * *

Two hours later I sat across from Paul at a coffee shop close to campus.

"Greer wrote some great books while dating Jonathan," I said. "*Swingline* and *The Book of Deuteronomy* are two of my favorites. *Deuteronomy* was probably the best. I read them over and over, my covers tented over my head, and a flashlight in hand." I smiled at the memory. "True, *The Girl Who Sang* wasn't as stellar as her other books, but every author has a book or two that didn't shine quite as brightly as the others, right? Usually that was no one's or everyone's fault, right?"

Paul was grinning at me. "You're so darn cute when you're deep in thought."

I stuck my tongue out and snapped my fingers in his face. "Focus, please. I need you to be my advisor for a minute."

While I'd told him about Rachel's allegations, I hadn't told him about Rachel's threat to eliminate me if I didn't commit to proving Jonathan killed Greer. True, he was the most likely suspect, but as a documentary filmmaker I needed to have some level of objectivity. Rachel seemed possessed by a vengeful rage that made the hair on my arms stand at attention. I felt a little uneasy not sharing this with Paul, but how do you tell your lover that you were maybe, possibly, probably threatened?

"Of course, Ms. Masterson. It is true that every author has one book that isn't as good as the rest. Carry on," he said, straightening in his chair, but continuing to grin at me.

I rolled my eyes. I couldn't be mad at him, but I did need him to be a little bit serious. He cleared his throat and went on, his voice taking on his advising tone. "Yes, Rachel hated Jonathan. But she'd also had no proof about what he'd allegedly done to Greer. From your notes, she said she'd never seen bruising, and she'd never gotten a call from Greer asking for help. All she said was Jonathan acted like a big baby and distracted Greer from her family, friends, and writing career. Love will do that to you." As if to illustrate the point, he reached out and stroked the back of my hand.

He'd only touched my hand, but my skin tingled all over. Thoughts became indistinct—fuzzy. True, love could be a powerful distraction.

"I see what you mean." My voice was disgustingly breathy and my body suddenly didn't care that I needed to have a serious conversation with Paul instead of riding him like a Kentucky Derby winner. *Down, girl*, I said to the fluttering heat building inside me. To Paul I asked, "Do you think I should reinterview her? Get her to be more specific about the abuse?"

Paul shook his head. "You don't have a lot of time. Move on to the agent. What was her name?"

I looked at my notes. "Bethany Allen, of the Barry Allen Literary Agency," I said. "She's his daughter."

"Yeah, move on to her. See if she can be specific about anything she saw between Greer and Jonathan. She would have noticed things at book launches, signings, and meetings," he said. He tapped the pages I'd given him when we sat down.

"I like your questions. They're direct and can lead to insightful answers. Maybe even unexpected. Those are the best kinds of answers." He looked at his watch. "I have to run. I have another advisee to meet."

My skin prickled with jealousy. I didn't like it when other people cut our moments together short. "Where are you meeting them?"

"The office," he said, smiling, probably amused at my jealous tone. "I'll tell Dave you said hi."

I narrowed my eyes. Dave Zukko was my stiffest competition in the program. Everything he filmed came out magically beautiful. My films had to be reshot and re-edited at least three times. I hated him. "You do that," I said.

Paul laughed, playfully tapping me on the nose. "I'll see you later."

I knew better than to expect a kiss. We were too close to campus, and we couldn't afford to have his colleagues realize that I was more than just a favorite student. Still. A peck on the cheek would have been nice.

Tables in the coffee shop were hard to come by. When a guy saw Paul leave, he started hovering around waiting for me to leave too. I hate people who do that. Pisses me right off. I got my laptop out and pointedly looked at him as I opened it and typed in my password. It was as good as sticking my tongue out. Air whooshed out of his nostrils like a bull threatening to charge as his eyes narrowed. An enormous wave of satisfaction swept over me at his disappointment.

The coffee shop had been my second home for a while now. There was something about the space that let my brain do its thing. I had fired off an email to Bethany the minute Rachel had given me the agent's email address. I held my breath as

I opened my account, hoping to see the dark bold print that heralded unopened mail.

Most of it was junk. An invite to a party thrown by another film student, which I trashed immediately. I did not need to socialize with my competition. The last email was from a person called BLAR1953. At Hotmail. Who still used Hotmail? I hesitated, my cursor arrow hovering above it. I could see the email started with, "I don't know what you think you're doing . . ."

Some sort of scam? It didn't sound like it. But scammers are tricky. I weighed my options between not opening the message and missing out on something crucial, and opening it and having spyware sucked into my hard drive.

Then a new and terrifying thought hit me. OMG. Was it from Paul's wife? She went by her maiden name, but I couldn't remember what that was. Oh, shit. I started to hyperventilate and shut my laptop.

It can't be her. She couldn't possibly know. *Calm the fuck down, June.*

After a hard mental slap, I opened the laptop again. "I'd better not be giving myself a virus," I muttered, clicking on the email.

No salutation. Just straight to the point.

I don't know what you think you're doing, but Rachel says it would be worth talking to you. I do not approve of airing our laundry for the world to see, but I would rather be a part of this process than excluded from it. You may come to my house tomorrow at ten o'clock. 115 Waverly Place. Yours, Blanche Larkin

My chest tightened as bells began to ring in my ears.

I have no idea how long I sat immobile with shock. I came back to my senses before I started drooling on myself and sent a reply.

Dear Ms. Larkin,

I would be delighted to have you as a part of my documentary about your daughter. I will be at your house by ten a.m. tomorrow. Yours, June Masterson

This time when I flipped my laptop shut, I actually got up from my table. I was buoyant. The gods had chosen to shine upon me—and I desperately needed to prepare. Tomorrow was going to be a big day. I signaled past another alpha male who was angling for my seat to a mousey-looking woman swimming in a brown sweater behind him. He and his gigantic backpack were blocking her way.

"Hey, miss," I said. "Would you like my seat?"

Her eyes lit up, and she nodded. "Yes, thank you! I have a ton of reading to do."

Alpha Male's mouth flattened out into a thin line and his eyes were furious. "I was waiting for that table," he said.

"Too bad," I said. "I'm giving it to her."

"Bitch," he said, banging me with his backpack as he moved past.

"Troglodyte," I shot back. Typical male student in New York for you—oozing with low-level aggression and mediocre cursing.

"Thanks for the seat," the woman said.

"No problem." I slung my messenger bag across my body and headed back to my apartment.

I decided to text Paul the good news on the way home. I was pumped. I had gotten an interview done and another scheduled for tomorrow. Now I only had Jonathan and Greer's agent to hear back from.

Of my three initial emails, Jonathan was the one I really needed to email back with a yes. Maybe I was inflating how important Jonathan was to my project, but I wanted both sides of the story—and only Jonathan was around to tell his.

Chapter Six

Walking into Blanche's home, I understood for the first time what coming from old money really looked like.

Everything in the foyer screamed quality, from the wastepaper basket under the console table to the deceptively delicate-looking silver chandelier above my head.

I could tell she would never have anything as gaudy as a gold toilet. A butler was three paces in front of me, guiding me up white marble stairs and through a pair of French doors into a library. Or was it a salon? An office? I was poor and didn't have the vocabulary for this.

We entered a large room with sweeping views of a garden right out of a Jane Austen novel nestled into the city. The other walls were covered with shelves of books and art. The colors were white and navy blue, like Delft pottery.

Blanche Larkin sat in a white Queen Anne wingback chair reading the newspaper: the financial section. Impressive. I could barely make out the front page, much less a whole section that dealt with numbers. She wore a lavender suit. A white blouse peeked out around the lapels, and a thick silver chain hung around her neck. Her ankles were crossed and tucked demurely under the chair. She even wore heels—nude and more expensive than my computer. I didn't have a pair of nude heels. While they weren't normally my style, I'd priced a pair about a month before after seeing a Kardashian wearing them, and, forced to decide between the shoes and my rent, I'd reluctantly decided on the roof over my head. I was still bitter. Blanche's hair was a golden white. Not platinum blonde, but blonde hair that was being allowed to go white naturally. It was thick and glossy and perfectly bound behind her in a low bun.

"Madame," said the butler. "Miss June Masterson."

"Thank you, Gerald. Please bring us coffee."

The butler gave a sharp nod and a bow before disappearing from the room. Blanche folded up the newspaper and set it down on a white ottoman—or footstool to us normally funded people.

"Ms. Masterson." Her voice was all whiskey and leonine. Her eyes were blue ice chips that made me shiver as she raked me with an appraising look.

Since it was the only decent outfit I owned, I wore the same navy blue slacks and white tunic non-sweater I'd worn to interview Rachel. I now regretted not ironing my pants—not that I owned an iron.

"What is it that you want from me?"

"Thank you for seeing me," I said. My face felt hot. *Don't eat me*, I wanted to squeak. Instead, I cleared my throat and said, "I wanted to talk to you about your daughter."

She arched a perfect eyebrow as Gerald the Butler came in carrying a large silver tray loaded down with a silver coffee set and two delicate floral teacups. He set it off to Blanche's right on a table at elbow height—perfect for pouring coffee. Gerald poured, placed a lump of sugar in Blanche's cup, and handed it to her. He gave me an inquiring look and I shook my head. I was already nervous and highly caffeinated. Not the best combination for a tense situation.

"My daughter," she said, "is dead. Not you, nor your little movie, are going to change that." I hadn't expected that, and my face clearly reflected my shock. "Surprised that I don't believe in the power of a movie to solve all my problems?" she said, sipping her coffee.

"No," I said, truthfully, "surprised that you think she's dead."

Blanche set her cup back onto her saucer. "Why is that surprising?"

"Well, most parents hold out hope that their child is somewhere in the world. Or they explore every avenue until they find out what happened. You don't seem to be doing either." I tried to keep my voice neutral. I didn't want to accuse her of being a shitty parent and end this interview before it even started.

"You certainly speak your mind," she said, carefully placing her cup back onto the tray.

"I didn't mean—"

Blanche held up a hand. "Don't ruin it by apologizing. A mother knows when her child is gone. I'm sure Jonathan is responsible, but there isn't enough proof. There is nothing the district attorney can do, or so they tell me. So I have contented myself with ensuring that every business scheme Jonathan attempts fails utterly."

"You've made him destitute?" I was both confused and awed.

Blanche laughed. "He is hardly destitute. Somehow he keeps afloat. He lives in a semi-posh building and manages to buy overpriced Japanese whiskey by the crate. But," she continued with a dangerous note in her voice, "he doesn't control Greer's books, her image, or her money. The account in the Caymans the police found in his name was seized indefinitely. He will never have her again."

"Someone out there might know something that could prove Jonathan killed her," I reasoned. "Her car was found in a very public place. It's possible someone saw another car come or go from the lighthouse at about that time."

Blanche picked up her coffee cup again and took a delicate sip. "It's been twenty years. Wouldn't they have come forward by now?"

"Breaks in cases happen all the time. It's also possible that because of my film the police would be motivated to send evidence for more DNA testing. There have been huge leaps in science since her disappearance. Or maybe Jonathan let something slip once, and that person didn't realize how important that information might be, if he did do it."

"Of course he did it," she snapped. "Who else could have done it?"

"That's one of the things I'm trying to discover. I'm not only going to look at Jonathan, I'm going back to the beginning. That's why it's important that you are in this film. Why it's important you talk to me," I said, hoping I sounded logical and trustworthy. And competent.

She said nothing. Instead, her cool blue eyes regarded me over the rim of her cup. I cleared my throat and plunged on.

"Ms. Larkin, I am a huge fan of your daughter's work. Her writing is lyrical and her mysteries are delightfully intricate puzzles. Doesn't she deserve to have her books remembered? Doesn't she deserve not to be forgotten? You said you wanted to be a part of this. Wasn't that so the story would be told the right way?"

Blanche Larkin put her cup and saucer back onto the silver tray. Her eyes were hooded, impossible to read. Was I about to get kicked out by Gerald the Butler? My heart rate kicked up a notch. I had utterly fucked this up. I was a nobody film student from a small film school in Manhattan. She was never going to talk to me.

"Ms. Masterson," Blanche said, pulling herself up so she sat in her chair like a queen, her face taking on a haughty look. "I do want my daughter's story told the right way. In order to ensure that it is, I must be a part of this project. You will show me the interviews, and I will approve of what you will publish, or whatever it is you people do."

Show her the interviews? For her approval? No fucking way. But what I said was, "Ms. Larkin, with all due respect, you will not have approval rights to what I put into my film. I have a story to tell: Greer's story. I will not allow crucial information that could exonerate Jonathan or condemn others to be excluded from this film."

Blanche's eyebrows went up a fraction of an inch, and her haughty expression changed to one of mild approval. I believe I saw the corner of her mouth twitch, but I couldn't be certain. "I believe a first review of the material will suffice." She rose and I saw that, physically, I towered over her; however, there was no question of who was in charge.

"Gerald!" she called and Gerald the Butler entered the room so quickly I knew he'd been standing right outside the door, listening to our entire conversation. "Please remove the coffee. Ms. Masterson will need to set up her cameras."

* * *

Describing Blanche Larkin as being crafted from steel would be too pedestrian. She was made of solid titanium, with diamonds running through her blood. Our filming began at ten thirty in the morning and we didn't end until two that afternoon. The woman never broke a sweat or even looked the least bit fatigued. I, on the other hand, felt like I'd been run over by a bus.

Gerald had come in with "light refreshments" sometime after noon—a tray tastefully heaped with finger sandwiches and iced tea. Blanche ate one. I got two, but stopped myself from eating a third. I really, really wanted that third, but since Blanche had only had the one, I was afraid she would think me a glutton. Apparently, the rich saved money by not eating.

We plowed through the rest of the filming, and I prayed that my growling stomach wouldn't be heard on the tape. I would find out as soon as I got home and started reviewing the tapes from Rachel and Ms. Larkin. If I didn't faint from hunger first.

That's why I was sitting on a bench at Eighty-Fourth Street and Central Park at three in the afternoon scarfing down falafel and a Diet Coke. Passing out from hunger at my laptop was not going to get my film edited.

I realized now that I had made a mistake agreeing to let Blanche Larkin review the interviews. Would she want to see the whole interview or just my edited version? She hadn't specified. However, she had signed my waiver, which gave me editorial power over the project and prevented her from suing me if she didn't like it. But then again, she had lawyers who charged an hourly rate higher than my monthly rent. They would be able to weasel out of anything.

At home I pulled up Blanche's interview footage onto my laptop. I had varied between close-ups and a waist up shot. Her lavender suit was beautiful on screen. The different angles would look great when I got it pieced together. I clicked on one of the files and it flickered to life.

"Please tell us about Greer as a girl." I was off-camera, but my voice was strong and clear.

Blanche was smiling as she subtly lifted herself up so that her back was straighter than the chair she was seated in. It made her look proud of Greer in an oddly regal way. "Greer was easy to love. She was such a good baby. She hardly ever cried. She had big, thoughtful eyes. My mother called her an Old Soul. The only time she cried was when her grandfather held her, but he was a complete bastard, so we believed that she had been born a good judge of character."

"When did you first realize Greer was a talented writer?"

"She was probably nine when she started writing some little stories. We didn't know she was writing anything until the maid found a box of notebooks in her closet. They were full of little stories. I enjoyed reading them. I don't think she ever knew I read those . . ." A fond smile softened her face.

"What did you think when she was not only published at fourteen, but also a *New York Times* bestseller?"

"I was very proud. She was so young. I was happy to help guide her career. She needed me. It is a rare thing for a teenager to need her parents."

I'm sure my own parents would agree. If I ever called them again.

"How did you help guide her career?" I asked.

"I introduced her to an agent, Daniel Baumgartner, an old family friend, and his partner, Barry Allen, signed her to a contract. I pushed her first novel into publication. I made sure she formed a solid writing habit. I read and critiqued all her work. We were very close."

"You approved of a fourteen-year-old girl writing about murder? Her books are quite graphic in places." My own mother would have shit a brick if I wrote about the stench of decaying flesh or blood flooding a carpet like a leaking bathtub.

"I didn't like all the blood and the horrible nature of her books. Murder. Too violent for a lady. But I was proud. Parents generally like it when strangers praise our children."

"What did she think of her fame?"

"She didn't think too much of it at first. I think she thought it was nice. It encouraged her to write more."

"Did any of it worry you? Her popularity?"

Blanche shook her head. "Greer had a solid head on her shoulders. And she had me right beside her. She was just glad people liked her work. It wasn't until people started waiting for her at her favorite writing spots that she was bothered."

"Bothered?" Was that the rich people way of saying harassed?

Her thin shoulders gracefully lifted and then dropped in a shrug the French would have found elegant. "It was an inconvenience. Or an intrusion. We—she—was very private. I insisted she stay home. It was safer here. If she had just stayed home she wouldn't have gotten caught up with Jonathan."

"She moved in with Jonathan pretty quickly. From different accounts, she had an apartment with him about three weeks after they met. Why do you think that was?" Hearing myself ask this question, I felt the heaviness of it. Loaded, like a gun. I was waiting for her to go off—to become defensive about what kind of mother she'd been. But she'd surprised me completely.

"The sex, obviously. Greer had been an innocent young girl of eighteen when she moved out of the house. And where did that get her? She should have listened to me. I am her mother. I knew best. Men like him are, unfortunately, common." I made a note not to underestimate Blanche.

"You didn't like Jonathan or Greer's relationship with him?" *Well, duh.* A gimme question.

"No. I did not approve of Jonathan." The memory of the chill as she'd said his name had me shivering in my living room.

"What was it about him that you didn't like?"

"Jonathan Vanderpoole is an opportunist and a leech. She should have sent him back to the swamp he crawled out of." She said it with a sneer. I made a note to push in on her expression.

"So he was an opportunist. Do you think he is responsible for Greer's disappearance?"

Blanche almost rolled her eyes. I even rewound the tape to make sure. It made her feel more human. "I told her to never trust a man. Greer had talent. All these books came pouring out of her. That stopped when he came. It was his fault. He poisoned her soul. He poisoned her against me. All because he was born poor and common in Queens."

"Ms. Larkin, being born poor doesn't prove Jonathan murdered Greer. Also, being poor is not a crime."

Blanche's smile attempted to be kind, but ended up more patronizing. "It is not a crime. You must understand, people with our kind of money have to be careful. Social climbers are everywhere. It is easier to date and marry inside your own class."

There was a pause, and I could tell I was struggling to find a response to this bourgeois crap. "Isn't that, well, classist?"

Blanche was looking at me with pity. I wanted to scream. "That, my dear, is life."

"Was Rachel the right sort of person? From the right class to play with Greer?"

Blanche looks down at her hands and then back up. Instead of the tears I expect, her eyes are fiery diamonds. I can hear myself gasp on the film.

"He took her away from me. Even if he didn't actually pull the trigger—"

Wait. What? I stopped the tape and rewound it.

"Even if he didn't actually pull the trigger—"

Did Blanche *know* that Jonathan didn't kill Greer? Did that mean Blanche knew who the real killer was? Was she blaming Jonathan for Greer's death because she thought he was a rotten boyfriend? It seemed like an extreme reaction. Maybe in line for a rich person who did her spring wardrobe shopping at the runways of Paris and Milan, but I would hate it if I got blamed as collateral damage for something horrific that wasn't my fault.

I started the tape again. "—trigger . . . He killed who she was long before that night. She was the only thing I had, and he took her away from me. If it's the last thing I do, I will make him pay for what he did to Greer."

The video ended abruptly. I would need to fade it out, soften the transition to whatever my next shot would be. But her anger had made me jumpy and possibly careless. I would also need to edit out my gasp. At some point I'd have to show this to Blanche. I wondered what she would think of her own words, the venom as she spoke about Jonathan. Would she see weakness? Would she decide she was being indiscreet? Would she force me to censor her words? Would she hate it?

I shivered again at the thought of Blanche Larkin's glares of disapproval. She was nobody's fool and certainly not one to be trifled with. It seemed like Greer had been on a tight leash in that household. I knew what it was like to live with a controlling mother. To be watched and judged. To have your comings and goings monitored. But I wondered what it would have been like to feel that stare every morning at breakfast; to bring home a B on a test. What were the consequences of disappointing a woman like that?

Chapter Seven

~

Excerpt from
When She Was Seventeen
An Oberlin Hurst Mystery by Greer Larkin

*O*berlin was sure the slender shadow she had spotted slinking away from Dr. Parker's mangled body had been Margo Beauchamp, her clubbed foot making her gait distinctive. Her mother had kept Margo locked away: the family's distasteful secret, locked in the attic like the proverbial mad aunt. The terrible isolation, the abuse, had driven Margo to kill, to take revenge on all those who had wronged her. There was no telling what she would do to her mother if she found her.

The stench of cat urine was breathtaking. The acrid fumes burned her nose, her throat. "Is anybody here?" she called. No one answered. Not even the cat.

With soft, slow steps, Oberlin crossed through the living room and into the kitchen. Food was still on a single plate on the counter, flies buzzing around it, gorging themselves on a free meal that hadn't been fresh for days. Rot assaulted her nostrils and made her choke. She should run for help. She should call 9-1-1. She should do anything except for what she was doing now, which was continuing to move stealthily toward the bedroom.

The buzzing of flies was louder here. Oberlin opened the door and the scent of decay flooded from the room in a putrid gush.

Oberlin was far too late to deliver her warning.

Mrs. Beauchamp was very, very dead.

Chapter Eight

When She Was Seventeen is my second favorite novel of Greer's. Definitely in my top ten of all time. Probably even in my top five. I'd been reading it for the past hour.

Closing the book, I gave a happy sigh.

It's not like I'm not working on my project—it's called research. You get to know an author through their books, right? I needed to reacquaint myself with Greer. At least, that's what I told myself.

What I should've been doing was editing Rachel and Blanche's interviews. I also should've been calling Bethany's office after her nonresponse to my email. I looked at my watch; it was after seven in the evening. Bethany's office was closed. A phone call would have to wait until morning. I'd be able to finish Rachel's interview tomorrow if I got up early and worked on it all day. Then, maybe, I could flick through some of Blanche's interview in the evening.

I put the book down next to where my laptop sat on my behemoth coffee table, staring at me, accusing me of slacking. "You should be working," it said. "You should be reviewing the video."

I opened my soda and took a drink. When I looked back, my laptop was still there. Mocking me.

Fuck. An inanimate object was making me feel guilty. I was going soft.

"The clock is ticking," it said.

"Fine," I said and huffed, making my internet appear.

Maybe I should check the fan site to see if anyone has anything new. You know, to inform my notes and edits.

No doubt about it, procrastination was going to sink me.

I clicked open GreersGone.com anyway. I was PricklyPear on the site. This is what happens when you choose your avatar name when you're fourteen. But it was as good as any. I was at "Sleuth" level, which was the top ranking on the site. You had to have ten thousand posts to make Sleuth. It was a badge of honor. It gave a certain authority to my posts. People listened to me. I didn't want to throw that away because I'd outgrown the name.

The top post on the site greeted me with big blaring letters: NYC MEET-N-GREER-T.

Whoever came up with that title should be kicked off the site. What a horrible name for an event. I clicked on the post anyway, because it had fifty-two replies and over a thousand people had looked at it.

COME TO A LIVE, IN-PERSON EVENT!! IT'S BEEN ALMOST TWENTY YEARS SINCE GREER LARKIN DISAPPEARED. LET'S GET TOGETHER AND TALK ABOUT IT! MICHAEL'S ANNEX. TONIGHT!!!! 8PM!!!

My eyes were overwhelmed by the all-caps message and thousands of exclamation points. Someone needed to start drinking decaf. I scanned the message again. Michael's Annex was a ten-minute cab ride away. It could be fun. And it might be a good use of my time. Who knows? Maybe I'd get a lead on some footage of Jonathan and his arrests. Or other useful tidbits of information might float my way.

My phone whistled at me, signaling a text from Meadow.

Meadow: I wanted to remind you that the gallery show is Friday. Are you coming?

Me: Of course. I promised.

Meadow: Thank God. You'll officially be the only person I'll know there. That is, of course, unless your parents accept my invitation.

An icy chill gripped me. My parents were going? Oh, sweet Jesus, no. No way they'd come to The City. Hang on. *Dammit, Meadow!* She was trying to get a rise out of me.

Me: Nice try. No way they'd leave the commune. And if they did show up to Faye's show, I'd be heading out to buy some diamond-studded Jimmy Choos, because the end of the world was coming.

Meadow: Fine. Be that way. BTW, your mom got a cell phone. I'm sending you the contact card.

A rectangular icon popped up in the chat. I immediately deleted it.

Me: Good for her. Gotta run. Plans.

Ten minutes later I'd pulled a leather jacket on over my Nirvana T-shirt and laced up some red Converses. I'd almost gone for my yellow plaid Converses, but this seemed like a red shoe night. My phone, ID, and cash were stashed in my pocket as I exited the building to meet my Uber.

Michael's Annex was a warehouse-esque kind of bar. It was going for an industrial look, but the ceilings were low, making it look like the inside of a gnome's hut. Still, it had a certain charm. The bartender was a serious mixologist who replenished the bowls of nuts often.

It wasn't hard to spot the people who were there for the so-called event. A group of about twenty men and woman—considerably more women than men—had clustered five round tables together with chairs lined around the irregular shape. They chatted animatedly, doing their best to be heard over the music pumping out of the speakers.

Most of the women were in skirts and sweaters, while the men were in brown pants with patterned button-up shirts. They looked like a bunch of Lutheran ministers. I looked at my own retro grunge style. I was dripping with nineties angst and they were Stepford June Cleavers. I took a deep breath, pasted a toothy grin onto my face, and sat with them anyway.

"I'm Arielle. Vixen42 on the site," said the woman on my right. She was a redhead in a blue sweater set with a camel-colored skirt. She looked more like a kindergarten teacher than a vixen. I took this as proof that irony wasn't dead. "Which one are you?"

"PricklyPear," I said, trying not to cringe.

"Oh wow! You're practically a legend! Will . . ." She nudged the guy next to her with tiny round glasses and dark brown hair that curled over his shirt collar. ". . . This is PricklyPear!"

He beamed at me while holding out his hand. "Hey! I've read almost all your posts. You have such an amazing way of working her writing into your theories," he said. His hand was dry and warm as I shook it. "I'm WBJ on the site."

"And you give great advice," Arielle added, touching his arm in a flirtatious way.

I was warming up to the idea of meeting these people in real life—Will and Arielle weren't half bad. "Thanks. I've read some of your stuff too. What brought you to the site?"

I could tell I'd asked just the right question by the way Arielle's hazel eyes sparkled. "It was the fight she and Jonathan had at Battaglia's. There was a poster once who wrote that the maître d' said he could tell they were fighting about money, and then all that money shows up in the Caymans. I think she found out he was stealing from her and he was going to leave her. He had to kill her. It was either that or go to jail. My own husband—ex-husband, that is—skimmed a million dollars out of our accounts and was set to leave me with his secretary. You should've seen the murder in his eyes when my lawyers found out and the judge awarded the entire million to me. Believe me, people will kill over money."

Will's eyes were locked onto Arielle and her boob-accentuating sweater. "I think that's the key right there. 'Follow the money,' right? Well, they followed it and it led to Jonathan. What was it? Fourteen million?"

"Eighteen," I corrected. Money was often the motive for murder, and eighteen million dollars was a lot of motive. But there's a big difference between a murderer and a thief. "I can see that," I said. "I was also thinking that if I had eighteen million, I would head for the hills. Go to a country like Morocco or Samoa where I couldn't be extradited. Don't worry about killing anyone, just run for it."

"But then you'd never be able to leave," said Arielle. "You'd have to stay there forever. That could get awfully boring."

True. I knew firsthand what it was like to never be able to leave somewhere. Even a glorious island might feel claustrophobic after a while, like a honey trap for wasps. You don't know you're a goner until you're already stuck.

"I've always wondered how Greer didn't notice that money was missing for so long," Will said. "It was, what, a year and a half? That's a million a month! She was scheduled to see her accountant the week before she died, but the accountant said they never talked about any missing money. They talked about removing her mother as the beneficiary of the trust."

I sat up straighter, focusing in on Will. I'd never read that anywhere before. Not even in the harebrained theories page of the forum. "What paper was that in? Was that in the *Post*? The quote from the accountant?"

Will blushed scarlet. "No, it wasn't in the newspaper. Her accountant's my Uncle Morty. He's in a nursing home outside of Boston now. Alzheimer's. He told me that once when I visited him."

Arielle frowned at him. "But he's losing his memory," she said. "How can you be sure that's true?"

"That's one reason I didn't share it on the website. But he was lucid. I'm almost sure of it. He knew who I was and that the Dodgers suck." Shrugging, Will said, "I believe him."

So Blanche Larkin was about to be removed as the main beneficiary of the trust. "Did he tell you who the new beneficiary was going to be?" I asked. I had leaned in so closely I could identify the brand of beer he was drinking just from the smell of his breath.

Will's eyes dilated as he registered how close our heads were. A flick of his chin and we'd been kissing. "He—he wouldn't say. When I asked if it could've been Jonathan, he got all agitated. Then he went back in time, asking when Aunt

Patty was coming home from Cabo. Aunt Patty's his ex-wife. They'd been divorced for thirty years. His new wife's Linda. They've been married for twenty-nine years. I couldn't ask him any more questions after that."

"But it hadn't happened, right? Blanche still got all the money?" Arielle said.

Will shrugged. "I don't know. I'll try to ask Uncle Morty again, but I'm not driving to Boston until next month. Who knows how reliable he'll be by then."

Well, well, well. How about that? Blanche hadn't mentioned that particular nugget of information. I wonder how she felt about Greer wanting her own mother removed from the trust and a new person getting all of Greer's money. It was disappointing that I wouldn't get confirmation until next month. And Arielle was right. Who knew how much had slipped out of Uncle Morty's brain? I gave Will my number anyway. This was too good to pass up.

"I'm going to get a drink," I told Will and Arielle. "Save my seat?"

They nodded before hunching closer together, away from the space I'd vacated, continuing to talk about their money theory. Arielle moved her hand to rest on Will's knee as she tilted her head so that his mouth was close to her ear.

They were totally going to sleep together, if Arielle had anything to say about it.

The bartender worked his way toward me, wiping the counter with a white towel. "What'll it be?"

"A beer. A Brooklyn Lager," I said, knowing that I was wasting the opportunity to have the best cocktail of my life. But beer was lower in alcohol and I wanted to stay sharp.

"One Brooklyn coming up," he said, popping the top off the beer before handing me the bottle.

I was knocked from behind as I slid a ten over to him, sloshing some of the beer over the clean mahogany bar. "Hey, watch it!" I snarled, turning around to chew out the asshole who'd cheated me out of a sip of my overpriced beer.

Instead, I came millimeters from slamming right into a stick of a woman. Her blue eyes were wide and startled. She was petite like me, so that we were eye-to-eye, but my extra twenty pounds would have let me plow right over her with no problem.

"Sorry," I said, trying to move past her. The bar had gotten more crowded. It was going to be a challenge to get back to my chair.

"I heard you're June? Masterson?" she said, her eyes remaining wide and startled.

"That's true. PricklyPear on the site," I said. I held out my free hand to shake hers, but she didn't take it.

"You can't tell anyone who I am," she said.

I could feel my brow puckering in confusion. "Why not?"

"Because I'm Bethany Allen. Greer's agent."

* * *

"I appreciate your discretion. Some of those people can swarm like piranhas," Bethany said.

"Why were you there if you didn't want to talk to anyone?"

Bethany had asked if we could leave Michael's, and now we were ensconced in a booth at the bar inside the Occidental Hotel. It was quieter, with a Napoleonic vibe that was unsettling in its blood-red velvet plushness. I had been afraid to order a simple beer here. Reading Greer's books had taught me that a place like the Occidental demanded a vodka martini or two fingers of scotch over a gigantic, manly ice cube.

Bethany looked right at home in this world. She was liquid-limbed, with sea blue eyes and honey blonde hair that waved over her shoulder. I was positive her blouse was silk and her charcoal gray skirt was probably Chanel. Her shoes were limited edition Gianvito Rossis that cost twenty-five hundred dollars per shoe. I was in a leather jacket and a Nirvana T-shirt, like someone's black sheep cousin. Bethany had ordered martinis for us, but they didn't help me blend in.

Bethany rolled her eyes, waving away the serious tone behind my question. "I like to keep track of what people are saying about Greer. She may be dead, but I'm still her agent. I manage her work and her image. Fans who actually take the time to meet up in person are the most serious of them. Their opinions are the ones that matter most," she said.

"But you didn't even listen to them? Did you?"

"I heard enough to know that I needed to talk to you. Rachel emailed me, too. And I received your email, so I know this conversation isn't completely unwelcome." She took a sip of her martini, leaning back into the plushness of the booth. "So," she said, giving me a hard, appraising look, "you're doing a film on Greer."

"Specifically on her disappearance," I said. "It's been twenty years, yet it's still unsolved. Jonathan Vanderpoole has been the only suspect the entire time. I'm hoping to explore other suspects." *Like Greer's mother.*

Bethany's sculpted eyebrows jumped to her hairline. "I didn't think there were other suspects."

"You think Jonathan's guilty too?"

She laughed. It was high and golden and delicious.

"No, I don't think he did it. I think she committed suicide."

"Suicide?" I blurted out. The waiter turned to look at us with curious eyes. In a softer voice, I added, "Suicide? What? I mean, how? A body was never found."

Bethany's startled blue eyes looked misty. "The poor girl probably threw herself off the cliff by the lighthouse. She'd been depressed. Battling her own demons. I urged her to get therapy, but she never did."

"So you think Jonathan is innocent?"

Had I found one of the handful of people in the entire world who thought Jonathan Vanderpoole had nothing to do with Greer's death?

"Yes, I do. Is he a total saint?" Her blonde waves bounced like a model in a shampoo commercial as she shook her head. "Not at all. He wasn't a great partner for Greer. The two of them brought out the worst in each other."

"What's the worst?" I was practically salivating into my drink, hoping for more juicy details.

"Look, Greer was a lonely girl at the end of her writing career, with nothing in front of her. At the tender age of twenty-four. Writing was all she knew. She came out of a crippling writer's block to produce *The Girl Who Sang a Tune*, which was, let's face it, a flop. She just didn't have it any more."

"You were going to cut her loose?" I asked.

"Never!" Bethany's wide eyes gaped at me. "I would never lose Greer Larkin to another agent. *Deuteronomy* was a fantastic book. She was on her way back up, but I think she hit another block in her creativity. Another bout of undiagnosed depression, maybe. And that was it. She couldn't face it."

I looked down at my forgotten drink, pondering what Bethany had said. This was going to be amazing in my film.

I had Blanche as a possible other suspect, a theory that Greer committed suicide, and Rachel who vehemently proclaimed Jonathan had killed Greer. All I was missing was Jonathan, and some other supporting documents, but I could find those. I'd call the police officers in Virginia who investigated the case and get them to send me their files. I think the Freedom of Information Act applied. I made a note on my phone to check.

"I'll need to get everything you said on film. What day this week is good for you?"

Bethany's golden laugh peeled around the Baroque arches. "I'm not going to be in your film."

"But you—please? What you told me was amazing. This is an entirely new perspective." I was shamelessly begging and I knew it. Not a good look.

"Why should I do that? Rachel asked me to talk to you, and I have. But I see no benefit to putting my opinions out there for public consumption," Bethany said, taking another sip of her martini.

The gears in my mind clanked into overdrive. I had to get Bethany on video. I racked my brain to come up with a compelling reason, then something came to me. When in doubt, Oberlin Hurst always appealed to the villain's humanity. Bethany wasn't a villain, but I did need to convince her that this was important.

"For twenty years Jonathan's been the only suspect. It's affected his entire life. He's never been able to move on. What if this film—your appearance with your suicide theory— allows him to move out of the cloud of suspicion that he's been living with?"

She scoffed. "Why would I care about him? I barely know the man."

"Because it's the right thing to do? Because if Greer loved him and he really didn't have anything to do with her death, she'd want her friends to help him." Ugh. I did *not* look pretty when I begged, but this was too important for pride and vanity.

Bethany looked down at her drink, tracing the rim with a slender finger, deep in thought. I needed her to go on camera. Desperation made my throat go dry and set my nerves jangling. My hands shook a little as I gulped my martini to help settle me down.

"Fine," she said finally. "I'll do it." She opened her purse, took out her card, and slid it over to me. "Call my assistant, Stella. She'll set up an appointment."

Chapter Nine

～

The people on my commute back to the northern reaches of the city got to enjoy the spectacle of a tattooed girl, with a leather jacket slung over one shoulder, skipping into the subway like a four-year-old in a princess costume. Sure, the martini had cost fifteen dollars—too much for a shot of vodka and one olive—but I had Bethany Allen's card and her promise to sit for an interview. I just had to make sure Stella could fit me in sometime in the next week.

I texted Paul. "Awesome news! Just ran into Bethany Allen, and she has agreed to be in the film!"

Three little dots lit up on my screen, filling me with anticipation.

Paul: Great news. Who is she again?

Me: Greer's agent. She thinks it's suicide.

Paul: Really? That is interesting. We should talk about how that changes the structure of your movie.

Me: Of course. You can also walk me through how to convince a suspected killer he should talk to someone like me.

Paul: That'll be a piece of cake. He'll want to proclaim his innocence from the top of the Chrysler Building.

Me: Hmm. I emailed him and he hasn't emailed back.
Paul: Give him time. Where are you right now?
Me: In the subway going back home.
Paul: Come to my office hours on Tuesday. I need an
    update on your progress. Martha says hi.
Me: Hi to Martha. I will sign up for Tuesday.

I clicked off my phone. My lady parts had been charging up until he mentioned his wife. "Martha says hi" was my signal that she was around or it was unsafe to text. Always a cold splash of water when I read it.

Pushing Paul and his delicious mouth out of my mind, I changed into my pajamas. Part of my evening ritual was emptying my pants of the spare change floating around in them. When you're as poor as I am, you don't even let a nickel slip through your fingers. Tossing my jeans into the laundry, I started scrounging through my jacket pockets. My hand closed around paper. An errant dollar? Or maybe, if I was lucky, a five-dollar bill had appeared. But this felt different. I pulled out a scrap of notebook paper. Had Will slipped me his number? Poor Arielle. She'd had high hopes for her and Will.

But it wasn't Will's number. Scrawled across the paper, in block letters, was a note. The expensive martini in my stomach turned into lead.

The ink was heavy and black, making the block letters seem like they were shouting out at me. My hand trembled as the adrenaline pulsed out into my limbs.

LET SLEEPING MONSTERS LIE.
THIS IS NOT A GAME, LITTLE GIRL.

What in the fuck? Was I being threatened? And how had this gotten into my coat pocket? I searched the pocket again to see if there was anything else in there, like a handy business card with the name and number of my threatener, but didn't find anything else.

My knees began to feel as though they were made out of pudding. I angled for the couch, clumsily plopping myself down, my eyes still riveted on the message. "This is not a game." I was starting to make someone nervous. The trouble was, I didn't know how nervous. Of equal concern was the fact that I couldn't back out now. Two interviews were done. I'd made promises to both Rachel and Blanche that I'd find the truth. I'd been working my entire adult life to figure out what happened to Greer. If I backed out now, I would look like a coward.

I wasn't a coward, dammit.

Carefully flattening out the note, I slid it into the page of my journal. I'd need to work twice as hard. I started to write down all the people who'd been at the bar. Unfortunately, the description of "Lutheran minister" applied to all of them. Maybe if I called the bartender he'd remember who'd bumped into me.

Aaaand maybe not. There'd been tons of people there. I'd been there for less than an hour and ordered one beer. The chances he remembered me were slim to none. I pushed the tremors of fear away. I needed to move on and watch my back.

Maybe it wouldn't be a bad idea to add another lock to my door.

Turning to the next page in my journal I jotted down the information Will shared about the change in trust beneficiary. I'd have to find an independent document to corroborate this, or I'd get sued for slander. Or was it defamation? I'd taken notes on it in one of my classes, but I always got them mixed up. I promised myself I'd look it up later. Using my best pen-manship, I printed Will's name and online moniker too, just in case I needed Uncle Morty to notarize a statement. Would a statement from someone with Alzheimer's hold up in court?

Best not to think about it.

Before the details disappeared from my brain, I wrote down a summary of my conversation with Bethany. Suicide. Jona-than and Greer bringing out the worst in each other. Depres-sion. Writer's block. Once it was captured for posterity, I fired off a request for an interview to Stella, Bethany's assistant. I hoped she'd email back quickly. Bethany didn't sound enthu-siastic about the idea of going on the record. I wondered if she was going to blow me off. Why wouldn't she want to talk? Was she scared of Blanche? Because I couldn't blame her for that. Or were there things about Greer she wanted to hide? How much of an income was she pulling in as an agent of an author who hadn't published in twenty years?

I did a quick search of Bethany's website. She had only four other clients listed. I looked up those four on Amazon. Two-star ratings. That couldn't have been good for sales. One was a cookbook for kangaroo and rabbit called *All That Hops*. Yikes. Did Greer's disappearance have anything to do with Bethany's publishing slump?

After puzzling through Bethany's career, I decided it was impossible to know why having a client disappear mysteriously would affect her ability to attract other authors. Maybe she'd lost her publisher connections. Maybe she'd broken a mirror. Maybe Mercury was in retrograde.

I settled into bed. Before going to sleep I checked my phone one last time for a text from Paul, but there was nothing. My messages and emails were boringly mute.

Tomorrow will be better.

* * *

It wasn't. I spent all day reviewing footage, noting time stamps and quotes that I would need to tell my story. Then I started taping up scene sheets underneath my disappearance time line around the room. Sighing, I resigned myself to repainting the walls when I was finished with my movie. I wondered which store sold "coffee stain white."

My scene sheets would show me the story arc, helping me find any patterns or themes. So far it was just a frustrating jumble of anecdotes and points of view.

My inbox remained disappointingly bare for the morning. Not even an email from Old Navy, who had been my most frequent correspondent since I'd ordered one T-shirt three years before. Jonathan hadn't emailed me back yet, so I decided it was time to step up my game and find any clips or interviews I could use in place of an interview.

God bless the internet. I managed to find clips of his arrests and other visits to the police station in Virginia on YouTube. The clothing was almost comical—so different from the tight lines of today. And Jonathan sported sideburns on his long, lean face. No denying it—he was handsome. His jet black hair was carefully styled, and his gray eyes blazed as he followed his lawyer into the station. If I hadn't already read it on the web, I would've known he'd been a runner just from his frame and gait. Climbing the stairs looked graceful and effortless for him, while his lawyer, a blond man with jug ears, huffed and puffed.

In another clip Jonathan looked haggard. A beard was forming along his jawline, and he had bags under his eyes. His lawyer paused, with Jonathan stopped behind him, waiting as

Jug Ears made a statement proclaiming his innocence. A bar appeared under Jug Ears. His name was Ronald Peterson. A few keystrokes later, the internet coughed up his law practice website and email address. I sent him an email asking for an interview with his client, one Jonathan Vanderpoole. I had no idea if Mr. Peterson still represented Jonathan, but this was at least an attempt to prove that I was legit and not some wacko fame whore.

I clicked on another video. In this one, Jonathan had a microphone stuck into his face, and instead of saying "No comment," as I'm sure Mr. Peterson had told him to say, he actually made a statement. "I am in no way involved in the disappearance of Greer Larkin. I loved Greer. We were going to be married. We were going to have a happy life together. I wish you bastards and the police would stop hounding me. Get out there and start looking for her! Find her!"

Interesting. He sounded certain she was alive, but he also referred to her in the past tense. *Loved. Were.* Was it because he knew she was dead? Or because he knew that their relationship was over? The maître d' at Battaglia's had witnessed them fighting and seen Jonathan slap Greer. I surfed through the internet again looking for the maître d's statement—the same one line in every article. "Greer said something to Jonathan, Jonathan began shouting, they stood up, Greer shouted, 'it's over,' Jonathan slapped her, and she left."

The *Virginia Sentinel* also reported Jonathan had left a five-dollar tip on a two-hundred-dollar meal. It seems we could also add lousy tipper to Jonathan's myriad sins.

I could see how people thought the fight could've been about either their relationship or Jonathan's theft of her money. *It's over.* Two words. If only she'd really gone for it like Angelica

DiMatto when dressing down Chip Taylor in Greer's *The Calling of Oberlin Hurst*. Man! Now, that was a scene to be savored. And it was in no way ambiguous as to its meaning.

When I had exhausted the search engines, I scrounged through my own notes. Had the maître d's official statement to police ever been released? I would love to have that for my movie, but I couldn't find anything more illuminating that what I'd found in the *Sentinel*.

Maybe another GreersGone member would know. I decided to message Arielle and Will. There was a green dot next to Arielle's Vixen42 icon, which indicated she was currently on the site.

> Me: Do either of you know if the maître d's full statement about the fight was released to the media? I can't find it.

Thankfully, only ten minutes elapsed before Vixen42's response popped onto my screen.

> Vixen42: It wasn't released, but if you search his last name—Rossi—you will find that a friend of his niece posted that they had been fighting about the wedding. He seemed to think Greer was getting cold feet.
> Me: Ooo! Thank you! Searching now.

A chime from my phone interrupted me before I could start my search of GreersGone. Was it Paul? My heart skipped a beat, and then sped up when I saw it was Will. Did he have news from Uncle Morty so soon? Or was he replying to my question off-line? I wondered how his evening with Arielle had gone. I smirked remembering her hand creeping up his thigh.

Will: Where'd you go?
Me: I had to run. A friend needed to talk.

Not exactly a lie.

Will: Oh, cool. Hope your friend is okay.
Me: She is. It was fine. Sorry I didn't say goodbye.
Will: It's okay. I hope I see you at the next event. I think that maybe I'll try to see Uncle Morty next weekend to get him to tell us who was going to be the new beneficiary of the trust.

Eeeeeee! I squealed out loud. Looking around, I was grateful there was no one around to hear me.

Me: That would be amazing! And if it isn't too hard on him, can you ask him about the bank account in the Caymans? The one Jonathan set up? Maybe he knows how Jonathan was able to transfer the money without setting off alarms.
Will: Sure! I hope I catch him at the right time. Uncle Morty is a hoot when his brain is right.

A hoot? Who even talks like that anymore? Lutheran ministers, that's who.

Me: Me too. Well, I've gotta run. Nice chatting with you.
Will: See you at the next event.

He ended with a waving smiley-face emoji. I didn't reply. I didn't want to give him hope. Arielle was a nice woman who was probably more his speed. Plus, I was in a relationship. Was it weird that I'm being monogamous in a relationship with a guy who is married? Or was that typical of mistresses?

Hmm. *Mistress.* I didn't like that word. It made me feel like I should be swanning about the apartment wearing silk robes and garter belts. I didn't feel like a mistress. I felt like a girlfriend. It was like Paul's wife didn't exist for me. She was an oppressive, dangerous cloud, but she was *over there*. Not hanging right above me. I never wanted her hanging right above me, because that meant she was going to squash me like a bug. As long as she was *over there*, Paul and I were safe together, and I was his girlfriend.

I missed Paul. I wanted to talk to him. We hadn't been able to really talk lately. We'd both been busy. I missed the way talking to him made me feel. We connected on such a deep level. He was the only other person in New York who knew about my crazy childhood. He could understand because he had weird parents of his own. He also made me feel smart and funny—I was worthwhile when Paul was with me.

It was almost eight, so I picked up my phone to dial him, but before I could scroll to his number, it rang in my hand. The number was a New York area code, but I didn't know it. Could be a scam. Or it might be Bethany. I took my chances and picked up the call.

"Is this June Masterson?"

A man's voice, smooth and melodic. Not quite the baritone of Benedict Cumberbatch, but it had a pleasing, hypnotic resonance. Whatever he was selling, I planned to buy two.

"This is," I said, caution creeping into my tone.

"Jonathan Vanderpoole," he said.

I almost dropped the phone. "Hi," I said, my voice going up three octaves. "You got my email."

"I did. And my lawyer called me to pass on your message. What can I do for you?"

I couldn't tell if he was smiling, but his voice didn't sound angry. It was polite. Even friendly. I took a deep breath and went into my pitch.

"I'd like you to be in my movie," I said. "It's a documentary about Greer Larkin's disappearance."

"Why would I want to do that?" he asked. "I've been questioned by police multiple times. About twice a year an enterprising reporter comes along to ask me about Greer. You make reporter number three. I'm sick of talking about her. No one ever finds out what really happened, and I'm never cleared of any of these bogus charges."

Panic gripped me. He was going to hang up on me, so I just blurted out, "Because this time I might have new information."

"Really?" I could feel him sit up and pay attention.

Sweet Jesus. "It has to do with Greer's trust fund. I can't say more right now, because it's not confirmed, but it does give someone other than you a motive." I really, *really* should not have been telling him this, especially given that Uncle Morty was an unreliable fount of information, but I also needed Jonathan to want to talk to me.

"Someone else? Other than me?"

"Yes. So it would be helpful to talk to you and get your side of the story. On tape."

"If you do get confirmation on this new evidence, what are you going to do with it?" he asked.

"I'm going to turn it over to the police," I said, because that sounded like what a responsible citizen would do. In reality, I had no idea what I would, or could, do with Uncle Morty's statement.

"If I'm going to be in your movie, I want copies of anything you find that proves I'm innocent," he said.

That sounded surprisingly reasonable to me, so I agreed.

"I'm free tomorrow," I added, crossing my fingers.

"Tomorrow," he said, drawing out the word.

I clicked open my calendar. Oops! Office hours with Paul. "Uh, I mean Wednesday. I am free Wednesday. Can we meet at ten?"

"In the morning? Too early. I can meet you at one o'clock. How long is this going to take?"

"About three hours. Maybe four," I said, crossing my toes as well. I didn't want to scare him off.

"That will be fine. Should I bring my lawyer?" he said.

"No!" I yelled. "Uh, I mean, I'm not with the police, so there isn't really a need for—uh—anything like that." I didn't want Jug Ears to keep him from telling me everything. "It's not strictly necessary. Unless you feel you need him to read the waiver."

"I am capable of reading," Jonathan said and sniffed. "Okay. Wednesday. One. My house?"

"Great," I said. He gave me his address and the code to his front door before ending the call without a goodbye.

Hooting with glee, I jumped up onto my couch, doing a vigorous happy dance over the cushions. Jonathan Vanderpoole was going to be in my movie! He was going to tell me what happened that night! I was even going to his apartment to do the video.

My movie was coming together!

* * *

I was still buzzing with excitement the next day when I sauntered down the hall of the Sackman Building to Paul's office. I must have looked particularly joyful, because Dr. Katz, who taught postproduction, gave me an odd look as we met in the hall. His eyebrows climbed when I gave him a cheery smile. I guess I must have Resting Bitch Face most of the time.

Paul's door was open and he was seated behind his desk. He always kept his desk clean of clutter. He said an organized desk created an organized mind. Today, papers were neatly stacked to his right and his laptop was open in front of him. He was squinting at his computer, his brow crinkled with concentration. I hung back, leaning against the doorframe. I couldn't help but wonder what had captured all of his substantial focus. He was so handsome when he was in his creative zone, so deeply into his work that the rest of the world didn't exist. He had that same expression when we were in bed.

He worked without seeing me for another three or four minutes while I watched his long fingers deftly flash across the keyboard. My eyes traveled up to his high cheekbones that I loved to stroke. He had a thin but expressive mouth that could be soft and warm, then urgent, demanding. The memory of his lips against mine kindled heat in my chest.

Then he saw me. Today he wore a navy button-up shirt that made his eyes take on an even deeper blue tone. His lips curled up into an affectionate smile.

"Hi," he said, sitting back in his chair and letting his hands slide off the keyboard. "Come in."

"Hi," I said. "Do you want me to shut the door?"

"We'd better leave it open today," he said with a rueful twist of his lips.

That meant at least one of his neighbors was in. My smile slipped a little at the disappointment, but I shrugged it off and sat in his advisee chair. I laid a flash drive on his desk, letting my fingers linger. Some of our best moments in the past year happened on this desk.

"You look happy today. Everything going well with your project?"

"Yes," I said. "I brought you a flash drive with my edited scenes on it. The raw footage is in the Dropbox if you want to take a look."

"Great! Interviews going well?"

"Yes! Last night Jonathan finally contacted me. He's agreed to be in the film."

"Excellent. Now your film is coming together."

I had to agree. With Jonathan onboard it felt like this movie was actually going to happen. "Yes! He is The Accused, living under the shadow of Greer's disappearance for twenty years. Or maybe he is The Wrongfully Accused? They've never been able to find enough evidence to convict. Jonathan didn't want to do it, but when I told him I might have new information—"

"You have new information?" Paul cut in. "If you found evidence you have to turn it in to the police."

I'd already decided I wasn't going to be telling Paul about the threat that'd been shoved into my pocket. No need to worry Paul, right? Especially since whoever wrote this extremely theatrical and dramatic note clearly didn't know where I lived.

"I don't exactly have it. I met a guy whose uncle was Greer's accountant, and he told me his uncle mentioned that Greer was going to change the beneficiary of her trust." I was breathless with excitement.

Paul leaned across his desk. "Who was it going to be?"

"I don't know. He's got Alzheimer's and has trouble remembering things. But the nephew will ask him again," I said.

"He's positive about the trust thing? I mean, if the guy is losing his marbles, you need to be careful," Paul said.

"He's been consistent in his story," I said, even though I didn't really know that. I needed this to be true. I needed there to be a reason Blanche would kill her daughter and hide the body.

"Well, that's something," Paul said. His eyes flicked up above my head. "Something I can do for you, Pete?"

I turned to see Dr. Katz standing in the doorway. I gave him a little finger-wave and a smile. He returned it with a half-hearted wave of his own and said, "No. It'll wait," before disappearing back down the hall to his office.

I looked at Paul, unsure of what their little exchange was about. He shook his head, stopping the question that had been hovering on my tongue. "Anyway," he said, "where were we?"

"New evidence," I prompted.

"Yes. So, if this does turn out to be true, you'll have to pass this on to the police," he said.

"I promise," I said. And I meant it. Mostly.

"And, Pear Blossom," he said. "When you interview Jonathan, I want you to take a camera operator along."

I recoiled in surprise. "Why? I'm perfectly capable of running the camera and doing the interviews. I did it with Blanche and Rachel. I think you'll see that when you watch my scenes."

"I have no doubt that you're capable. However," he said, leaning forward, his eyes burning and serious, "he is suspected of murdering his fiancée. Yes, I know that we live in a country where you're presumed innocent until proven guilty, but you *will* have someone with you when you march yourself into his home. You will not be alone with him."

His face was deadly serious. His lips were drawn into a hard line as he leaned forward in his chair, in a way that made me afraid that if I said *no* he'd take me over his knee for a spanking.

Not that the image didn't have its charms, but it seemed this wasn't an opportune time. Better to just agree.

"Okay. I'll have someone with me."

"A man," he specified.

"That's rather sexist of you," I said, archly.

"Yes, it is. But this is the world we live in."

"I also have an interview request out to Bethany Allen. Do I need a camera operator for her interview too?" I snarked.

"Possibly. Don't push me."

I stuck my tongue out at him and dismissed myself. Paul promised to watch my scenes and get me an appointment in the studio for the voice-over work, but there was no goodbye hug or covert touches. I left feeling hollow and unsettled in the pit of my stomach. I texted him to check that everything was okay, but my phone remained stubbornly silent throughout the night.

Against my better judgment, I called Dave Zukko the next day. He was the best in the program—second after me, of course. He was also an arrogant, womanizing dick, and I'd rather stick a fork in my eye than ask for his help. But here we were.

"This can't be June Masterson calling me. Because June Masterson would never call me." I'd no idea he even had my phone number, much less had it programmed into his phone. But he must have, because this was how he answered my call.

I almost hung up on the cocky prick. But then I remembered that my other best choice was Joyce Bennet. Not only did she suck at camera work, she could never keep her mouth shut. My only option was to suck it up.

"Mark the day on your calendar because it's never happening again," I said, grumpy.

"So what do you need?" he said. "Because you wouldn't be calling me unless you were desperate."

Agreed. "Paul told me that I need to have another person with me to operate the camera for this interview I'm doing. And I'd like you to do it," I said. When he didn't respond, I gritted my teeth, adding, "Please."

"Why for this interview? What are you doing?" he asked, his voice dripping with curiosity. I hadn't told anyone what my topic was. Mostly because I'd changed it so often, but also because I didn't want anyone stealing my idea. Filmmaking was a cutthroat industry. Kill or be killed.

"Because it's with a guy who's a little shady. Paul is concerned for my safety, so he insisted I take someone along," I said.

"And you picked me?" I could see his incredulous, shit-eating grin in my mind, and I inwardly groaned.

"Yes," I said, my jaw clenched.

"This. Is. Awesome!" The joy in his voice was intolerable. I couldn't go through with this.

"If you can't do it, that's okay." I'd rather go by myself, facing the possibility of being a victim of a grisly murder than put up with his crap for an entire day.

"Oh, no. I wouldn't miss this for anything," he crowed.

Perfect.

I groaned out loud and he barked out a boisterous laugh. "Fine." I gave him the address and told him to meet me at a quarter to one. I didn't trust him to be on time.

"That's the Clarendon. It's pretty ritzy," he said. "Is this guy rich?"

"Probably." Blanche's promise to ruin him notwithstanding. "But you'll be running my camera, only. You won't be talking."

Dave laughed out loud again, so I hung up on him.

This was going to be a complete shit show.

Chapter Ten

❧

At twelve fifty-five, I was outside the swanky Clarendon Building a few blocks off Central Park tapping my foot, waiting for Dave Zukko, and cursing Paul. I refused to be late, dammit. Dave hadn't called me, nor had he picked up my calls. Argh. He was a total and complete jerk.

Screw him! He wasn't going to sabotage me. I started punching in the code to Jonathan's front door when a hand closed over my shoulder. I screamed, flinging my elbow backward in a wide arc. It collided with something hard that crumpled under the force of my blow. A huff of air brushed past my cheek, followed by a male grunt of pain. You don't mess with a chick in New York City.

I turned around, prepared to kick my attacker in the balls, but stopped when I saw Dave.

"For crying out loud," he moaned. "You hit me right in the gut."

"You're lucky I'm not shorter," I said, "or your family jewels would be bruised for a good three months."

"I doubt it. My senior year English teacher always told me I had big brass ones," he said with a cocky grin.

I set my mouth in a thin line. "Let's go. We're late."

"Give me a minute," he whined.

I entered in the code again, snapping, "We don't have a minute."

The giant brown and cream marble foyer felt luxurious. It looked like it belonged in a five-star hotel. Blanche's plan to keep Jonathan poor didn't seem to be going well. A woman in a uniform with her platinum blonde hair neatly pulled back into a bun stood at the concierge desk that commanded the entrance. I walked over to her while Dave hung back. She beamed at me with perfect, bleached teeth.

"How can I help you?" She was perky to the point of nausea.

I bit back a stinging reply, instead pasting on my friendliest smile. "I'm here to see one of your residents. Jonathan Vanderpoole?"

Her cheery smile never wavered, although I had expected to see it at least droop a little bit. He was under suspicion of murder, after all. "Of course. Can I have your name please?"

"June Masterson."

She looked down at the desktop for a minute to study something I couldn't see. Then she looked back up. "Of course. He's expecting you. He lives in Penthouse Suite A. Take the elevator to your left and go straight to the top."

"Thanks," I said.

"This is some kinda place," Dave said, taking it all in. "And this guy is supposed to be scary enough that you needed me to come along? Are you sure you aren't just gloating about hobnobbing with the bigwigs?"

I glared at Dave as we started rising in the elevator. "You can leave if you want."

He grinned at me so that I could see his teeth clear back to his molars. "Oh, I am not missing this for anything," he said.

"Great," I said without enthusiasm.

"What're you interviewing him about, anyway?"

"Murder," I said, as the elevator doors opened and we stepped out into blazing sunlight.

Squinting against the light, I could see that we were in a huge open room. Floor to ceiling windows lined the length of one wall, allowing the sun to flood the room. The white walls and light birch flooring intensified the light bouncing around the room. The furniture was Scandinavian modern— light-colored woods like birch and teak with soft off-white and celadon green fabrics. To our left was a kitchen sporting sleek, creamy cupboards with a solid backsplash in a gray mushroom color, with a cooking island in the same creamy tones. To our right was a long wall that featured—*Oh. My. God.* Was that an original Jackson Pollock?

I walked closer. The painting was a mass of drips and splatters. It was energy and life. Hypnotized by the waves of color, I caught myself reaching out to touch it. My mom would've known the name or number of this piece. She'd been an artist. Of all the homeschooling classes I'd endured, my art education was the most complete. I was almost sorry I wasn't talking to her. She would've loved this. I looked around, nervous to be caught almost touching the priceless painting.

But we seemed to be alone.

"Where is he?" Dave said, seemingly as puzzled at our lack of host as I was.

Unease fluttered through my stomach. I'd expected him to greet us, but there was no one here. "Hello?" I called into the bright stillness. "Mr. Vanderpoole?" When there was no response, I called out, "Jonathan?" as I stepped further into the room.

"Are you sure he knows we're coming?" Dave asked, his voice low.

"Well, the smiley lady downstairs sure knew," I said with more certainty than I felt. I tried again, walking even farther into the great room. "Jonathan? It's June Masterson."

I was rewarded with the snap of a door far off to my right, followed by the padding of feet on the wood floor. Jonathan came walking past the Pollock, barefoot, wearing tan chino pants with a casually rumpled blue shirt, the sleeves rolled up to reveal muscular forearms. According to my records, he was supposed to be fifty-five years old, just ten years older than Paul, but where Paul's blond hair was beginning to be streaked with gray, Jonathan's was still black. His face had character, but didn't seem old. Not how I pictured a man who'd spent the last twenty years weighed down by a cloud of suspicion.

"Sorry. I was just finishing up a business call." He stuck out his hand to me and gave us a warm smile. "Jonathan Vanderpoole."

"Good to meet you," I said. "This is my camera guy, Dave. He won't be talking," I turned to give Dave a pointed look. He winked at me, so I added, "At all." I turned back to Jonathan with a please-like-me smile. "Is there somewhere you'd like to be filmed?"

"How about in front of the skyline?" he said, gesturing to the windows bursting with light.

"It'd have to be somewhere without light behind you, which will make you look like one of those people trying to hide their identity. Ideally, we'd like the light highlighting your face."

Jonathan looked perplexed for a minute. "So, not the skyline."

"No," I said. "Do you have somewhere else?"

Jonathan looked around his apartment trying to find a spot that didn't have the sun coming from behind him. As he pivoted, Dave spoke up from behind me. "How about in front of your painting?"

Jonathan gave the artwork a critical look. "Yes," he said, slowly. "I think that might work. It will need some adjustments, though."

Fifteen minutes of huffing and grunting later, Dave and I had the sofa and coffee table pushed over to sit in front of the painting. We'd tried the armchair there first, but Jonathan didn't think it looked balanced considering how large the painting was. Then we tried a settee with an end table. That was no good. I hoped the sofa worked for him.

"How's this?" I asked, praying it met his requirements. I didn't have the energy to cater to a *prima donna*.

"I think so." He cocked his head, squinting at the arrangement. "Yes," he said finally, "let's try this."

I heaved a sigh of relief. "Dave, can you get the camera set?"

"Sure, *boss*," he said, with an especially obnoxious emphasis on the word boss.

I cut him a look that said "Fuck right off," before turning back to Jonathan.

"I'm going to be asking you a lot of questions about Greer—about the timeline of her disappearance, about her behavior, and about your behavior. If I ask anything you don't like, just tell me. I'll be editing this, and I can remove sections of our conversation. Please remember, this is your chance to tell people what happened and why you had nothing to do with Greer's vanishing. The more you tell me, the better you're going to look."

He nodded like a schoolboy whose teacher was prepping him for a major test. "No problem. I have nothing to hide, since I didn't do anything wrong."

Dave gave me a thumbs up and I turned to Jonathan. "Ready?"

He sat on the couch, slung one arm over the back of it, and crossed his legs, setting his ankle on top of his knee. "Ready."

"Great." I hoped I was ready. *No pressure.* I nodded to Dave. He switched on the camera, then winked at me again. I glowered at him as I asked my first question.

"Tell me about the Greer Larkin you knew."

"I was Greer's guardian angel, and whoever says different is a lying bitch."

* * *

Jonathan had charisma that flooded the camera lens. He'd missed his calling as a television personality, that's for sure. His voice was a relaxed purr coming out of my speakers. I moved the film forward a few frames, until I got to the part I wanted. Jonathan was leaning forward a little, saying, "Greer Larkin had a dark side. Unsurprising for a person who wrote mysteries, I guess, but it was deeply dark. And that darkness? Well, it came from her childhood. It came from her mother."

The darkness quote from Jonathan would make a great contrast to the segments from Rachel and Blanche I was using to introduce Greer. Rachel had called her "Kind and gentle. A true friend." Her mother had said Greer was "Smart as a whip. Gifted. Giving and loving. She always donated money to a scholarship fund for children who were exceptional writers."

Light and dark. Plus, Jonathan was not so subtly blaming Blanche for whatever darkness lay inside Greer. I'd seen a glimmer of anger during her interview, but only when she talked about Jonathan. I thought of the petite, elegant woman surrounded by opulence, with who knew how many resources at her disposal. There was danger there, but how dark could Blanche be?

I zoomed forward again.

"Greer had a difficult childhood," Jonathan said. "It was the 'poor little rich girl' syndrome—a mother too busy with her wealth to be there for her. No father at all, but she had all the nannies, plus the best help money could buy. She resented it. Didn't anyone ever wonder why a twelve-year-old girl was writing grisly murder scenes? That isn't normal."

He had a point. No one batted an eye when preteen Greer Larkin had presented her mother with a short story about a man who pushes his mother down the stairs so he can inherit the family fortune, but is brought to justice by his fifteen-year-old niece. How did a little girl like that start writing about the sickening crack a broken neck makes as a body bounced down the stairs? There was more darkness in Blanche's house than I thought.

"But Greer had a gift. And as soon as her mother realized her gift could make millions, she stopped being too busy with her charities and properties and began managing Greer's life. Greer had to write as soon as she got up. She couldn't set foot outside until she had at least fifteen hundred words on the page. Her mother pulled her out of boarding school and got her tutors, so that meant no distractions and no friends. Except for Rachel, but that's because Rachel's dad was in the publishing business. But no one else was permitted inside Greer's life. Mommy Dearest made sure of that."

A vision of Greer looking longingly out her bedroom window at the people passing by on the street filled my imagination.

I could imagine the anguish she must have felt seeing kids skipping down to the park while she was locked in her room until she'd met her word quota. She must have felt desperate to get out. I could relate.

I'd been boiling with envy watching Meadow and Sage pull out of the yard to go into town. Meadow had always claimed it was boring. They'd had to stay at their booth at the farmers market in order to sell the vegetables we'd picked that day. But I knew she was lying. Sage would be talking a mile a minute about the chickens and geese being sold, the dogs that came by, and the free samples the bakers would give him and Meadow. After he'd told me about the wagon of puppies for sale that a family had been pulling around the market, I knew that I had to go and see what town was all about.

That was the first night I'd sneaked out. It was everything I'd longed for and more, even with most of the stores closed. I hoped Greer had gotten that chance. The whole scenario left a bitter taste in my mouth. I could see why she'd jumped into Jonathan's arms and away from Blanche.

Then I forwarded to a third clip I knew I wanted for sure, about the fight in the restaurant that ended in the infamous slap. Juicy drama for sure.

"That was simply a misunderstanding. She thought I'd had too much to drink, which I hadn't. Greer told me once we'd finished the bottle of wine we were done, but I'd planned on having a celebratory glass of champagne with Greer to finish out our meal. She didn't want to. I tried to explain my feelings, but she overreacted—nerves about the wedding—and before I knew it I'd lost my temper. I apologized when we got home and we were fine. We had a nightcap and went off to bed."

Jonathan shrugged like it was just another typical day. Nothing to see here, folks.

I wasn't sure. His answer felt like it came too easy, like it was scripted. Is that what happened when you had to tell the same story over and over to the police? But this was twenty years later. Were there any changes from his police statement? I made a note: *Get Jonathan's police statement.*

Near the end of our three-hour interview was the last clip I knew I needed. I had to scroll quite a ways. Finally it was there, the toss of his head in laughter. I rewound and started from just before.

"What do I think about Rachel?" He threw his head back, giving a high, wild laugh that didn't sound right coming from his mouth. "Rachel is a sad, sad person. Frankly, I wouldn't be surprised if she's the one who killed her, if Greer is really dead. Rachel loved Greer. And not in a friends-only kind of way. She *loved* her. She always had. But Greer didn't feel the same way. She was totally hetero, you know? Plus, she loved me. A bizarre little love triangle, don't you think?"

Love triangle? Rachel? In love with Greer? What in the actual fuck? Rachel hadn't mentioned anything about having feelings for Greer, and I hadn't gotten a whiff of anything other than a protective sisterly vibe. But this wouldn't be the first time I'd been lied to. It wasn't even the millionth. My parents had been lying to me my whole life.

"Rachel was even stalking Greer. About a year before Greer went missing, she finally had had enough and got a restraining order against Rachel. It was just after Rachel had followed us to a club. I caught her trying to drag Greer to a taxi. Greer slapped her, and the next day we went to a judge to get the order. Rachel had to stay one hundred feet away from Greer from then on."

"Did she?" I asked.

"Stay away?" he said. He considered the question, his finger tapping his handsome pursed lips. "For the most part. There were some moments she had to be around. She worked at the publishing house that put out Greer's books. If Greer had to go to the publisher's offices, Rachel would be there. I went along to make sure there were no problems. I couldn't really afford to. My nightclub needed me to be more hands-on. Rachel is why my club failed. Greer needed me to protect her, and that was more important. Her work was always more important than mine."

Then his face, which had been relaxed and friendly all day, went stony, and anger flashed in his eyes. "Greer needed me, so I put everything aside to give her what she needed. I sacrificed everything for her. And what's the thanks I get? I'm accused of hurting her. I'd never hurt Greer. She was my whole life. Why can't anyone see that I was hurt too?"

Chapter Eleven

It wasn't until later that I realized I'd made a huge mistake. I'd forgotten to ask about the money.

It was moronic of me to miss the chance to get Jonathan's explanation for *the* major motive against him in the case. But he'd held up Blanche's and Rachel's motives like delicious cupcakes, and I had lunged for them like some kind of toddler. I could've kicked myself.

He'd sounded so sincere in his love. He'd given all his time to Greer's well-being and career. I'd been so overwhelmed by the special love that fostered such sacrifice, I'd forgotten he was suspected of embezzling millions of dollars from Greer and was, therefore, the best suspect of the lot. How embarrassing to make such a rookie mistake. Worse, I'd have to admit to the awful Dave Zukko that I'd fucked up, and I wasn't about to do that.

I needed to redeem myself.

My mind flipped back to Lutheran minister Will and his Uncle Morty. Uncle Morty was essential to this case, and no one else had spoken to him that I'd heard. He could be the link that breaks things wide open! It would give me the big score I needed that would distract Paul from my blunder.

I hopped onto GreersGone and messaged Will.

Me: I need to see Uncle Morty. Would it be okay if I visited him?

His dot wasn't green, telling me he wasn't online, so I'd wait for who knew how long. I couldn't afford to pace my apartment in nervous contemplation or sit refreshing my message box like some kind of psychopath. Instead, I decided to dig into the meat of Rachel's interview and start getting some of her interview clips mixed with Blanche's to begin my— Greer's—story arc.

I was so deep into The Zone, I didn't hear it when my message window chimed at me. It wasn't until I stopped to warm up my long-forgotten coffee that I noticed the message blinking.

Will: I don't know. He's old and gets confused easily. You want to talk to him about money, right?

Me: I do. Can I tell you a secret? And you promise not to tell anyone?

Will: Yes! I swear I won't say a word.

Me: I'm filming a documentary about Greer's disappearance. I think your uncle could be really important. I'd like to film him before the Alzheimer's erases everything.

Will: Holy cats! That is seriously cool! Yes, I will let you talk to Uncle Morty, but I need to be there with you.

Me: Great. Give me his address and I'll meet you there. Tomorrow at 10:00 AM?

Will: Perfect!

Now, I could have asked him for a ride or offered to carpool, but I didn't want to be in a car for that long with a guy

I didn't know. Sure, I'd fought to interview a suspected murderer alone in his apartment, but I was reluctant to hitch a ride with a guy who literally used "holy cats" as an expletive and dressed in loafers and earth tones. I read Greer's books. I knew there was a fine line between "genuine nice guy" and "no one ever suspected him of being a serial killer." I wasn't sure which side of the line Will was on.

The address he'd given me was in Roslindale, Massachusetts. Googling it, I found it was a very southern suburb of Boston. I'd have to get up early, which was practically against my religion, but this was for Greer. Sacrifices needed to be made.

I booked the tickets and laid out my best jeans, cleanest T-shirt, and a pair of green canvas Cariuma sneakers, then set my alarm for three in the morning. I spent the rest of my day writing interview questions for Uncle Morty. With Alzheimer's you never knew what version of the person you were going to get. I made the questions open-ended and decided to allow him to wander through his recollections of Greer, hopefully guiding him to the day when Greer had come in asking him remove her mother as the beneficiary of her trust.

Still blinking the sleep out of my eyes and on my third cup of coffee, I departed for the train that whisked me away to Boston. The subway jostled me into alertness, and by the time I hit the front door of Uncle Morty's nursing home at 9:55 AM, I was ready for action.

Will must've been excited about his uncle being featured in a movie, because he was standing by the nurses' station holding a box of chocolates. Lord, I hope he didn't think this was a date. Still, it wouldn't have been the weirdest date I'd been on. When he saw me, he gave me a big wave.

"Hey, there! You found it!"

The home hadn't been hard to find. It was the only building in an oasis of green space amid Boston's urban sprawl. "I did," I said, matching his enthusiasm. "How about we go and meet Uncle Morty?"

Uncle Morty lived in what looked like a fancy college dorm room with a small kitchenette and a bathroom. The walls were a soothing sky blue and the furnishings were white. Pictures of family members covered the walls, each with a label under the picture giving the name of the person and the year the picture was taken. Memory aids.

Uncle Morty sat in a navy blue BarcaLounger wearing gray sweatpants and a World's Greatest Grandpa T-shirt. His face lit up when we entered the room. "Now isn't this a surprise! You didn't tell me you were coming."

Will blushed. "I did call, but it was late yesterday. I brought you chocolates."

Uncle Morty took the white box from Will's hand. "Ooo! I love chocolates!" He looked at me. "Hello, pretty lady. Am I supposed to know you? Sometimes my memory isn't so good anymore."

I felt a little sad. Here was a perfectly nice man, excited to see his nephew, and he knew that his memories were slipping away from him. But he didn't seem to let that get him down because he beamed at me like I was his favorite person in the world.

I stuck out my hand. "No. We've never met. I'm June, a friend of Will's. I'm here to meet you."

"Well, Will, your taste level has certainly gone up." He gave my hand a tight squeeze and winked. "If he hasn't asked you out on a date yet, put me on the list above him."

"Uncle Morty!" Will laughed. "June is a friend. She is making a movie about Greer Larkin and we're here to ask you some questions."

"You want me to be in a movie?" Morty looked doubtful.

"I sure do," I said, with as much enthusiasm as a car salesman.

"I don't remember so good sometimes. Today I'm doing pretty good. I knew Will without having to ask. You threw me for a loop. I have to admit I was pretty relieved to hear I wasn't supposed to know you."

"Well, let's give it a shot. I won't use anything that is embarrassing to you, and I'll leave if it gets too much."

"Let's do it. I always felt bad about Greer. Nice girl. Always sent me chocolates for my birthday. Say! Do you want a chocolate?"

"I could go for a piece," I said, smiling.

Uncle Morty was hard not to like. His enthusiasm for everything drifted around him like perfume. I could feel my own mood lift with every breath I took.

He struggled a bit with the plastic wrapping, so Will helped him strip it off. Then he opened the lid and took a big sniff. "Ah! I love the smell of chocolate. When I was a kid we only got chocolate at Christmas. The smell still reminds me of my mom and dad and the crunch of snow under my feet." He held the box out to me. "Ladies first."

I took a small dark chocolate dome and popped it in my mouth.

"What kind was it?" he asked, eyes bright.

"Raspberry cream," I said. "It's really good."

Uncle Morty took the one in the center and groaned in delight as his teeth bit through. "Maple! That really is Christmas. Will?" he asked, holding the box out to him.

"No, thanks. I brought those for you."

"Suit yourself. You don't know what you're missing." As he fumbled with the lid, I saw him flick a chocolate with his thumb into the palm of his hand. As he turned to put the box on the table next to him, he slyly popped the chocolate in his mouth. Uncle Morty had just palmed out a chocolate from his own box. Pretty slick moves for a guy in his eighties.

He caught my awed look and gave me a wink. I winked back. Uncle Morty was *cool*. I couldn't wait to get him on film.

"Can you give me your name and what your job was, for the camera?"

"My name is Mortimer Bartholomew Collins and I was Greer Larkin's accountant."

"How long were you Greer's accountant?"

Morty thought for a minute and I got nervous that might be a memory that had slipped away. "She came to me in 1993, just after she'd turned nineteen. She wanted me to start paying her bills and keeping track of her royalties and the like." *Whew.* Sharp answer, full of details. Uncle Morty was having a good day.

"How did she know about you? How did she find you?"

"I guess she asked around. I was the accountant for a lot of authors, so I know about publishing money. You wouldn't believe the kind of money some of these people were getting for advances back then. High five figures and into mid-six-figure territory. And then it rushed back out again, just like the tide. Oh, some were frugal—used it for living expenses and to fund their next book. Some of them used it for champagne and caviar. All I could do was shake my head."

I could only imagine what Morty had seen.

"What was Greer spending her money on?"

"Well, she had a special situation. Some of her money went into a trust she and her mom controlled, and some of it she could spend all on her own. The trust was put in place by a grandparent, and her mom insisted a third of her money kept going into that trust. But a lot of her money just went rushing back out again. I had bills from her condo, art galleries, hotels, booze, food. She was a party girl. Not a bad girl, though. She was young and having fun."

"So she sent you her bills?"

"Some. The places she went more often knew to bill me directly. She wasn't in any trouble, though. The trust paid for the condo and a basic living allowance, but she blew through that in about a week. The other three weeks were from the movie and book royalties. She was fine until she stopped writing. Then the trouble started to happen. For, like, four years? No advances. The royalties went down. No movie contracts. I was getting nervous. I started calling her, but that guy of hers—what was his name?—he gets all angry. Tells me to just fix it. But how can I fix it? I'm not putting my own money up for her. I got my own family to feed. Patty didn't like it."

Will broke in. "It was Linda, Uncle Morty. Linda was your wife then."

Morty waved off Will's correction. "Yeah. *Linda*. She didn't like it at all. Wanted me to fire them, but how could I fire them? Greer was a good girl. She'd just gotten caught up in the high life of her success. She'd level out pretty soon. And she did! A new book came out and she was fine again. All the bills paid. That was when I moved my offices to Highland Street."

Will cleared his throat. "Uh, Uncle Morty? You moved your offices to Highland Street in 1985. You were already there in the nineties."

Morty's brow puckered and he went quiet for a second. "Oh? Okay. That's right. Before Highland I had been on Oakmont."

"Oakdale," Will corrected.

Morty waved him off, annoyed. "Right. That's what I said. Anyway—"

I needed to get this interview back on track. Will's corrections were throwing Morty off. "What did you think of Greer's mother, Blanche Larkin?"

Morty's face lit up. "That woman was a firecracker, and make no mistake, she said what she meant and she meant what she said. I would've liked to make her my third wife."

Will snorted. The nurses must've had to watch Uncle Morty like hawks. I never knew my grandparents since they died before I was born, but I hoped they were like Morty. "I've heard that Greer came to you about removing her mother's name as the beneficiary of the trust. Do you remember that day?"

Morty shook his head. "I don't remember her wanting Blanche's name off the trust."

Will gasped. "But that's what you told me!" Will was going to have to shut up or I was kicking him out of the room. It'd take me hours to edit out all his interruptions.

Morty snorted. "I told you she was having some troubles with her mom and didn't want me to take orders from her anymore. She was turning twenty-five soon anyway and about to get married. Her husband would've become the main beneficiary automatically."

"So Greer was happy to leave her mom's name on the trust?" I asked before Will could indignantly correct Morty again.

Morty looked at me blankly. "Whose name?"

"Blanche Larkin's name. On the trust." *Come on, Uncle Morty. Keep it together.*

He scratched his head. "I'm not sure she was happy about it or not. It was just a waiting game. I do remember that Greer wanted me to run every transaction through her. She didn't want me to just pay the bills like I had been. She was actually starting to grow up and pay attention. I was impressed."

Me too. And what had she seen? Who in her life was she doubting? "Do you remember why the change?"

"I think she'd been having trouble. The . . . uh . . . advances. There were problems. I can't remember for sure."

Uncle Morty started fidgeting in his chair, agitated. I jumped in to soothe him. "It's okay. I have a few more questions. Can you tell me about the money in the Caymans?"

Another blank look. "What money in the Caymans?"

Okay, we just need to fill in a blank or two and he'll remember. "Eighteen million of Greer's money had been moved from her accounts into an account in the Caymans in the name of Jonathan Vanderpoole. One million a month for eighteen months. Do you know how that happened?"

Uncle Morty looked at Will. "I'm . . . not sure . . . The Caymans? Where are they? Is that in Boston?"

"They're a group of islands in the Caribbean. You used to set up accounts for people there from time to time," Will said.

Uncle Morty looked back to me, his expression dazed. "Did I? I don't remember that. I went there once with Patty. Or was it Linda? And you say I put some of Greer's money there?"

I tried to shift him to something he might remember before this interview could spiral out of control. "Did Jonathan ever ask you to give him some of Greer's money?"

It worked. His eyes snapped back into focus. "I wouldn't give it to him. I may not remember about some islands, but I do remember him. I did not like him. Came in demanding that I give him fifty thousand dollars. He wasn't on Greer's accounts and so I wouldn't give him money. Called me a wimp. I was in 'Nam, motherfucker. I'll show you who's a wimp! Gave him a black eye. Proudest day of my life."

"Holy shit," I said.

"Holy shit," Will said.

"Fuckin' a!" Uncle Morty said, pounding his fist on the arm of the chair.

I was mentally celebrating having Uncle Morty in my movie when he leaned forward and grabbed my wrist in a vise-like grip. "Ow! That's my arm!" I yelped.

"Greer! Don't go back to him. He's not worth it. Just leave!" His blue eyes blazed with anger and his teeth were bared.

Will crouched down next to him, and said, "This isn't Greer, Uncle Morty. This is June. My friend June."

Uncle Morty clamped down harder on my wrist. "Greer, I'm telling you. They're no good for you. They want too much. You've got to get out!"

He wasn't angry, he was scared. Scared for Greer. "I will. I promise."

"Uncle Morty!" Will bellowed, trying to peel his uncle's hand from my wrist.

"Promise!"

"I won't go back!"

Relief relaxed his face and then he let go and collapsed back in his chair, his eyes closed. "Good, good." Opening his eyes, he looked around at us, like nothing had happened. "Where were we?"

My brain reeled around like a Tilt-a-Whirl. "Uh. The money in the Caymans. You didn't put the money in for Jonathan."

"I don't remember. My memory isn't so good anymore."

I steadied my voice. "If you didn't put that money into an account for him, who do you think did?"

Uncle Morty folded his arms across his chest. "I don't think that's any of your business, little lady."

"But, Uncle Morty—" I began.

He wagged a finger at me. "A nice girl like you shouldn't be involving yourself in a dirty business like this."

"Is this a dirty business?"

"Oh, yes. This is a very dirty business indeed."

Chapter Twelve

Uncle Morty wouldn't say much after that. He'd gotten more and more confused as the interview went on until I decided to put us all out of our misery and shut it down. He asked me who I was again and if I was dating Will. When I said no, he asked me to put his name on the list. Again. He was still charming, but this time his enthusiasm for life left me a little sad. In a shockingly short amount of time, Uncle Morty would be nothing more than a shell of his former self. It wasn't fair.

But Uncle Morty had been worried for Greer. Worried that some "they" would harm her. They implied more than one person. So Jonathan *and* Rachel? Sure. If hell had suddenly frozen over. Equally unlikely would be Jonathan and Blanche working together. Rachel and Blanche? More likely. Even possible. If Meadow were in a bad situation, I'd for sure work with her parents to save her. We'd move heaven and earth for Meadow. How far would Blanche and Rachel go?

Will had been a perfect gentleman. He drove me back to the train station and gave me a hug goodbye. I'd felt as bad for him as I had for Uncle Morty. But I was grateful to have met the old geezer and had the fleeting thought that I might be able to call Will a friend.

That evening on the train I turned on my phone and found I had a string of texts from Paul. They contained a variety of words and phrases, but all of them boiled down to: *call me.*

I hadn't thought of Paul for the entire day. That never happened. I thought about him constantly. But today . . . nothing.

Searching for Greer had taken over my life. I missed him, missed us. When we were together I felt like the only person in the world. I mattered. I didn't feel like some kid who had been raised by loony parents on a God-forsaken commune in the middle of the woods on the side of a mountain.

Paul had also felt isolated as a child. He'd been raised on a farm in Kansas. He'd stuck out like a sore thumb when he moved to New York to try to make something of himself at Columbia Film School. He knew what it was like to fake your way through the appreciation of pop culture references.

My first day at film school had been an orientation meet and greet. I'd been surrounded by people talking about Captain America and Iron Man. I'd never seen those movies. I'd barely read the comics. I felt stupid. I didn't belong at a film school. I thought I'd be okay when I heard someone discussing *The Handmaid's Tale.* I'd read the book and really liked it. But they'd been talking about the television series, which differed from the book enough to expose me as never having seen it.

It's not like I'd never seen a movie. I had been to college, after all. But I hadn't been watching the same movies as these people. Meadow and I had sneaked into movies all the time, but it was late at night. I remember my first. It'd been a two-dollar showing of *Star Wars.* I still got shivers thinking about it. The music. The story. The effects. The actors. All of it perfect. I felt just like Luke, burdened with a family who wanted to keep me where I was—stuck in an unhappy and boring life. I could be so much more than just a farm girl running through the woods. I needed to escape. For months I waited for my Jedi mentor to rescue me, but no one ever came.

After that, I made Meadow sneak out with me to the two-dollar movies whenever they were showing. But those movies were old classics like *Casablanca* and *The Wizard of Oz*, not modern films. They only showed those at night—after ten. Meadow had been allowed to go into town from time to time. She'd come home to tell me which movies were playing. She also started to bring me back entertainment magazines. It was from reading one of these that I learned there were people who did this for a living—made movies and told stories. And they *got paid for it.*

It was a quirk of fate that I ended up doing documentaries. My parents did their best to homeschool me, but I missed out on a lot of historic events and important people. It was a short film about the life of Genghis Khan in my History 101 class at college that inspired me to switch from entertainment to documentaries. It turned out I liked telling true stories.

Paul's childhood wasn't too different. He had also been raised by quirky parents. Like me, college had been his escape.

It had been Paul who'd saved me from the *Handmaid's Tale* discussion. The most handsome professor in the program asked me questions about the book, while steering me toward a quiet alcove so I could pull myself together. I looked into those deep blue eyes—bluer than any others I'd ever seen—and lost myself.

Two years later when we'd picked our thesis project advisors, I made it my mission to be paired with him. It turns out he'd been as obsessed with me as I had been with him. Sometimes I kicked myself for not being bolder when we'd first met. We could've had three years together instead of just one.

I called Paul. "What's up?"

"Where have you been?" He sounded pissed and it took me off guard. "You missed office hours. You don't pick up your phone. I've been worried sick."

"Sorry! I was in Boston."

"You didn't mention that to me. What where you doing up there?" He was calming down, but his words still had a sharp edge to them.

"Interviewing Greer's accountant. He was giving me information on the trust fund and the account in the Caymans."

"And? Did he know anything?"

"He's got Alzheimer's, so sometimes he did and sometimes he didn't."

"Lord. You wasted your time on an accountant with Alzheimer's?"

"It wasn't a waste," I said, defensive and stung. "He had a lot to say. He hated Jonathan, for one thing. For another they were spending a lot of money really quickly. He also said this was a dirty business for such a nice girl."

I didn't tell Paul that there had been a moment when Uncle Morty had thought I was Greer. I didn't tell him about the fear in Uncle Morty's eyes or how his voice trembled as he begged Greer to leave Jonathan.

"Well, he's not wrong. Are you coming home now?"

"I'm on the train as we speak."

"Great. Text me when you get home."

"Promise."

Uncle Morty had been afraid for Greer's life. Yet she'd stayed. Was that because she loved Jonathan? What did she see that others didn't?

Love was funny. It could make the sanest of people do the most insane things. I'd never have let any of my other boyfriends push me under the bed and then stay there while he fucked someone else. But Paul was different. I loved him. If I didn't love Paul, I wouldn't be following all these rules to protect him. If I didn't love Paul, it wouldn't hurt so much when we were apart. Right?

What would I do for Paul? Kill for him? Jonathan said he loved Greer. He also said Rachel loved Greer. Then there was Blanche. Agatha Christie once said, "A mother's love for her child is like nothing else in the world. It knows no law, no pity, it dares all things and crushes down remorselessly all that stands in its path." Blanche was definitely capable of crushing people without pity or remorse. How far had that love pushed them—any of them? To what lengths would they have gone to keep Greer for themselves?

Could Jonathan or Rachel have killed Greer in a fit of passion? Or perhaps Rachel had met Greer in the early morning at the lighthouse, as the sun was just lighting the sky. Perhaps Rachel, knowing the wedding was coming, begged Greer to leave Jonathan—to choose her. Maybe Greer said no. Maybe Greer said more than no. Maybe she'd been mean and cruel. Rachel could've snapped. It wouldn't have taken much. A shove. A well-timed hit. Then it was just a matter of pushing Greer over the edge of the cliff and into the water.

I pictured myself and Martha meeting at that lighthouse. Would I push Martha into the water? Could I have hit her in the head with a rock, just to win the man I loved?

No.

At least I didn't think so.

What would people do for love?

I texted Paul.

Me: I'm home.

Me: What would you do for love?

Paul: Interesting question. Have you been drinking?

Me: I am stone-cold sober. Running a thought experiment about Greer. Could unrequited love drive someone to kill?

Paul: It would depend, I think, on the person and who they are inside.

Me: Rachel was in love with Greer, according to Jonathan. Would the idea of Greer getting married spur her into making a declaration? And would being rejected drive her over the edge?

Paul: That's hard to know. Anything is possible, though, if she was desperate enough.

Me: What would you do if I started to see someone else?

Paul: Am I going to have to kill Dave?

Me: lol. No. Just a hypothetical question. Thought experiment, remember?

Paul: lol. Well, I wouldn't like it. At all.

Me: You wouldn't?

Paul: You are my world. I don't know what I would do without you.

Paul: I need you. Can I see you tonight?

Me: Yes.

Paul: I'll be over in twenty.

* * *

You know that euphoric feeling when the guy you love the best in the world not only rocks you to an orgasm that rips a scream from your throat so loud your voice is raspy afterward, he also takes you out for dinner at a legit nice restaurant? I highly recommend it. It's better than Disneyland.

The tablecloths and napkins were real linen. There were glass wineglasses on the table—for water and for both red and white wine—and three forks and two spoons. And candles! And ferns! I bet the chef spoke with a French accent.

My one good outfit was a little wrinkled from its recent unprecedented usage. It had gone from being crammed into the back of my closet to being the belle of the ball. Even wearing the nicest thing I had, I felt underdressed. That wasn't quite true, I felt . . . inelegant. The other ladies were all in dresses or pantsuits with flowy trousers and artistic tops. I was just in pants and a sweater.

I felt out of place and awkward, just as I had at that first departmental meet and greet. But it was amazing to see how some people could live. The precision of the waiters. The jewels that hung from women's ears. The effortless grace of the men. It all reeked of wealth, which was an unfamiliar smell.

Paul was in a navy suit with a lighter blue paisley patterned shirt open at the collar, looking at me like I was the most beautiful girl in the world. My worries about not being dressed right started to fade as I smiled back at him.

Or, more likely, beamed like an idiot.

The menu in front of me was completely in French. I did not speak French other than *merci*.

"I should bring Meadow here next week for dinner. It's really expensive, though," I said.

"You still have dinner with your cousin?" Paul said.

I nodded. "About once a month. Sometimes less than, sometimes more. It depends on our schedules. The woman she is dating is having an art show next week. I was going to go."

"I thought you were cutting your family off completely?" he said.

"Meadow is different. She worries about me." *She especially worries about how I'm in a relationship with a married man.*

"Sometimes you just have to move forward. You've always told me how much you hated how controlling your parents were and how isolated you felt. You can be a totally different person now. You don't have to be that girl from the commune anymore," he said.

"I don't think I am. It's just, well, Meadow understands how difficult it is to be here, out with people in the real world."

Paul reached over and stroked my hand before raising it to kiss my palm. "Welcome to the real world, Pear Blossom. You can have anything you want from the menu. Just enjoy yourself."

"Maybe you should order for us?" I said. "I don't know anything about French food."

Paul laughed. "What kind of meat do you feel like having? Fish? Beef? Chicken?"

"Beef sounds good," I said. I had developed a taste for beef after leaving home. My parents were hard-core vegetarian. I was decidedly not. And if I was going to eat anything fancy it was going to be beef, since that was always out of my budget.

"Okay. There are a couple of good choices here," he said. The waiter approached and Paul rattled off our entree choices with a few other things I couldn't understand. "You're going to love it. I—" Paul's voice choked off and his face went pale. His eyes bulged as he started sputtering. Finally he croaked out, "Jesus. She's here."

"Who's here?" I asked, turning in my chair.

Paul grabbed my arm where Uncle Morty had gotten me in his vise-like grip earlier, making me wince. "Don't turn around to look! Martha just walked in. She's with some of her colleagues. I think she might be taking a client out."

I gasped, turning anyway. If I was going to take a bullet, I wanted to know what direction it was coming from. There she was. Dressed in a suit that was probably tailor-made for her hourglass figure. It was black (like a lawyer's soul) with a white silk blouse that V-necked down, revealing creamy pale skin. She wore a pearl rope necklace and matching earrings. They probably cost more than my education thus far.

"I told you not to look," Paul hissed.

I whipped my head back around, my own eyes now wide and bulging. "What do we do?" It came out high-pitched and squeaky, like a panicking mouse about to be caught by the cat. "Maybe she won't see us?"

"We have to leave," Paul said. "Oh shit! Get down!" He stood, reached across the table, and shoved my head down where it could be hidden by the fronds of a large potted fern. "Go!"

"Where?" I hissed.

"Anywhere!" he said, trying not to move his lips. "Just go!" He was waving his napkin.

Or waving the white flag of surrender.

Two tables over, a waiter was making a Caesar salad, table side. He had a big cart with a white tablecloth draped over the top. I slumped down to my hands and knees and crawled between the tables to that cart. I waited until the server went to set the salads on the table before I made my move. Gingerly, I edged the cloth aside. The bottom of the cart was empty, with the exception of a bottle of oil, some garlic, and a jar of anchovies. I crawled inside it, waiting to be pushed to safety.

The waiter came back to the cart. There were a few murmurs before the wheels started to slowly roll. He paused and then, giving a grunt, started wheeling me and the anchovies out of the dining room.

I knew we were in the kitchen when the noise through the cloth became louder, punctuated by the clang of pots crashing down onto the stove. The cart stopped in the middle of the noise. Then the tablecloth was pulled back, and I came eye to eye with a very startled young man in a starched white tunic. "What in the heck?"

"Hi," I said, giving him a finger-wave. "Thanks for the lift." I bolted out of the cramped space to sprint through the kitchen and out the back door.

A half-hearted "Hey!" followed me into the night air. I made it around the corner, back to the front of the restaurant and paused to look through the window.

Martha was now sitting in my chair, smiling at Paul. They were holding hands and Paul was talking to her. I could tell from the movements of his head and the way she beamed at him in adoration that he was telling her he had been waiting for her. *Surprise! Ditch your client and eat with me.* My heart broke a little as my vision became blurry from the tears welling in my eyes. She was going to get my fancy dinner.

It wasn't fair! She was never there for Paul. *I* was the one who listened to his hopes and dreams. *I* was the one who encouraged him when he felt his new documentary was going nowhere. *I* was the one who was there. *She* was always at the office, working until late into the night, defending crooked corporations that could pay her outrageous fee. My tears became hot and angry.

Rule Number Six: Never let your lover take you to his wife's favorite restaurant.

I felt like I was watching other people living the lives I wanted for myself. A kind of bitter envy settled down on my shoulders as I watched them toasting each other with the wine Paul had ordered for us. His eyes didn't even flicker over to where I was standing in the window.

I felt a tap on my shoulder and looked up into the surprised face of the maître d'. "Are you okay?" he said, following my gaze to where my lover now sat with his wife.

"I think I'd like a cab, please," I said, wiping away my tears with as much dignity as I could muster.

"Of course," he said sympathetically. I wondered how many mistresses he saw gazing through the windows at their lovers. Enough to know to be kind.

The last thing I saw before I got into the cab was Martha being served the dish Paul had ordered for me.

Chapter Thirteen

～

Excerpt from
The Calling of Oberlin Hurst
An Oberlin Hurst Mystery by Greer Larkin

Moonlight danced off the quivering blade lodged in the door. The night had been blissful, crescendoing from the wobbly knees of hopeful infatuation to mind-bending surges of ecstasy. It had been her first time. Oberlin had not been his first, though. His hands had been too deft, his body too knowledgeable.

But all that frenzied joy had begun to drain out of her as soon as she had seen the knife. The blade was long and slender. A stiletto, the name surfacing up from her subconscious. It was delicately pinning a note made with letters cut from the newspaper to her door.

GEORGE FREEMONT IS DEAD. IF YOU WANT TO KEEP BREATHING YOU WILL DROP IT.

A warning. Oberlin began to shiver, from both fear and excitement. She was on the right track and someone was taking notice.

Chapter Fourteen

The flowers were delivered to the front door by ten AM the next day. Men. Thinking the most humiliating experience of my entire twenty-four years could be erased with daisies and roses. This was going to take jewelry. And groveling.

I'd had to go down to the lobby to get them. Typical. I burned with a renewed fury. Why couldn't he show up with flowers at my door? Why did I have to go all the way downstairs to get them? As long as I was down there, I picked up my mail, delaying with the hope someone would come through so I could give them the unwanted flowers. Great. My electric bill and another letter for Maya Davenport. Angrily, I shoved the letters into my back pocket. I bet Maya Davenport never allowed herself to be humiliated by a man.

Paul texted me an apology. Twice. I ignored him. I was hurt, and he was going to suffer. That's just how my family does love.

Love. A small word, but so powerful. It could be cruel or joyous. What wouldn't we do for love? Like crawling through a five-star restaurant to save Paul from having his nice life ruined.

The lows that love could bring us to.

If Rachel had indeed been in love with Greer, what wouldn't she have done to rescue her from a bad boyfriend? Or *to* her if that love had been slapped back in her face?

I loaded the picture of Greer onto my computer, her hand coming toward Rachel, an angry sneer on her face. Rachel was already recoiling from the blow. But what happened before and after this picture? A member of the fan site once posted that they'd witnessed Greer slapping Rachel. They'd said that Rachel had been screaming at Greer after dragging her outside the club where she and Jonathan had been dancing.

"You are going to leave him if it's the last thing I do on this earth!"

Greer hollered back, "Leave me alone. I'm not going anywhere with you."

"You're being a moron and a waste of my time."

In short, Rachel had had it coming. After the slap, the forum poster reported a bouncer had intervened to break up the fight. I could see a hulking form in a black T-shirt on the left side of the frame.

A waste of my time. Was Jonathan right? Had Rachel been carrying a torch for Greer for all those years? Rachel and I had to meet again. I *should* have been emailing Jonathan, rectifying my colossal blunder, but I wasn't ready to call Dave Zukko and admit I needed him one more time. I gagged, imagining how he'd gloat. *No thank you.*

I also should've been calling Stella, demanding Bethany Allen keep her promise of an interview. The first email I'd sent to Stella had gone unanswered, much to my annoyance. But I didn't have the energy for that kind of fight today. I typed out my request to Rachel—today, if possible. It was Saturday, so Rachel might not be checking her phone. Maybe she was the one person in the entire city of New York with a healthy work–life balance.

And maybe not.

My computer dinged, announcing the arrival of Rachel's reply. Of course we could meet today. How about at eleven at the Heavenly Goods Bakeshop in Yonkers? I typed back that was fine and I'd be bringing my tape recorder.

I was early. Or rather, I was on time and she was late. This was New York, where being late was an art. The Heavenly Goods Bakeshop smelled divine, like cinnamon and sugar and warm chocolate with a hint of coffee. I got a churro and a mocha before commandeering a table by a long row of windows where I could see the street. About ten minutes later, Rachel came bustling into the shop. Her breath puffed out in quick, steamy clouds as she wheeled a purple rolling suitcase behind her. When she sat down in the chair across from me, she was out of breath and her cheeks were pink.

"Sorry. I decided to bring you something at the last minute. It took me longer than I thought to find it. I'm getting a coffee," Rachel said, bouncing back up and over to the barista.

She returned with a large coffee and a pear croissant. "Did you have questions about anything I said?" she asked. Her cheeks were still pink, but she looked less winded and harried.

"It's actually about something Jonathan said," I explained, placing my little Sony digital recorder on the table. Rachel eyed it as I clicked it on, but said nothing, so I continued. "Jonathan said that you hated him because, well, you were in love with Greer."

Whatever she'd expected me to say, it wasn't that. Her croissant was poised halfway to her mouth, about to take that first bite. She put the pastry down and got very still. With her hands placed flat on the table, she said quietly, "What did he say?"

Now my cheeks turned pink. I did not relish digging up trash that might hurt Rachel. "He said that you were in love with her. That you wanted her for yourself and were jealous. He said that you were stalking her until she got a restraining order against you. He thinks you were trying to get her to leave him and that . . ." I cleared my throat. ". . . Perhaps you went a little too far."

Color flooded over Rachel's collarbone and up her neck while red spots formed on her cheeks. "That piece of shit!" Rachel seethed. "He wouldn't know love if it bit him on the ass."

"So it isn't true?" I asked. "We can film you refuting it. But how would he even come up with something like you being in love with her?"

Finally, Rachel took a deep breath and let it out slowly. "Well, I am gay and he's a homophobic idiot," she said. "But we were never lovers. We were friends! Practically sisters. We'd been friends almost our whole lives. Of course there was love there," she said.

"Tell me about the fight," I said.

She leaned back and crossed her arms. "I already told you about that. In the interview."

"You told me that you wanted to talk to her, but that she was drunk and didn't want to leave," I said.

"Right."

"But is that true? Is that what it really was about? Because people don't take out restraining orders against someone who was only killing their buzz," I said. "There are reports that you called Greer a moron and said she'd wasted your time."

Rachel sat quietly, looking out the window with such intensity I felt compelled to follow her gaze. She was watching people passing by on the sidewalk. Couples holding hands. People typing on their phones. A bike zoomed past.

When she finally spoke, her voice was rough. Rachel never took her eyes off the passing people as she sat with her hands folded in her lap. "I never said Greer was wasting my time. I said she was *wasting time*. We had only minutes before Jonathan was going to see she was missing. We didn't have time for her to fight with me. Jonathan is . . . not a nice man. He . . . used her. He took her away from us and started her drinking and then, eventually, using drugs."

"Drugs? Like what kind of drugs?"

"It started out with sleeping pills," she said, still not looking at me. "Greer'd always had a hard time going to sleep. She told me her mind was full of characters always trying to have the last word." Rachel barked out a mirthless laugh. "She just wanted some sleep. Then the doctor stopped prescribing them. He said he was afraid she was growing dependent on them. He recommended melatonin instead, but it didn't work, so Jonathan got her some Valium and Percocet. We never knew where he got the drugs. Probably at the nightclub. Then they stopped being only for bedtime. Greer would take them whenever she felt stressed or anxious. They worked for a while to keep her calm, but when those stopped working, he switched her to quaaludes. Jonathan would ration them out to her. He would give Greer a few after she did an event. She hated book signings. She was terribly shy."

Alcohol? Drugs? Being controlled through addiction? *My God*. That poor woman. Jonathan's a monster. "She probably had an anxiety disorder." That Jonathan took advantage of.

Rachel finally looked at me, her eyes still far away. "She probably did. But the point is, Jonathan had her. She was addicted. And he gave her those pills as rewards for being a good girl and doing as he said. She'd give him anything he wanted to get those pills. Money mostly, but he also loved art. Art is a great investment and a great place to hide wealth. Then, when she was so doped up she couldn't write, he started to give her uppers too. But that didn't work because all she wanted to do was go to a club and dance it off."

I thought of the Jackson Pollock on Jonathan's wall. My mouth tasted sour as I considered that Greer'd given it to Jonathan so he'd give her drugs. Ironic, considering Pollock had been an alcoholic who'd died because of his addiction. I swallowed the sourness and asked, "And that's what happened when she slapped you?"

Rachel nodded. "She was high all the time. Blanche and I were worried. We knew that if Greer kept going down that path, she'd overdose and die one day. We tried to talk to Jonathan. Blanche actually offered to pay him off to leave her. But he wouldn't do it. He . . ." She swallowed hard. ". . . He *laughed* at her. He said the only way Greer was leaving him was if she died."

"What happened at the club?" I pressed.

"I followed her there. I couldn't stand it anymore. I was going to drag her off to rehab. Once she was sober, she would see that he was using her. She told me I was crazy, that for the first time in her life she was happy and free. I—I slapped her. In the club. Then I hauled her away by the arm as she whined, trying to wriggle free. Jonathan had gone to the bathroom, probably to fuck some girl, so he wasn't there to stop me.

"But then, when I got her outside, she kind of woke up. She started screaming and cursing me out, whacking me with her purse. She managed to slip away from me, we fought, and she slapped me, screaming at me to go away and never come back. Then she got the restraining order."

"Did you still follow her?" I asked, gently.

"I didn't dare. There was nothing Jonathan would have liked more than to have me arrested and thrown in jail." The bitterness in Rachel's voice made me want to hug her, but I sat there instead, letting my coffee grow cold.

"Did you love Greer Larkin?" I whispered.

"Yes," she whispered back.

* * *

The silence stretched out between us. I knew a tortured heart when I saw one. Rachel had loved Greer. Very, very much.

"Did Greer love you, too?"

"Once she did. I think she did, anyway. But before anything could come of it, Jonathan appeared. Larger than life and twice as fun. Greer was chafing under her mom's strict rules. Any teenager would be, especially if you were earning the kind of money she was pulling in. Jonathan was a carnival she could run away and join."

"I'm sorry," I said.

Rachel gave another dry chuckle that was more like a cough. "Thanks. But I know we were still friends, even after the restraining order. Greer came to see me and dropped this off." Rachel patted the suitcase beside her. "I think she was finally realizing that Jonathan was using her. I think she was getting ready to leave him. So she brought the things that were her most valuable possessions to me—her notes and journals."

Suddenly, that purple suitcase looked a lot more important. I stared at it, seeing if it would give me any hints as to what

I might find inside, hoping I would suddenly develop X-ray vision. "When did she give you this?"

"About six months before she disappeared, she showed up at my house. Out of the blue. She didn't come in or say anything, really. Just asked if I would keep this for her for a little while and not tell anyone," Rachel said. "And I did. Until now."

"Did she seem nervous? Scared?"

Rachel shook her head. "It was really quick. She just shoved the suitcase at me and took off. I think she wanted to make sure no one saw us together, so I guess she could have been nervous."

She pushed the purple case over to me. In awe, I laid a hand reverently on it.

"I looked through it once, right after she disappeared," Rachel said. "It's a jumble of notebooks and loose papers. There could be a clue in there somewhere, but I couldn't make sense of it." Rachel looked up at me, her deep brown eyes troubled and teary. "I'm hoping that you can."

Chapter Fifteen

～

My conversation with Rachel left me shaken. Jonathan had seemed so open and honest—so *nice*. But the details Rachel had shared removed any doubt from my mind that Jonathan had controlled Greer with drugs.

I also had no doubt Rachel loved Greer. The cloud of loss drifting around Rachel reminded me of one of the waiters I'd interviewed who'd been grieving his lost wife.

It also meant she had an even bigger motive for making Jonathan look guilty. She could put the man who lured the love of her life away from her in prison. That kind of revenge would taste extra sweet.

I looked at the purple suitcase perched on top of my mammoth coffee table. I hadn't opened it yet. I still hadn't quite wrapped my head around the idea that Rachel'd given it to *me*, hoping I'd find the magic clue that would expose the mystery. Should I be turning this over to the police or should I unzip it and dig in? I could hear Paul's voice in my head. *Turn it in! This is evidence!* Part of me agreed with him.

But another part of me said, *I will be God-damned if I am going to listen to a man who made me crawl through a restaurant so that he could feed his wife my dinner!*

The zipper was a little stiff from years of sitting unused, but I yanked until it submitted to my will.

Rachel wasn't kidding when she said the suitcase was full of papers. The lid sprang off like a literary jack-in-the-box. Lunging at the stack to keep the papers from cascading out, I ended up shoving some out instead, making them waterfall onto my floor.

Hastily circling my coffee table, I bashed my shin on a corner, again. Seriously! This coffee table was out to kill me. I limped around, lowering myself to the floor in order to sift through the mountain of paper without putting a crick in my back. Some had dates with clear beginnings, while other pages looked like they started mid-sentence. I recognized one as an excerpt from her book *When She Was Seventeen*.

Oberlin moved through the underbrush, "Buttons!" she called. "Buttons, come here! Good boy!"

Oberlin Hurst, her amazing detective, was about to find the body of Mr. Grady, the caretaker of her family's estate. Definitely the "Book" pile.

I picked up another page.

I know I shouldn't take the pills he gives me. I shouldn't be drinking the wine he serves me. But I have to. I itch. I itch so badly. It's an unceasing prickling of little bug feet crawling over my skin. I want to peel my skin off, scratch through the surface, and get to those nasty creepy-crawly spiders that are racing across my back and up and down my arms. I need those little pills. Those little pills scratch my itch.

This one seemed vaguely familiar. There was an alcoholic wife in *The Girl Who Sang a Tune*, but this is a completely different voice. It's in first person, for starters. Plus, it's desperate and fevered. Was it another book she'd set aside at some point?

Or was it a journal entry? Was this proof that Jonathan was drugging Greer? There weren't any names, just "he" and "I." Reluctantly, I slid it into the "Don't Know" pile.

Really, all these pages looked like they could have come from one of her novels. I grunted in frustration. There were *so many pages*. My chest tightened as pressure built in my ears like a drowning victim. All of these couldn't be from her books, but how could I tell? Surely, Greer must have given an interview at some point about her writing process. Did she make journal entries of the characters as part of creating them? Or were there bits of other books that never went anywhere?

There were two places that might know.

The first was Bethany Allen, Greer's agent. She hadn't emailed me back yet, but maybe if I had a specific question I'd get a response. After that message had been sent off into the ether, I fired up GreersGone. I'd have to be careful about how I asked my question. I didn't want the entire community to know I was working on this documentary. Once the nutsos found out, I'd be inundated with wild theories and alternative facts. Then the Nice People would start sending helpful suggestions on how to make my movie "perfect." Reading those posts would be a waste of my time, and I didn't have any to waste.

After a couple of minutes of writing and deleting, I posted this message: *Do any of you know if Greer was ever interviewed about her writing process? Like, how she came up with her stories and developed her characters?*

Because of my standing in the community, I was sure this post would get both attention and responses. I almost added, "Do you know if she kept journals?" but I thought that would give too much away. I'd have people blowing up my inbox asking if I (a) had journals written by Greer Larkin and (b) was trying to prove authenticity. Then (c) how much would it take for me to sell those journals? They might even track me down to my apartment. The internet was a crazy place.

Two minutes later I had a reply from QueenB. Ooo! Exciting! She'd been a member even longer than me. She rarely posted, but when she did it was juicy.

> QueenB: There may be an article from really early in her career in some magazine. I doubt it's online. You trying to write your own mystery?

I frowned. Not as helpful as I had hoped.

> PricklyPear: Not writing my own mystery. Just curious about how she wrote such three-dimensional characters. They all feel real to me.

There. A good, yet vague reply. I took a quick shower so I didn't hover over my post like a helicopter mom. When I came back, it thrilled me to see pages of posts.

> <3Greer4ever: Mom was notoriously controlling of her appearances. Wouldn't let media near her.
> QueenB: Well, after Greer gave away the location of her favorite writing spots, people came flocking and ruined them. I doubt she'd want to answer any questions about how she wrote after that.
> Vixen42: People were respectful, IMO. No one approached her when she was writing.
> QueenB: Says a person who probably approached her in Roxy's Cafe, asking for an autograph or picture. <Eyeroll>

OHurst: @<3Greer4ever Mom wasn't that controlling. For half her career she was living with Jonathan. How much longer can we continue to blame Mommy Dearest?

Vixen42: I never approached her! I may have seen her while having my own cup of coffee at Roxy's, but that's completely different.

QueenB: Oh, please.

<3Greer4ever: There was more going on behind the scenes than anyone knew. Mommy Dearest had her talons deep in Greer's hide. If only Joan Crawford were still alive to play Blanche in the movie.

Vixen42: @QueenB It's hardly my fault if Greer and I happened to like the same cafe.

OHurst: @<3Greer4ever HA! You have at least one thing right; there was a lot more going on behind the scenes. #WhatDoesJonathanKnow

QueenB: We all know that Jonathan was trying his best with a broken, traumatized girl. @Vixen42 If the shoe fits, Barbie.

<3Greer4ever: The travesty here is how many times Jonathan was dragged into the police station, in front of cameras, for questioning about his whereabouts, relationships, diet, bowel movements, etc. And never any charges filed. Total exoneration!

OHurst: @<3Greer4ever He's never been exonerated. That's a legal term for when a conviction has been reversed. He's never been charged or tried and can, therefore, never be exonerated.

<3Greer3ever: @OHurst Oh? Are you a lawyer? Care to post a picture of your legal degree? Being not charged

is totally the same thing as exoneration—it can also mean to informally absolve someone from blame. I can use Google too, Columbo.

Vixen42: @QueenB I'm more of a Cinderella type. #Blingbling #Foundmyprincecharming

OHurst: I work closely with the legal world. Just because Jonathan was never charged doesn't (a) exonerate him or (b) mean he is innocent. That man is in NO WAY innocent.

QueenB: @Vixen42 So you know your way around a mop? Sending you a DM. I can use a new cleaning lady.

<3Greer4ever: "Work closely with the legal world?" Hookers also "work closely with the legal world." You wanna come by and suck my dick?

Vixen42: Bite me, QueenB.

WBJ: There's a movie being made?

<Post Locked by Moderator>

My eyes widened as they traveled down the thread. Well, that devolved quickly. And I got no answers. Plus, word of my movie might have leaked. I didn't know who OHurst was in real life or how they would've heard about my documentary, but I was going to hunt them down if they started blabbing. I clicked back to the main board and breathed a sigh of relief when I didn't see a thread about a potential Greer Larkin movie. Thankfully, the group had treated OHurst's words and WBJ's question as a nothing remark. Shutting my laptop, I looked at the heaps of notes, sighed again, and sat down cross-legged on the floor, going elbow deep into a forest of paper.

At the end of the night my legs were numb and my brain was cramped. The "Don't Know" pile was woefully larger than my "Journal" or "Book" piles. I didn't have a chance to read through them all. This was a skimming and sorting mission only. "But soon, my pretties, I will read you," I promised before going to bed.

*　*　*

Nothing was making any sense. I was alone and it was dark. The wind was whipping my hair into my eyes. The briny smell of the ocean made my nose wrinkle. I was waiting for someone, but I didn't know who it was. A message had been slipped under my door. "Meet me at Kilmarnock Lighthouse at 3:00 AM."

So here I was. On time while they were late. Standing at the edge of a wood, looking out onto a small sandy beach. The moon danced on the water, full and buoyant. Something was out there. I strained to make out the shapes in the moonlight. A boat? A dolphin? I jumped and whirled around at the snapping of a twig. Two hands grabbed me. I tried to scream, but he covered my mouth with his. I brought my knee up, hard and fast, right where it counted.

"Ahhh!" a voice screamed.

I jerked back, tumbling out of bed, my ass colliding with my hard wood floor. I had been dreaming.

But someone *was* in my bed with me.

And they were screaming.

"Jesus Christ! It's me! It's only me."

Popping my head above the edge of the bed, I turned on my bedside lamp.

"Paul?"

He'd stopped yelling and lay very still, curled up into a ball on top of my quilt.

"What are you doing here?" My heart threatened to beat out of my chest.

"I came," he wheezed, "to see you. To apologize."

I picked myself up off the floor to stand over him, my mouth agape. I stuttered around looking for something to say before landing on, "You could have called." Not the poetry I'd been going for.

"I tried. You wouldn't pick up," he said, uncurling himself to sit up.

That was true. "Because I didn't want to talk to you." My heart rate was approaching normal speed and the shaking in my hands was lessening.

"You got the flowers?"

My eyes involuntarily drifted to the beautiful bouquet of roses and daisies sitting on my kitchen counter. "Yes." Obviously.

"Did you like them?"

"That's not the point, Paul," I snapped. I did very much like them, but I wasn't going to let him know that. I was still mad. "If I wanted to talk, I would have texted you."

He got up onto his knees in the bed, a crooked, chagrined smile on his face, and looked at me through his lashes with those sapphire blue eyes of his. I could feel my will to stay angry crumbling. Still, I did my best. Then he reached up to gently stroke my cheek with his fingertips. He took my head in both his hands. "I am so, so sorry. I was wrong. I panicked and I was stupid. I will never put you in that situation again. I should have protected you. Pear Blossom, can you forgive me? Please, forgive me." His teary eyes searched mine, desperate to see some sign that forgiveness was coming. His face was etched with worry, dark bags blooming under his eyes. His normally sleek hair was a tousled mess. He looked wretched.

My throat thickened as warm butterflies started to flutter through me. Hot tears began to well up as my amethyst eyes locked with his blue. I nodded as those tears started to spill over. I swiped at them, but Paul began to kiss them away. "I'm sorry," he crooned. "I am so, so sorry."

That night we made love. Slowly. Gently. For hours. He stayed for the entire night and served me coffee in bed the next morning. He was warm and firm, and when his arms wrapped around me as we snuggled in the bed with our coffee and the Sunday news, my whole world came together. I have never felt as complete as I did at that moment. He kissed the top of my ear and nuzzled my neck.

I held off spoiling the moment for as long as I could, but eventually curiosity got the better of me. I had to ask. "Where does your wife think you are?"

"A conference in Boston," he said, continuing to lay tender kisses on the sensitive spot where my collarbone met my shoulder. "This whole day belongs to you."

"Really?" I couldn't believe it. This was only the third time that I'd gotten to spend an entire day with Paul since we'd started our relationship. Usually it was a few hours or maybe even a half a day if Martha was out of town. I clapped my hands like a kid who has just discovered the biggest Christmas gift under the tree was for them.

Turning, I wrapped my arms around him and pulled him into a kiss. My lips were hungry and demanding. Paul responded with equal hunger, much to my complete and total satisfaction.

*   *   *

"What do you want to do next?" he asked. "Because I'm going to need some time to rest after that."

I giggled, scooting closer to him, and put my head on his shoulder. He was warm and smelled like cedar and good sex. "We can talk about my film, if you want," I said.

"Alright," he said, kissing the top of my head. "I watched the clips. They look good. I can see where you're going with the narrative, but it's still loose enough to fit in a surprise."

"Well," I said, my eyes sparkling, "I got a surprise. It turns out that Rachel was in love with Greer. For years."

I felt Paul shift, and when I looked up at him he was looking back, eyes wide, and a faint smile playing around his lips. "You're kidding."

"Nope. Jonathan told me she was, and when I confronted her about it yesterday she admitted it. Not only that," I said. "Rachel tried to drag Greer away from Jonathan at a club. That's when Greer slapped her."

"And the restraining order was issued," said Paul, the pieces clicking together in his head.

"Exactly. But here's what no one knew. Greer was an addict. She was on pills and alcohol almost all the time. *Jonathan* was her dealer. Rachel said he kept her compliant that way."

"No fucking way." Paul sat up, dislodging me from his shoulder, forcing me to sit up, too.

I tucked the sheet around myself, replying smugly, "Yes fucking way."

"Please tell me you got this all on video," he said.

I bit my lip. "Actually . . . no. I have it on audio. It was an informal meeting. I thought it was just going to be her saying Jonathan was crazy and we could set up another time to video. I didn't know she was going to drop a house on me." I crossed my arms, feeling defensive. "We can do it as a voice-over?" I had meant it as a statement, but it came out as a squeaky question.

"Get it on video. Call her up and get her back on camera," Paul said. "No one knew Greer was on drugs. I wonder if there were pills in her purse and that's why they didn't release the contents."

"Maybe. Blanche Larkin is rich enough to ensure some kind of privilege. But it would be in the case file."

"Then we need to get that case file." The thrill of the hunt made Paul's eyes bright. He grabbed my phone off the nightstand and handed it to me. "Call the police."

I dropped my phone like it was a poisonous spider and sprung out of bed. "I can't call the police *naked*!" I said. "I have to get dressed."

Paul started laughing. "Is it okay if I stay naked?"

"No!" Imagine being naked and calling, not just a single police officer, but an entire station full of police officers. Scandalous! I picked up his shirt and threw it at him. "Put this on."

He was still laughing as he slipped it over his head. "If I had known you were going to make me get dressed, I would have kept my mouth shut. The police can't see you on the phone."

I stomped into the bathroom with a bundle of clothes in my hand. It was only yoga leggings and a T-shirt, but it was better than nothing. Once I was dressed and fueled with another cup of coffee, I picked up the phone again.

The internet was a wondrous thing. In less than two minutes I had the number of the Northumberland County Sheriff's Department, the name of the captain (Franklin Lewis), and their address. I could even see what their headquarters looked like from satellite images.

I took a deep breath. "Well, here we go."

I dialed and the phone rang. Once. Twice. Three times. Finally there was a pause and a man with a smooth, friendly southern accent said, "Hello, Northumberland County Sheriff. How can I help you?"

"Hi," I said. My voice was wavering. I cleared my throat, mustered up my courage, and said in a clearer, stronger voice, "I'm a film student doing a documentary about the disappearance of Greer Larkin. I was wondering if you could send me a copy of the files?"

I was watching Paul for cues and he mouthed, "Her case files."

"I mean, her case files."

"I'm sorry, ma'am," he said in a very polite drawl. "We cannot release the files of open investigations, and Ms. Larkin's case is still open."

"Can I speak to Mr. Hoyt Bedford, please?" I asked. He'd been one of the officers who'd arrested Jonathan the first time.

"Hoyt Bedford?" he asked. Then he chuckled. "Ma'am, Officer Bedford has been retired for about ten years now."

"Oh," I said, not able to think of anything else. I hadn't thought he'd be retired already. On the tapes he seemed like a young man.

I hung up and plopped down on the bed next to Paul.

"So?" Paul asked.

"They won't release the records. The investigation is still open," I said, plopping down on the bed next to Paul. "They wouldn't even give me the number of one of the officer who had been a lead investigator. He's retired."

"You can still get his number."

"How?"

"The internet is a vast and wondrous place."

He was right. There's nothing I can't find on Google. We booted up my computer and started searching.

"They said he was an avid fisherman. Let's see if the library website offers lectures on fishing. He could've been a presenter at one."

Sure enough, Hoyt Bedford had given a lecture on fly fishing in 2015 at the Northumberland Public Library. His contact information was printed neatly at the bottom of the flyer.

"Sneaky," I said.

"That's why I get paid the big bucks."

"Well . . . no time like the present."

Lieutenant Hoyt Bedford, retired, picked up on the first ring. "Hello," he barked, his voice grating like a gravel crusher.

"Mr. Bedford, I'm June Masterson and I'm—"

"I'm not buying anything!"

"No, Mr. Bedford, I'm a—"

"And I'm not sending you money!"

"No, Mr. Bedford, I don't want your money," I said, a desperate edge to my voice. Paul began to laugh, shaking the bed. I frantically waved at him with the international symbols for *shut the fuck up*. "I want to talk to you about Greer Larkin."

There was a pause.

"Greer Larkin." His voice scraped over her name. "What do you want to know about Greer Larkin?"

"I'm filming a documentary about her. I want to find out what happened. Did she disappear, was she killed, or was it suicide? I'd like it if you could tell me what you think. I'd also like to know if there were pills in her bag. Opioids or anything else addictive?" I held my breath.

He paused again. "The contents of the purse are part of the case file. The files of open cases can't be released," he said with great deliberation.

"Could you just tell me if there were? I have a source who says Jonathan Vanderpoole was controlling Greer Larkin by keeping her addicted to drugs."

"That would be Rachel Baumgartner," Bedford said, amusement frosting the crushed gravel of his voice.

"How did you know that?" I asked, stunned.

"Because she told me that too. Twenty years ago," he said.

"So was she right?"

"Miss—what did you say your name was?"

"Masterson. June Masterson."

"Ms. Masterson, I can't tell you what we did or did not find at the scene. However, I can tell you that I had no reason to suspect drugs were involved."

His meaning washed over me and I smiled. "Ooohh."

"Exactly," he said. I could hear him smiling. His voice was a little less gravel and more river-washed pebble. "Is there anything else I can't answer for you?"

"Do you think she threw herself off the cliffs?" I asked.

I heard a deep, wistful sigh. "I don't know. We haven't discounted that theory, but there wasn't a note at the scene. If you find out, though, I'd appreciate you telling me."

The lack of a note didn't mean Greer hadn't committed suicide, but this was a definite hole in Bethany's suicide theory. Surprised that Bedford was in a sharing mood, I made my move. "Is there any way I could see your notes?" I asked. "They aren't strictly part of the case file. Or would you be in my movie?"

"Well, I'll think on the other stuff, but I won't be sending you my case notes. Not today, not tomorrow. Not ever."

"I understand. Can I come and see you?" I asked.

"Do what you want. It's a free country. I'm not promising I'll be in your film, though."

"Okay. Can I get your address?"

He rattled it off at top speed and I wasn't sure he wouldn't slam the phone down if I asked him to repeat it, so I prayed I'd gotten it right.

"Thanks a lot, Mr. Bedford."

"My pleasure, little lady." He paused. I thought he was going to hang up, until he said, "Odd thing. We know that Greer and Rachel hadn't seen each other for over a year."

How did he know that? Rachel had told me that Greer had given her the suitcase only six months before she disappeared. I did not, however, correct him.

"What's odd about that? They had a fight. Greer had a restraining order against Rachel." I asked in my most nonchalant tones.

"You'd think that Greer would clean out her car more often. Or maybe she didn't vacuum a lot and that's why we found Rachel's hair in the car. Gotta go. Rain's gone and the fish will be biting."

And then he hung up on me.

My Spidey sense tingled. Rachel's hair had been found in the car. Meaning Rachel had been in the car. I knew, for sure, that Greer and Rachel had seen each other six months before

Greer disappeared, but Rachel had said Greer delivered the suitcase to the front door, not that Rachel had been in the car. And what had made Greer break her own restraining order to give her one-time best friend a suitcase full of scraps of writing? Was she suspicious of Jonathan? Was Blanche trying to get her to move home where she could control Greer's writing output again? Who didn't Greer want to have those papers? It certainly wasn't Rachel.

"Well, that went well," I said, only halfway meaning it.

"He didn't say no," Paul said. "We can go down to Virginia, if you want."

Hoyt Bedford had to be in my movie, and I needed those case files. It was harder to say "no" to a person's face than to a voice on a phone. "I think we have to visit Virginia. We can stop by the police station and then find Officer Bedford. But first," I said, "how do you feel about going to church?"

Chapter Sixteen

❧

You might be surprised to learn that lightning did not strike me dead when I walked into the church.

It could be because the church was no longer, technically, a church. My promise to Meadow that I'd be at her girlfriend's art show brought me to the front steps of a former Catholic church that was now an avant-garde art gallery in the heart of Brooklyn Heights.

Brooklyn Heights is an artsy neighborhood just south of the famous Brooklyn Bridge. It's a hipster's paradise and, more importantly, a place where Paul's decidedly uptown wife would never have a reason to visit.

Keeping his promise to make the whole day mine, Paul walked in next to me, arm wrapped around my waist. From the way people looked at me, I knew I was glowing. I was in jeans that were ripped at the knees, a butter yellow T-shirt that screamed "I'm a fucking ray of sunshine," and my black leather jacket. Paul looked particularly handsome in dark jeans and a forest green, untucked button-up shirt.

"We won't have to stay long," I said. "Just long enough so that Meadow doesn't feel alone."

"We can stay as long as you want," he said, kissing my temple. "This is your night."

Rainbow fairy lights hung from the flying buttresses of the church, adding a festive air to the cavernous space. Paintings hung on the walls and pillars, with a spotlight trained on each canvas. The pews had been replaced with tall cocktail tables, and a bar sat on the altar.

"They're all definitely going to hell," Paul said. "Do you want a drink?"

"Is the pope Catholic?"

We grinned at each as we walked up the aisle to get Manhattans at the altar-bar. We turned, drinks in hand, to survey the gallery. It had dark gray stone floors and light gray walls. Stained glass windows were trimmed with walnut planks. Walnut wood pillars outlined the congregation like soldiers on watch. The stained glass told different Bible stories—stories I hadn't heard until I'd moved out of my parents' nonreligious home.

Paul gestured to the paintings filling the space. "So, which ones belong to your cousin?"

"It's her girlfriend, Faye, and I'm not really sure." I scanned the crowd looking for Meadow's golden hair, but she found us first.

Waving at us, she mounted the stairs. "I'm so glad you're here," she said, hugging me. She shook Paul's hand and said, "I'm Meadow. Good to meet you." Meadow's flowy slacks were the color of a sandy tropical beach and her white silk blouse hugged her curves.

"Meadow, you look gorgeous," I said.

She gave me a deprecating smile. "Thanks. I need a drink," she said, grabbing a straight bourbon from the bar.

"Where's Faye?" I asked. "Which ones are hers?"

Meadow pointed with her glass to our right. "She's there. Her series is called 'Gloria, Angela, and Nina.' They're portraits of famous feminists done in the style of religious icons. Complete with gold leaf." I looked down to see Faye, her hair in purple dreadlocks and her golden ochre skin highlighted by a golden cocktail dress that highlighted her amazing legs. She was surrounded by people, talking animatedly with her hands and smiling widely, basking in the triumph of her show.

"She looks so happy," I said.

Meadow smiled fondly at her. "Yes, she does. They're really quite good. People are loving them. Oh! We got the best news! An art critic will be showing up at some point to review the show. This could be her big break. My girlfriend could be the next Georgia O'Keeffe."

"I guess you decided to make it official? She's your girlfriend now?" I said, teasing just a little.

Meadow blushed. "What can I say? I decided to give love a shot. We should go say hello. I told her I wouldn't be long. Oh!" she exclaimed, snagging a glass of champagne off the bar. "I promised her a drink."

Meadow led the way through the crowd to Faye. As we got closer, I became enthralled with Faye's paintings. One was of Rosa Parks, her famous round, brimless hat like a golden halo, hands folded in gentle determination on her purse. Another was of Gloria Steinem, her long hair curtaining around her like the Virgin Mary's veil, her big brown eyes loving and innocent. But if you looked closely, the lines around the mouth told of an iron will that would never stop fighting. I gasped.

The paintings had a beautiful simplicity to them at first glance, but the more I continued to study them, the more ornate they became. The reflections of light on the window of Rosa's bus seat danced, but when you looked closer you could make out faces: Martin Luther King, Jr., Harriet Tubman, Medgar Evers, John Lewis, and Jesse Jackson. I looked back at Gloria's picture and found, hidden in the swirls of her shirt, a fish riding a bicycle and a clenched fist. I laughed out loud at Faye's brilliance.

I couldn't believe Faye had even one moment of doubt about her talent. These were incredible.

Handing Faye her champagne, Meadow gave her a kiss on the cheek. "Look who came!" she said, pulling me closer.

Faye let out a little scream of joy and gave me an enthusiastic hug. "You're here. I was so excited when Meadow told me you were coming." She stepped back, looking up at her work. "I'm almost afraid to ask, but how do you like it?"

"I love it! It's the most amazing show. You're going to sell out. I'm never going to be able to afford your work," I said, and I meant it. I wouldn't be surprised if she wasn't getting astronomical offers for her pieces.

Faye leaned in, whispering to me, "See that woman over there looking at my Nina?"

I glanced over to see a young Black woman in a long emerald green dress staring up at a portrait of Nina Simone, her hard, accusing eyes heavenward, a collar of blue jewels draped down her neck. In one hand she held a large iron skeleton key, and in the other a scepter.

"She hasn't been able to take her eyes off of my Nina," Faye said. "I modeled her after Rubens's portrait of St. Peter. Nina Simone's song 'Sinnerman' had the line 'I run to the rock' in it. Get it? Peter is The Rock? There's a lot of symbolism hidden in that one. She can look forever and not find it all."

"I guess she'll have to buy it then," I said.

"She'll have to pay a pretty penny. The more praise I get, the higher my prices are going." Faye gave a playful wink as she took a sip of her champagne.

"As they should!" I reached back for Paul's hand. "Faye, this is my friend Paul. Paul, this is the up-and-coming artistic sensation, Faye Reynolds."

Paul took her extended hand. "These are amazing. I might have to buy one."

"Well, you can have your pick. Let me know which one and we can negotiate." Faye gave him a warm smile.

"Well, then I guess I should see them all," Paul said, smiling back. He turned to me and asked, "Do you have a favorite?"

"Ooo, I don't know. I think I need to see them all too," I said.

Meadow linked her arm with mine. "Let me steer you around, then. I'll show you my favorite one first."

We left Faye to her adoring fans and explored her other paintings. Her work was incredibly good. The three of us had settled in front of a portrait of Simone de Beauvoir as Mary Magdalene. She was seated at a wooden table holding a glass of red wine, her hair tied back with a golden scarf, and her smug, satisfied smile harboring a secret that she wasn't about to tell. Her eyes were kind and gentle, yet they taunted me. They dared me to ask what her secret was so she could laugh, yet keep her silence.

"This is the one I would buy," I said. "Simone." As I studied the painting, I saw the grains of wood in the table come together to make a skull. That was her secret. Or one of them. There'd be more to find, but I wouldn't get to discover them today.

A woman ran up behind Meadow squealing, "The art critic is here!"

We stood on our tiptoes and swiveled our heads around to find him or her. Not that we'd know what an art critic is supposed to look like. It's not like they wear a badge.

What we did find, however, was Martha. She stood across the church, examining some abstract art in primary colors. She wore an off-the-shoulder navy cocktail dress that flared out at the hips and hit just below the knee. Her blonde hair hung down to her shoulders in thick waves. She was a knockout.

Damn her.

"What the fuck is she doing here?" I asked, my mouth going dry. You'd think a thirty-five-year-old woman who had the whole of New York City to herself for an evening would be anywhere but here.

"Oh. Shit," Paul said, ducking down. "Her friend Damaris is an art critic. She must be the critic reviewing the show, and invited Martha to come along since I'm out of town. I'm so sorry. What are we going to do?"

My mouth was stuffed with cotton. I slammed down the rest of my drink, but my tongue still felt like sandpaper. "We need to get out of here," I said to Meadow, my voice raspy.

"Follow me. There's a back way out," she said.

As we passed by, Meadow whispered something to Faye. Faye looked at Meadow, eyebrows raised to her hairline before scanning the room. I mouthed *I'm sorry* as Paul grabbed my hand and we started to dive through the crowd. I was grateful I'd decided on Chuck Taylors and jeans rather than complicated heels and a dress. Not that I even owned a dress.

Paul yanked me along behind him, weaving through the crowd like Steph Curry on his way to dunk a basketball. I ricocheted off of people like a pinball, knocking them into tables and spilling their drinks. My feet were starting to stumble over each other, catching in the crevices of the stone floor.

"Wait!" I said. "I'm tripping. I need to—"

But it was too late. Pain bloomed through my leg as I went down on one knee. Paul didn't even break stride. His momentum jerked me forward, causing my chin to collide painfully with the stone floor. The people above me gasped. One said, "Well, *that's* gotta hurt."

Paul dragged me along behind him for another three steps. I swore as the artful rips in my jeans got larger. I hurriedly tried to pull myself up, but my right shoe had become wedged under the feet of one of the cafe tables loaded with glasses in various stages of consumption. As I jumped up, my weight and momentum catapulted the table three feet behind me, sending the half-empty glasses crashing to the floor.

The sound of over fifty glasses sent hurtling to their deaths on the stone floor of a church was magical. The crowd went completely silent. Almost a hundred pairs of eyes looked over to the scene of destruction. Thankfully, I was upright. However, it was all too obvious that I was the cause of the beverage massacre. I looked around to find Paul peeking out from behind the bar, his horrified eyes staring at me. Meadow was in front of the bar, eyes the size of saucers, her hand covering her mouth.

"Uh, sorry," I said. "I tripped. Stone floors, you know."

I looked back to where Martha had been. Her hand was pressed to her chest, while her mouth made a perfect "O" of horror. She'd seen me, but there was no flicker of recognition in her eyes. *Thank God.* Her friend, a woman in black cigarette pants, a black button-up tunic top, and black ballet slippers wore an identical expression. Faye was at their side, eyes bulging.

Several people dressed all in black descended upon me. One shoved me out of the way, while the others began whisking away the debris. People went back to their conversations. Faye shot me a worried glance before she turned her back to me, guiding Martha and her friend toward Rosa.

Meadow approached me slowly, her face white and her mouth in a thin line. "Are you okay?"

"I don't know," I said. I did a quick body check. My chin felt raw, but with the amount of adrenaline pumping through me, I don't think I would've felt a bullet. My legs were going to receive more fresh air than before, but nothing seemed to be broken.

"This wouldn't have happened if you hadn't brought him."

"Really? You're going to do this now? His wife is *right there*."

"It's never the time."

"I'm fine, by the way."

"Good. Come on," she said, grabbing my arm.

I shook her off, saying, "Maybe I should do this on my own power."

She gave me a single grim nod and led me up to the bar. "Go to the right. That will take you to the back entrance," Meadow said.

Paul was no longer behind the bar. I looked around for him until Meadow elbowed me and pointed into the dimly lit hallway. "This leads past the sacristy and then a room marked 'storage.' I think it was the choir room. Turn left at the next corner, then follow that hallway until you reach a door. That's your exit," she said.

I gave Meadow a hug. "Thanks. Sorry about all that. Tell Faye I absolutely love her work. If I could afford it, I'd buy one right now."

Her color was returning, but her face was still grim. "I'll tell her. But, Pear? How much longer can you keep this up?"

I hugged her again so I wouldn't have to answer.

"You're going to drop that," Meadow said, pointing. One of the pockets on my purse was ripped open. A letter for Maya Davenport was threatening to fall. I'd brought it along with the intention of popping it into a mailbox.

"Thanks."

I knocked the letter to the floor, my hands too shaky from the adrenaline rushing through my system to properly grab it. Meadow picked it up. "Maya Davenport? How? What is this?"

"You know her?" I was hoping she'd say yes and I'd finally have a reason I was getting this poor woman's mail.

"No." Meadow said, the word jumping from her mouth.

Hmm. That was a bit fast and a bit harsh. Meadow knew more about Maya Davenport than she was saying.

"I was going to return it to sender. I forgot on the way here," I said, carefully gaging her reaction.

"I'll do it. There's a mail bucket here at the gallery."

Yeah, She knows something. A lifetime together had taught me a direct attack was doomed to fail. I'd have to ambush her when she wasn't ready for it. Our next dinner together would be the perfect opportunity, especially after a glass or two of wine. "That'd be great. I'd really like to stop getting her mail."

"Have you been getting a lot of her letters?" Meadow asked, her eyes studying the return address.

"Yeah. A couple every month. I feel kind of bad," I said, shrugging. Best to be casual so she'll fall into my trap later.

"I got this. You worry about yourself." Meadow's eyes flicked from the letter to where Paul lurked in the shadows. Her frown deepened.

"By the way," I said. "I'll be going to Virginia for a couple of days. I'm going to interview one of the officers on the Greer Larkin case."

"Wow! That seems huge." I nodded and she gave me another hug. "Good luck, Pear."

I gave her a saucy salute before heading into the corridor. Paul took my hand as we hurried out into the dark together.

We'd escaped, our secret still safe, but Meadow was right. How much longer could I keep this up? In Greer's books the affairs between husbands and mistresses never lasted, and in more than one of her books one or both of them ended up dead when the mistress wanted the man all to herself.

Rule Number Seven: No matter how much you love him, you'll always have to share him.

Would he ever be truly mine?

Chapter Seventeen

⁓

Excerpt from
Swingline
An Oberlin Hurst Mystery by Greer Larkin

*"**I** forbid it!" Verity Hurst's brown eyes sparked with an electric fury.*

"You can't forbid me," Oberlin raged, incredulous at her mother's angry declaration. "I'm eighteen. I'm of age. You were married when you were eighteen."

Her mother tsked. "To a man of quality. Not some ruffian from Cheapside, for God's sake. If you want to get married, why not someone like Lord Kimberley-Hughes? He has money and a title . . ."

"This isn't the 1880s, Mother. No one cares about that." Not to mention Lord Kimberley-Hughes was a depraved pig who Oberlin wouldn't inflict on her worst enemy. "I love Eddie. And he loves me."

"Eddie," her mother spat. "He could at least call himself Edward. But, no . . ." She shook herself, clearing her head from a particularly nasty image. "Absolutely not. I will not have you throw yourself

away on a man more than twice your age who makes less than half what you are worth!"

"Kimberley-Hughes is definitely twice my age," Oberlin countered.

"I meant a poor man. He's so . . . common. And he owns a pub! For God's sake, Oberlin!"

"You are such a snob! A horrible bigoted snob! I am leaving. And Eddie and I are getting married!" she screamed at her mother's equally enraged face. Oberlin felt her blood boiling in her veins. Why couldn't her mother understand! Oberlin didn't want a loveless marriage based on social standing and bank accounts. She wanted Eddie, who never made her feel like a failure, who always made her feel like she was worthy. She didn't want to spend the rest of her life apologizing for coming into a marriage with nothing more than a cheque book.

"Over my dead body!" Verity screamed.

"If that's what it takes!"

Chapter Eighteen

~

B efore he'd left to return to his wife from his fake conference, Paul urged me to talk to Jonathan again. "You need
to give him a chance to refute what Rachel claims—that he
used drugs and alcohol to control and dominate Greer. It's only
fair."

"Should I take Dave again?" I asked, my lip curling in
distaste.

"Of course."

I ground my teeth so hard I was in danger of breaking a
molar. "I do not need protecting."

"Pear Blossom," Paul said, his eyes growing dark and his
tone serious, "this is a man who has possibly killed his fiancée,
who is now being accused of controlling her by getting her
addicted to drugs. Things are getting dangerous. You're absolutely taking someone along with you, and if has to be Dave
then so be it."

I narrowed my eyes, snorting breath out of my nose. "Fine,"
I said, my tone low and dangerous. "But then you are coming
with me to Virginia. I'm not spending two or three days with
Dave at a motel in the backwoods."

Paul's expression softened as he laid a hand on my cheek. "I'll see what I can do. No promises, though."

"No promises," I repeated.

In too many of Greer's books, promises lead to bad things. In *Swingline*, as soon as Eddie promised to protect Oberlin he failed, resulting in her kidnapping thirty pages later.

So I have Rule Number Eight: No promises. Ever.

"Oh, and Pear Blossom?"

"Yeah," I said, already sulky about Dave nosing into my work again.

"Watch yourself around my office. Katz is getting suspicious. At the faculty meeting he suggested instituting a policy to leave our doors open during office hours or whenever we meet with students. You know, what with MeToo, and all."

"Maybe he's actually concerned about the harassment of students."

Paul's voice was bleak. "He looked at me while he said it."

After he'd gone, I moped around my apartment. Not even Netflix and a vodka gimlet helped. My apartment was tiny, with a coffee table that took up most of the floor space, so it shouldn't feel empty. But whenever Paul left to go back to his regular life, the space felt cavernous.

My mind, on the other hand, was way too roomy. It was swimming with joy over the day and night we'd just had, happiness for Faye's impressive art show, despair about Professor Katz's subtle accusation, anger at having to call Dave-fucking-Zukko for help again, terror at almost being discovered by Martha, and frustration that, for every step I made forward in my movie, I always had to take two steps backward.

Frustrated, I threw the sheets over the bed and beat the pillows back in place, then scrubbed at the dishes with such fervor I was surprised I didn't crack the plates. Feeling not that much better, I resigned myself to planning out my next steps for the documentary.

First, I'd email Jonathan to ask for another interview date. Next, I needed to email or call Rachel to ask that we film everything we talked about at Heavenly Goods. Then I should probably contact Greer's mom to show her what I'd gotten so far. I wanted to ask about the drug allegations, too.

I was looking forward to none of these calls. So what I ended up doing first was searching for hotels near the Kilmarnock Lighthouse. There were your typical chains, and then what looked like a mom-and-pop place called the Kilmarnock Inn. The prices were good, so I left that page open on my browser.

It was then, with a deep, deep sigh, that I texted Dave. *Free for a second go-round with Jonathan on Tuesday?*

To my intense irritation, Dave texted back immediately, saying that he'd make time to go with me, just let him know the time and the place.

"Great," I texted back and threw my phone down with a groan. Now I was stuck with him. Just perfect. Everyone loved Dave, but his cocksure, sloppy, God's-gift-to-women attitude drove me bonkers. *Grrr.* I wanted to slap his smug smile off his face. I sucked in a fortifying breath, embracing the doom, and promised myself that things wouldn't get worse.

Jonathan I handled with an email. I asked if we could continue our interview, not indicating that I'd royally fucked up by forgetting to ask him really big, embarrassing questions. I suggested we meet on Tuesday and, remembering that he was not an early riser, offered one o'clock.

Rachel, on the other hand, would require a phone call. I did some deep breathing to get rid of any residual mortification over my second complete fuck up, and dialed her number. To my amazement she picked up after three rings.

Who actually picks up a phone call anymore?

"Hi, Rachel," I said. "It's June Masterson."

"Hi, June. What's up?"

"I need to get you in front of a camera to talk about how Jonathan controlled Greer with drugs," I said. Maybe I was too blunt, because she was silent so long I had to ask, "Hello? Rachel?" to make sure she hadn't hung up on me.

"I'm here," she said. "I don't know if I should. I don't exactly have proof."

"But you did see her on drugs, right?"

"I suspected she was taking drugs, but I never saw her actually take a pill or anything like that."

What? But hadn't Rachel said she had proof? Or had at least witnessed her on drugs? I meant to say all this, but all that came out of my mouth was a weird groaning sound and then, "But—but—but—"

"Look," Rachel said, "I'm sorry. I can't go on camera. But maybe if you get proof, I will. Did she write anything about using drugs? Maybe there were pills in her purse or car when she disappeared. The police never released what they found, you know."

I swallowed hard. "I'm going down to Virginia. I'll see if I can get the list."

"Great. If the police can confirm drugs were found, I'll go on camera with what I told you. You have to understand, Jonathan would sue me for everything I'm worth if he knew I'd said he was controlling her with drugs without proof she was even on drugs."

A dull buzzing sound filled my head. In a faraway voice I said, "Sure. I understand. I'll get right on that."

"Great!" Rachel said, and hung up.

I could only stare at my phone, cursing how utterly fucked I'd just become. Jonathan isn't just going to sue Rachel. He's going to sue me too. I'd never have a job in the movie industry. My name would be mud. Well, I'd still interview Jonathan. Dave would be there, and I'd at least bring him down with me.

* * *

Goddamn Dave Zukko to hell. Today he'd been on time, early even, and was waiting for me inside the lobby of Jonathan's building. Ms. Chirpy, the concierge, had recognized him from last time and let him in. They let me stand out in the cold wind, punching in the number wrong twice before getting it right, and then lug in the gear by myself while they flirted with each other. He was leaning forward, elbows on the counter, grinning at her. Ms. Chirpy batted her eyelashes, giggling at some stupid joke Dave had just made. I refuse to think that Dave was actually witty. As I finally got through the door, I saw Ms. Chirpy slide him her number. Now we were on the elevator, and he was whistling. *Whistling!* Loudly. In an elevator!

"Could you just shut up for a minute?" I hissed.

"Bad mood, Masterson?" Dave asked, his voice dripping with amusement. "Or is it a hangover? I know there's a party girl inside there somewhere. Nice knock on the chin, by the way."

I glared at him, self-consciously touching my scabbed chin. "You could have helped me instead of flirting with the concierge, you know."

"Looked like you were doing fine. Plus, I know how independent you are."

I ground my teeth and growled at him. "It was windy and cold and this stuff is heavy. I shouldn't have had to ask."

He blew out a long, low sigh. "I can't win with you. I'm here to help you film, but you don't actually want my help. Then you want my help, but you can't tell me; I'm supposed to just know you need it. I'm not a psychic, June."

I was getting ready to smack him when the elevator interrupted me with a *ding!* I pasted a sunny smile on my face before I once again stepped out into bright white light. I was going to be cheerful, dammit. Cheerful and professional.

I looked around, taking in the sharp whiteness of it all. It hurt my eyes a little. Maybe this was what it was like to go "into the light" when you died. A blinding light and then a white room with Scandinavian modern furniture where you waited until St. Peter could get to your name.

Jonathan greeted us in white linen pants, an untucked sky blue linen shirt, and bare feet. He sipped from a mug of coffee, giving off the Zen aura of a catalogue model. "Welcome back," he said. "Can I get you a cup of coffee?"

"No," Dave said. "We're fine."

So now he was speaking for me? I don't think so, buddy. "I'd love a cup, please," I said, giving Dave a pointed look.

He shrugged and took the camera bag off my shoulder. "I'll go set up then. Same place?" he asked Jonathan.

"Yes, let me know if you have trouble moving the sofa," he said. "Come into the kitchen, June, and we'll get you that cup of coffee."

His mugs were a flat black color. I asked for cream, just so I could see the coffee in the mug. "Sugar?" he asked, spoon poised over the cup.

"Sure."

He dropped in the sugar, giving the liquid a quick stir. "Now, what are we going to discuss today?"

I wasn't sure how much I wanted to prepare him. A good surprise is always great for a film. I also didn't want him to shut us down before we'd even begun. "Well, I've spoken to some other people, and I wanted to give you a chance to respond." That sounded bland enough, I thought, but still gave him enough information.

"Who painted me in a worse light? Blanche or Rachel?"

"I can't really . . ."

"Rachel, then. Because Blanche barely cared about me." I tried to maintain my neutral expression while he sipped his coffee. "What, exactly, did they say about me?"

"I'd rather wait to ask you on camera, but it's nothing that you've been charged with, and most of it is hearsay." *So far.*

Jonathan took so long to answer, I started to sweat. Had I told him too much? Or not enough? Was he going to kick us out? I heard Dave grunting and then came the scraping of a large piece of furniture sliding across the wood floor in the next room.

Jonathan stared at me with his gray eyes, but I couldn't read his expression. He didn't look mad, but he didn't look happy either. Finally he spoke. "You haven't touched your coffee. Oh, and I'd like to read those notes," he said, walking back around to the living room. I quickly took a sip and followed him out.

Dave had the sofa in place and was putting the camera onto the tripod. "You could have helped."

"I'm not a psychic," I told him. "If you want help you have to ask."

Dave shot me a black look while I gave him a genuine shit-eating grin. With my mood suddenly improved, I sat down on a chair, took a rewarding swig of my coffee, and put my interview tablet on my knee. Dave clicked the camera in place, turned it on, and gave me a nod.

"I'm ready whenever you are, Jonathan."

Jonathan made himself comfortable on the sofa underneath his Pollock. "I'm ready," he said. His eyes locked onto the camera and his baritone voice became richer and more commanding than it had been in the kitchen.

I nodded to Dave and he started to film.

"One question—or, really, accusation—that kept coming up was the embezzlement." His mouth tightened, but Jonathan started nodding as I spoke. "Investigators found an account in the Caymans with eighteen million dollars in it. All in your name. How can you explain that?"

"I can't explain anything about the money. I had no idea that account even existed." Jonathan's eyes were wide and innocent.

I narrowed my own in response and forged ahead. "How can you not know that for a year and a half, a million dollars a month was being siphoned out of Greer's accounts? Even if you didn't have legal access to Greer's accounts, you would've known it was missing." I couldn't keep the incredulity out of my voice.

Jonathan's innocence turned into sheepishness. "Greer and I weren't the best at managing our money. You have to understand, at the height of her popularity, the money was *pouring* in. She had one book that had already been made into a movie, with two more books optioned. We couldn't keep track of all the bills—what was coming in and going out. After we almost got evicted from our apartment for forgetting to pay the mortgage for six months, we hired an accountant. He took care of things like paying the bills, getting the taxes filed. He would have been the one to notice anything."

"So a million dollars just . . . slipped through the cracks every month?" I was living so close to the bone that I was literally picking up pennies off the ground. To not notice that *a million dollars a month* was leaving the account? That excuse smelled a lot like bullshit. "I spoke to Greer's accountant. He told me you came to him once demanding fifty thousand dollars."

"That man is a kook. He was half in love with Greer himself. He'd say anything to smear my good name. He probably put the money in there himself to make it look like I did it. I bet there wasn't even an account until after Greer disappeared. He doctored his files to make it look like I was stealing."

"He said he gave you a black eye, trying to get you to leave."

"And I should have filed charges. He's a menace. Believe me, I didn't take any crap from some crazy accountant."

"If he hated you, why would he put money under your name in the Caymans, knowing that, once you were proven not guilty, you'd have eighteen million dollars free and clear. Why take the chance?"

"I don't know. He's crazy. When I first heard about the money, you know what I thought? I thought that Greer had been putting it aside for me. She had a fear of dying early. She worried about me. We weren't married yet, and she knew that her mother would inherit the big trust. Blanche had those talons of hers deep into Greer's trust fund. That was one reason why she'd buy me art." He gestured to the Pollock behind him. "So I wouldn't be left destitute in case the worst happened."

"You have to admit, eighteen million dollars hidden in the Caymans is a big motive," I said.

Jonathan nodded emphatically, his gray eyes wide. "It is. I understand why the police suspected me, but I'm clearly not guilty. I'm another victim here. My Greer is gone and the police can't figure out what happened. All they can do is look at me and wonder about money, which I knew nothing about, by the way. I've said it before and I'll say it again—I had nothing to do with it. I'm as much a victim as she is. More, because I'm still alive, yet not able to fully *live*."

"It'll be no surprise to you that while making this documentary I've spoken to other people about Greer Larkin. One person has suggested that Greer was not happy in her relationship with you," I said, moderating my voice to be low and calm.

"That would be Rachel and Blanche, no doubt," he said. He sounded almost amused about it.

"Can you tell me more about the kind of relationship you had?"

"We loved each other. Deeply. We were soul mates. She depended on me and I depended on her," Jonathan said, smiling into the camera.

"So you never fought?"

"Hardly ever. Sure, we had disagreements, but they were never major. Mostly we bickered over restaurants."

"Restaurants?"

"I liked spicy foods and she didn't. Greer had a delicate stomach."

"Did she take medication for her stomach issues?" I asked, gently stepping into the subject of drugs.

"Yes, she was on a couple different medications. She had anxiety. I've never talked about it in public before. We tried to keep Greer's life private. She was a very private person. I told the police, of course, because that might be one way of tracing her, if she was still alive. She needed her anxiety medication, and she had to see a doctor before her next refill."

"Jonathan, we've heard that she may not have been taking only anxiety medications. People have told us that she was taking illegal drugs and illegally prescribed opioids." I referred to my notes. "Valium, Percocet, and quaaludes, to name a few."

Jonathan was already shaking his head. "She wasn't taking anything like that. Yes, she took Valium for a little while, but it made her feel nauseous and dizzy, so her doctor switched her to Wellbutrin, I think. It's been a long time since I had to think about this," he said with a self-deprecating smile. "But she never took illegal drugs."

I had my answer, and it was a good one, but I plunged onward. "People told us that she was addicted to both legal *and* illegal drugs. They also said you were her supplier, that you used the drugs to keep her compliant and prevent her from breaking off your relationship. They say you used her addiction to keep her isolated away from her friends and family."

Jonathan gave a chuckle and shook his head. "That just isn't true. Greer and I were in love. We were going to be married. And for the last time, she wasn't addicted to anything."

He looked away from the camera and smiled at me. I smiled back and a tiny wave of nausea rolled over me. I frowned slightly, shaking my head to clear it. "Given the opioid crisis that we are facing now, knowing now how addictive drugs like Valium and Percocet are, isn't it possible that Greer became addicted accidentally and you, as a loving fiancé, were just giving her what she needed?"

Jonathan was already shaking his head. "No, no, no. That's not possible. I protected her. Her mother was a controlling, manipulative bitch. She wanted Greer under her thumb and her fingers on all the money Greer made. Her friend, Rachel, would do, and say, anything to keep us apart so she'd have Greer for herself. But," his voice hitched and tears were standing in his gray eyes, "but I loved her. I let her be free. I let her be what no one else would let her be. Herself." Bending forward, Jonathan began to sob.

I gestured at Dave to cut and we sat still as statues while Jonathan cried in long, rending sobs. I started to choke up when another wave of nausea hit me. As I stood, the room rocked. "I will—I need to go to the bathroom," I said and hurried down the hallway without waiting for Jonathan to give me permission.

When I found the bathroom, I closed the door and turned on the water taps full blast before I vomited in the toilet.

Chapter Nineteen

❧

"**I** *cannot* believe you left me in there with a crying, grown-ass man," Dave said. "Not just crying, *sobbing*. Sobbing like a baby." He huffed. "The only thing that made it better was you barfing in a sobbing man's toilet."

I still felt clammy and weak. "At least I got what I wanted before he kicked us out."

"Yeah. A full denial about the money and your addiction theory. Which helps you how, by the way?"

"I just need to get Rachel on camera with her side of the story, then I've got a good 'he said/she said' scenario. Plus, I'm heading to Virginia to get a list of what was in that purse. If she had any drug other than Wellbutrin, then I know Jonathan's lying. It's win-win." The brisk air, along with the knowledge I had another shot at proving Jonathan tried to control Greer with drugs, were making me feel better.

"Yeah, win-win. But if you're getting the flu, you're going to be flat on your back for a week. You're going to be so far behind schedule you'll never catch up."

"I'm not getting the flu. I just got a little nauseous," I snapped.

"Maybe Mr. Innocent put something in your coffee," he said, with a hint of malice.

"Oh. My. God. People don't actually do that in real life. You need to stop watching true crime shows," I said.

"Maybe you're pregnant!" Dave chortled. My stomach rolled again and sweat broke out across my upper lip. "Ha! We know it's not that, since you don't ever date anybody."

"Yeah." I laughed weakly. "I'm for sure not pregnant."

But I immediately started doing calculations. What day was it? When had my period last appeared? Seven, fourteen, fifteen, eighteen. Ugh. I couldn't count while Dave was still chattering in my ear.

"You're sure."

His skeptical, knowing tone sent a ripple of panic to join the nausea rolling around in my stomach. "Of course I'm sure," I said, trying for casual and failing miserably. "Why wouldn't I be sure?"

"Because you've been sleeping with Paul Logan."

My feet welded themselves to the sidewalk and I came to a screeching halt. "What did you say?" I whispered.

Dave turned to face me, nose to nose. "You, June Masterson, have been carrying on with your married professor."

"You know?" I whispered again. I couldn't make my voice any louder. Something was wrong with my throat.

"Of course I know. I figured it out two months ago when you came out of his office hours appointment with your shirt on inside out."

Oh. Shit.

"Does anyone else know?"

Dave shrugged. "I'm not sure. I haven't told anyone, if that's what you're asking."

My stomach unknotted slightly. "Thanks."

"Sure. But you know this is insane, right? You know he's never going to leave his wife, right?"

My turn to shrug. "We've never discussed it. We're fine as we are."

Dave snorted. "Yeah, I bet."

"What's that supposed to mean?" I asked, defensive.

"It means love shouldn't be 'fine.' People in relationships make plans for the future. If he's not discussing it with you, then there's no future."

Narrowing my eyes, I considered punching him in the throat. "You don't know *anything* about it."

Dave continued on like I hadn't said a word. "What is it about him, anyway? Is the sex that great? You know, if you're caught, you're always going to be 'that girl who slept with her professor,' right? Your entire career will be over before it's even started. Plus, he's *married*. Sleeping with a married man is just wrong, June. It's wrong on so many levels."

"It's also none of your business," I said. Why did Dave even care? It's not like we were friends. Why couldn't he keep his nose out of my business? It's not like I didn't know sleeping with a married man was wrong, but there was a voice I couldn't ignore deep in my soul, telling me Paul and I were destined to be together. With Paul, I felt grounded and whole. I felt lost without him.

Dave better keep his fat mouth shut. If he ruined this, he'd get to see, up close and personal, what the wrath of a pissed-off woman looks like.

"Look, as much as I'd love to see you fail, thereby securing my spot as the number one filmmaker in the department, I don't want it to be because you made a bad choice about who you slept with." Dave's mouth formed a thin, grim line, and his eyes grew serious. He lifted his hand, as if he was going to put it on my shoulder, but then seemed to think better of it, and his hand drifted back down to his side.

The truth is, I knew that he was right. My relationship with Paul was risky for me too. The woman always got the blame and the man walked away free. I also knew that if my mother were to find out I was sleeping with a married man, she would leave the commune for the first time in over two decades in her Volkswagen Vanagon to give me a hard slap and a lecture. Dave's concern was touching, if misguided.

"I know what I'm doing. And I don't think you'll ever have to worry about being the best." The corner of my mouth twitched into a ghost of a smile, which he took as a sign that I wasn't going to kill him.

"If your stomach bug ends up being a twenty-four-hour thing, maybe you could make it to Ashby's on Saturday. A bunch of us are getting together for drinks," he said, offering a proverbial olive branch.

"Don't think so," I said automatically.

"Come on. It'll be fun. You never go out."

"And if I show up I'll be arrested for murder, because all your friends will die from shock."

Dave gave a deep belly laugh, his brown eyes twinkling. "See? I knew you could be funny on purpose."

I gave him a jab in the ribs, but couldn't help smiling despite the small waves of nausea rippling through my stomach. At my subway stop I said, "Thanks, Dave. I hope I don't need you again."

"No problem," he said, handing the camera bag to me. I started down the stairs when he called, "Hey, June?" I turned my head back as he said, "My movie is going to crush your movie." I flipped him off, which inspired a guffaw out of him, and continued down into the bowels of New York.

At four thirty in the afternoon, rush hour's in full-swing. The swarms of humanity, wrung out and stinking from a hard day's work, crowded the swaying car, making me feel even worse. I opened my phone to the calendar to see if I'd noted my last period. Of course, I hadn't. It would've been shocking if I'd actually been that organized. Cursing myself, vowing to keep better track of such an important event, I passed by Walgreens. I slowed to a stop and stared at the door.

Five minutes later, I left the shop, shoving a pregnancy test into my bag. The cashier had been so absurdly cheerful I wanted to punch her. Instead, I gave her a pained smile before rushing out into the crowded streets.

My heart raced, and I felt sicker than ever, sweaty and faint. *Had Jonathan put something in my coffee?* A fleeting thought I pushed hastily aside. He'd only added sugar and cream. He'd also put sugar and cream in his cup, right? Or had he?

My brain told me puking into the gutter seemed like a great option, but I held off until I could get home and vomit in peace. My hands were so shaky I could barely hold the keys to my building. I managed to unlock the door, only dropping my keys once.

The mailman was in the lobby. My mailman hated me. I picked up my mail about every other week, or when he couldn't latch the box shut anymore. I avoided him like I owed him money. "Hey, Box 204. Take your mail. I can't fit anything else in there."

"Thanks," I said, grabbing my mail and bypassing the unreliable elevator to climb the two flights to my apartment.

It was slow going, slower than normal. Relieved, I finally reached my floor and began walking down the hall. As I got to my door, I focused on getting my door key out for a quick, easy entry into my apartment and my bathroom. I lifted my head only to come eye-to-eye with the blunt end of a very sharp knife.

My keys clattered to the ground. Then so did I.

Sometime later, I opened my eyes to find my eighty-year-old neighbor's shriveled face inches away from my own. I let out a "Ha!" of surprise and scrambled up onto my butt.

"Are you okay, dear?" Mrs. Bukowski breathed at me, making my head swirl as the alcoholic fumes leaked out of her body. Mrs. Bukowski was a gin-fueled, bingo-playing grandma who'd lived in the apartment across the hall since the Nixon administration. "I was about to give you a good, old-fashioned slap to bring you around."

"No, Mrs. B, I'm fine," I said, grateful to have woken when I did.

"Interesting note you've got up there," she said.

"Note?" I looked up. There was indeed a note impaled at the pointed end of the knife sticking in my door. "No worries, Mrs. B. Just a friend playing a joke. Ha-ha." My laugh was so wooden it had splinters.

"You've got weird friends, my dear," Mrs. Bukowski muttered. "You dropped your mail."

On top of my handful of takeout menus and furniture store ads was a letter addressed to Maya Davenport. "Hey, Mrs. B, do you know if a Maya Davenport lived here before me?"

"No, dear. No one named Maya has ever lived here."

Weird. Maybe I should Google her. "Well, thanks, Mrs. B. I think I'll be okay."

The smell of gin started to dissipate as I got back onto my feet. I gave Mrs. Bukowski a little finger-wave as she closed her door. I yanked the knife out of my door and brought it, and the note, inside.

The note was like something straight out of the movies. They'd cut each letter from magazines and glued them to the paper. It's a little hard to take it seriously, because it felt so Hollywood. However, that didn't mean my heart wasn't beating about a hundred miles an hour and I wasn't pumping enough adrenaline through my veins to power most of New Jersey.

GREER LARKIN IS DEAD. IF YOU WANT TO KEEP BREATHING YOU WILL DROP IT.

The knife went right through the O of "to," making a thin slice about an inch long. It was a really nice chef's knife—Wüsthof. I knew those were really expensive. Way out of my, or a classmate's, budget. This one was six inches long, with a slightly worn handle. Someone liked to cook and chop vegetables with this knife. Still, a six-inch chef's knife is an odd choice to stab into a door. In the movies, it's always some kind of Bowie knife or stiletto.

Who on earth used a small chef's knife to pin a note to a door?

I have to admit, I should've been more scared, but mostly what I felt was bafflement. However, did I secure both my locks and shove a chair under the doorknob? You bet I did. My finger also spent some quality time hovering over Paul's name as I thought about calling him. I would love to have him come to my rescue, to wrap his arms around me and make me feel safe. But then I'd have to tell him I'd been threatened by an anonymous note, which would make him freak out and demand I go back to uncovering the hidden talents of New York's wait staff. No, thank you.

Plus, there'd be yelling about touching evidence and not calling the police. It's better for everyone—well, better for me—if I pretended this never happened.

I'd have loved to pretend the nausea wasn't happening, either. At long last, I heaved to in my bathroom, ridding myself of what seemed like two days worth of food. Mercifully, I felt a lot better as I climbed into my bed.

Things were different in the dark, however. My body was rigid as the night began to fill with unnerving sounds I'd never noticed before. My ears strained to hear the telltale click of a key in my lock or the rattle of my doorknob turning. Just as I would finally shut my eyes, some new squeak had me bolting upright and sweating. In the end, I put all my pots and pans on the chair under the doorknob as a makeshift murderer alarm and spent most of the night willing the door to stay closed.

* * *

If jumping at shadows were an Olympic sport, I'd have been getting gold medals all week. It didn't help that I'd barely slept, or that I'd dropped food in favor of straight caffeine consumption. Give me enough coffee and I'd rule the world—wasn't that the saying? I was well on my way to proving it.

I'd wanted to call Paul the second I saw the knife in my door, but I stopped myself. Part of it was because he would've shut down my film, but I also didn't call because it was Against the Rules. Rule Number Nine: You don't call your lover at home when he's with his wife. Even if it's an emergency. Even if you're really scared. His wife needed him.

But a tiny voice deep inside couldn't help piping up. *But you need him too.*

I had to get out of town, if only for a couple of days, so I could reclaim some semblance of normality or balance in my life. I desperately wanted Paul to come with me. The threatening note and knife were hidden under my couch, but I kept pulling them out. The note called to me. IF YOU WANT TO KEEP BREATHING YOU WILL DROP IT.

Then there was the part declaring Greer was dead. How did they know? Had they killed Greer? I'd been with Jonathan right before the note was knifed into my door. I highly doubt he'd been able to get here from across town before me. Traffic in New York is no joke. I don't think he even knew where I lived. So if the killer was the one threatening me, then that automatically meant Jonathan couldn't have killed Greer.

That fact would be inconvenient for a lot of people. The forum members of GreersGone would blow up with speculation—about me, the threat, and what the timing meant. Rachel would call me a liar. Blanche, well, I shudder to think what Blanche would do.

Blanche already called—twice in fact—asking to see the footage I'd collected so far. The second time was more of a command than a request. Sleep-deprived as I was, I wasn't in a state to defend myself or my work from any attacks she might make. I also might slip up and talk about the threat I'd received. When I finally did call, I chose a time I hoped she wouldn't be home. When Gerald confirmed her ladyship was away, I breathed a sigh of relief and asked for her to call me back.

The whole week went by without another threat sliding under, or through, my door. No phone calls with heavy breathing. No one following me as I darted into the market for food or down the block for Chinese. Not even an anonymous text with the script, "you've been warned . . ."

Still, this would be the perfect time to go to Virginia. I'd avoid Blanche, feel safe enough to get a ton of sleep, and have an excuse for a couple of days away with Paul. Well, perhaps I wouldn't be getting *a ton* of sleep.

I called Paul at his office, asking if he would, please, escort me down to Virginia either tomorrow or the next day. I kept my tone and language formal. In case Professor Katz was listening, I wanted this to sound like a request from a student for their advisor's help, not a rendezvous of two lovers. There was a smile in Paul's voice as he answered.

"I'll have to check my schedule, but I think leaving the day after tomorrow will be fine. I'm happy to go support you during the interviews with the police. Send me your itinerary and make the hotel arrangements."

Thirty seconds later I got a text from Paul. "Checking to see if I can leave for two days. Need to have someone cover my class. Will get back to you."

Okay. Cool. Of course he needed to find a sub for his class and check with his wife to make sure he wasn't leaving at a bad time. He's always so cautious about our relationship. He had to be or he'd lose his job and any hope of making another film. Especially with Professor Katz gunning for him.

But I needed him. My vulnerability was screaming like skin rubbed raw. I needed to feel protected. To feel worth protecting.

*　　*　　*

Two hours later the text came.

"Book the room."

I did a happy dance before starting to pack my bags. I upended my shoulder bag, cleaning it out so I could repack with only what I needed, when a pink and white package clattered to the floor and slid under the couch.

Getting on my hands and knees, I put my head on the floor to reach under the couch. As I pulled out the box, the threatening letter came out with it.

DROP IT, the note said. A pit opened up in the bottom of my stomach, letting all the happiness I'd felt about having two whole days with Paul in a place where his wife would never, ever be, fall through it. Someone wanted what happened to Greer Larkin to remain a mystery. Wanted it badly. Badly enough, maybe, to follow me to Virginia.

I let the note fall onto the coffee table in order to focus on the other unwelcome thing I'd pulled out from under the couch—a small package with bold pink letters declaring this pregnancy test gave results six days sooner than other tests. My stomach sank to my shoes as spots swam before my eyes.

The pregnancy test.

How on earth could I have forgotten? Having a baby is the number one life-changing moment for women. Was amnesia a symptom of pregnancy? Because that was the only justification I could come up with that didn't end with me being a garbage human being.

Finding a note threatening my life knifed to my door had flooded me with panic, choking any thought of pregnancy out of my mind. All week I'd been watching my door for signs of invasion, attributing the low levels of nausea swirling around my body to a lack of sleep and food, along with overdoses of caffeine and adrenaline.

But what if I'm nauseous and tired for a completely different reason?

Lord in heaven. It doesn't matter how many rules you have, there is one ultimate rule that you never, ever break. You never get pregnant.

Five minutes later I was pacing around my room, looking at the timer on my phone every three seconds, not daring to look at the narrow, white stripe of plastic on the counter. I couldn't believe this was happening. Paul and I used protection every time—without fail. One minute left. I was going to die in agony of suspense. I should text Paul. But then I'd be telling him I might be pregnant. He'd freak. Would Paul want the baby? Did *I* want the baby? Would I be left to raise our child by myself? Would he leave Martha? Would we become a real family? Did he even like kids? He and Martha didn't have any. Why was that? What would it mean for him to be only mine? Or would I lose him forever? He might tell Martha all about us. I didn't want that. Not just yet, anyway.

I bit my lip. I wished I could be sure that telling Paul wouldn't ruin everything.

Thirty seconds left. I'd text Meadow. Not about the test, of course, but about Faye's show. Did she sell Simone? Did that woman buy her Nina? And for how much? I'm sure the show was a huge success—after I'd broken about a thousand dollars worth of glasses and escaped through the back door of a church, running from my lover's wife. I sighed. I'd have to apologize for that. I'd have to more than apologize. This would take groveling.

I could call Bethany's office. Again. For someone who was willing to be part of this film, she was exceedingly hard to contact. Each time I had to leave a message with her assistant Stella it was harder and harder to hold onto my temper. It's not like she'd dodge my messages. Would she?

Behind me my phone sounded with chimes and whistles. Without thinking, I leaped to stop it. A big zero stared up at me. It was time.

I didn't want to look, but if I waited, would that invalidate the test? Would I end up having to go through all this again? I couldn't bear it. I'd rip my apartment to shreds if I spent another three minutes like that.

"Okay," I said out loud. "You're going to have to put on your big-girl panties and look. Real quick. Then it will all be over." *Or just beginning.*

I walked over to the counter, the little strip of plastic coiled like a snake waiting to bite me. Before I could see whether there were two lines or only the hoped for one line, I closed my eyes.

"I'm going to count to three, then I'm going to open my eyes to look. No chickening out. One. Two." I took a deep breath.

"Three."

Chapter Twenty

⁓

Interstate 95 out of New York takes you directly to Virginia, with no side roads. It can actually take you all the way to Miami if you choose to stay on it and don't, as Paul and I did, get off at Fredericksburg and go east until we hit the Chesapeake Bay.

Paul's mood was buoyant. "I bet we can get some crabs here. Have you ever had crabs?"

"No," I said, watching an impressive amount of greenery flash by the window. I felt oddly pensive. I should've been just as elated as Paul, especially since I wasn't carrying his baby. The test window had remained blessedly blank. My initial relief had been replaced by heavy clouds full of What If. "Are they even in season now? It's almost February."

"Oh well, we'll find something else fun to eat," Paul said breezily.

I glanced down at the book on my lap. I'd brought one of Greer Larkin's books with me. A sort of security blanket. *The Girl Who Sang a Tune* was about a man found dead on his yacht off the coast of Virginia. He was, of course, alone on his yacht, with no sign of anyone else, apart from four staff members, having been on board. Plus, there'd been a storm during the night, making it unlikely for the murderer to sneak onto their boat and then escape. Oberlin Hurst, a boarding school classmate of the man's daughter, starts poking around, first suspecting the man's wife, then uncovering his mistress, and ultimately revealing that his mistress is pregnant with his child.

It's a juicy book with ripping dialogue and tense stand-offs. I admit I felt an affinity with the mistress, more so now, even though my pregnancy test had been negative. The mistress genuinely loved the victim and had been content to remain in the shadows. The wife knew about her, practicing a "don't ask, don't tell" policy. Did Martha know about me? Was she content with the arrangement as long as I was also content to stay in the shadows?

In the end it'd been Oberlin's friend who killed her father after finding out about his mistress and the impending arrival of a sibling. She'd disguised herself as a member of the staff, hoping no one would recognize her since she'd been at boarding school most of the time.

I wanted to talk to Paul about the pregnancy test. I wanted to know what he'd do if I did get pregnant. We were having sex, after all, and there was a real danger of getting pregnant, no matter how elite the condoms. But I also felt it would be a significant moment in our relationship. Once I opened my mouth and said the words, I couldn't take them back. And those words would change things; they would change *us*. That scared me. The chance that we'd unravel was too great. I looked out the window, watching the landscape rush by.

A door opened in my head and a small voice said, *If you were sure he loved you, you'd know if he'd be happy.* But I beat the voice back and locked the door. Paul loved me. I was sure. Well, pretty sure.

As we put the city farther behind us, knots started to loosen from my shoulders, the acid in my stomach stopped churning, and I found Paul's good mood infectious. I happily read snippets of my book between Paul's musings about what coastal Virginia would hold for us.

"After we visit Officer Bedford, we can go by the Kilmarnock Lighthouse to take some B-roll footage and plan your voice-overs. The internet says there's a barbecue place pretty close to there. How do you feel about ribs?"

"Sounds great," I said. "I'd like to get to Kilmarnock early in the morning so we can get some dawn light shots, though. We can film Mr. Bedford in the afternoon with indoor lighting."

"Perfect," Paul said, nodding. "Then we can get some evening shots of Kilmarnock and head to the police station."

"Maybe we should switch days," I said, the gears in my head clicking together. "When I get the case notes, I can plan a better interview for Bedford." Plus, I needed to know for sure if there had been pills in Greer's purse.

Paul was nodding again. "Yeah, I see that. Let's do it your way instead. But what if they say no?"

"I'll come up with something," I said, trying to keep the desperation out of my voice. I really needed to see the list, but I didn't want Paul to know how far I was willing to go to get it.

*　*　*

Quaint hotels are the bread and butter of coastal towns. I'd picked a Victorian inn that was as close to a bed and breakfast as I was comfortable getting. Noise tends to travel in old houses, and housekeeping might comment if your bed hadn't been slept in. The inn was beautiful, full of tall columns, wraparound porches, and white gingerbread woodwork. A huge Persian rug and a pair of tufted leather sofas made the entry feel cozy. A grandmotherly woman, with snow-white hair and a flowered apron, introduced herself as Joyce Compton and gave us our keys.

"Breakfast starts at six and runs until nine. Wine is served in the lounge after four," she said in a warm, chocolate chip cookie voice. "Enjoy your stay."

Our rooms were right next to each other, numbers 38 and 39, on the third floor of the inn. We had a spectacular view of the ocean. Wild and violent, spraying up white foam as it crashed into rocks at the edge of the world. The setting sun colored the water orange and gold, making it look deceptively warm. There weren't many tourists at the ocean in late January. The beach looked lonely and bleak.

Paul bounced into my doorway. "Dinner?"

The faint wrinkles that lined his eyes had smoothed out. His smile was broad and his eyes flashed with glee. He seemed more boyish. "Have you thought about where you want to eat?"

"I hear there's a good Italian place around here," I said, crossing to him and laying my hands on his chest. "It'll be amazing to go out for a dinner where we don't have to look over our shoulders." Crawling out of that restaurant had been humiliating. I vowed never to do that again. Here I didn't have to worry about Martha.

He wrapped his arms around my waist, pulling me closer. "It'll be amazing," he said, giving me a long, luxurious kiss.

"Let's go to Battaglia's. Maybe some of the staff will remember Greer and Jonathan," I said.

"Work, work, work," Paul said, his hands working lower.

"Well, this is a work trip," I said, playfully.

"As long as we can play later," Paul said, kissing the tip of my nose.

"Of course." I gave him a quick kiss on the lips. "Let me get my jacket and we'll go. I'm hungry."

The drive from New York had taken over seven hours, during which we'd barely stopped. We'd wanted to get to the inn before it got too dark. Now, antique streetlamps lit the way to Paul's car, making the old-fashioned downtown feel romantic. We held hands, and he opened my car door for me. This sign of chivalry made me feel fluttery inside. I gave him a quick kiss as I got into the car. I was floating inside, elated.

Battaglia's Italian restaurant was about five miles south of the inn, outside of town, and on the side of the highway. The parking was ample, with very few cars in the gravel lot. Christmas lights wrapped around the evergreen trees flanking the front door. A young woman dressed in a black cocktail dress hugging her in all the right spots met us at the door. I felt incredibly underdressed in my jeans, long-sleeved T-shirt, and leather jacket.

She didn't seem to notice, however. Without batting an eye, she said, "Good evening. Two for dinner?"

"Yes, please," Paul said. "At a quiet table, if you don't mind."

"No problem." Pulling out my chair, she handed us our menus and said, "Your waiter will be right with you."

"This is a nice place," Paul said. He was right. It was done in metal and wood, with white walls and diaphanous white curtains creating romantic alcoves. White linen tablecloths covered square tables while metal and glass chandeliers hung above them. I'd never been to a restaurant that felt so magical and intimate. Granted, I hadn't been to a lot of restaurants, period, but Greer had been here, maybe at this very table. Had Greer found Battaglia's just as magical? Or was it just another restaurant to her? She'd probably eaten at more restaurants by the age of ten than I had in my whole life. But those'd been under the watchful eye of Blanche. Or had Blanche insisted she stay home and work, like my parents?

"It is," I agreed. Our fellow diners, about eight other couples, were also dressed in jeans and casual shirts, which immediately made me feel better about my wardrobe. I also decided I really needed more than one nice outfit, and maybe a dress. Meadow'd be over the moon. She'd demand to shop with me, ensuring I'd end up trying on every outfit in the store. The image gave me a warm feeling, bringing a smile to my lips.

The menu was filled with pastas, antipasti, fish, main courses, and, God be praised, dessert. Like every serious woman, I picked out dessert first. Cannoli, obviously. It was homemade and came dipped in Swiss chocolate. There was a crab risotto that looked good, but then there was a mushroom ravioli with a rabbit ragù that had my mouth watering.

"I don't know what to get," Paul said. "This food looks amazing."

I agreed, but somehow we made our choices and Paul picked out a bottle of wine to complement our dinners. Together we scanned the waiters, looking for someone who looked old enough to have been working here twenty years ago, but every-one looked my age or younger. No way they would've over-heard the argument or seen the slap, even in utero.

"I don't know, Paul," I said. "These people are all really young. They aren't going to know anything."

"Maybe there's some folklore about it. Something big like that? They're going to talk about that for years."

I swirled my wine. "Maybe they'll know where we can find the old maître d'. I'll go and ask our hostess," I said, pulling my napkin off my lap before heading to the front of the restaurant.

Worry and curiosity flashed across her face before being replaced by a wide, toothy smile. "Is everything okay at your table?"

"Everything's fine," I said. "I just have a question. I'm a filmmaker working on a documentary about the disappearance of Greer Larkin. I understand she and her fiancé were here for dinner the night she went missing and they'd had a fight. Is there anyone here who could tell me what happened?"

Her mascara-heavy eyes grew large. "Oh! I've heard of that. Yeah, that was a big thing around here. Lots of press and police. They even had dogs. But no one ever found anything."

"Did you ever hear about the argument?" I asked, hopes high and climbing.

She nodded and said, "Sure, everyone did. I grew up around here. I was, like, two when it happened, but people talk about it. The guy—Jonathan—slapped her and she took off."

"He did," I said. "But did anybody ever say what they were fighting about? The newspapers said the maître d' overheard part of it, but there've been conflicting stories in the press about the actual topic."

She bit her lip. "Gosh. No, I don't know for sure what was said."

"Was it about money? Or another woman?" Domestic fights generally fell into those two categories. I was trying to lead the hostess down a primrose path to remembering.

"I just don't know," she said, apologetic.

Dammit. Still, I refused to be deterred. "Do you know if the maître d' still lives in the area?"

"Well, actually, he died about seven or eight years ago. Sorry."

My face fell as my heart deflated. "That's okay. If you think of anything, I'm staying at the Kilmarnock Inn tonight. Here's my email," I said, writing it out on the back of the manager's business card in my most careful printing. "If you've got any more information, please email me."

"I sure will," she said. I thanked her again as I went back to my table.

Paul watched me walk back to him, sipping his wine, his eyes all over me. I shook my head, and he gave me a sympathetic shrug.

"She'd heard about it, but didn't have any idea what the fight was about," I said. "I tried to jog her memory by asking her about money or another woman, but no go." I bit my lip in disappointment. I figured the fight would've been legendary, the story passed down from generation to generation at the restaurant. But maybe the staff saw more bizarre things on a daily basis than a man slapping a woman.

"Oh well. Nothing ventured, nothing gained. The fight might have simply been an unlucky coincidence."

"You have to admit the timing is suspicious."

"Of course. However, couples fight. Then they make up."

"So, Jonathan and Greer just *happened* to have a very public fight and then some other person just *happened* to kill or kidnap Greer that same night? That is the unluckiest coincidence in the world."

"All I'm saying is, it could've been anyone. Heck, Blanche or Rachel could've done it. It's an easy drive from New York."

I heaved an exasperated sigh. "I get that, but having a fight about money or another woman right before your fiancée disappears is not a good look."

"Don't make the mistake of locking onto one person. Keep your mind open. Get the footage and then build the narrative."

I hated that he was right. And he knew it, because as an olive branch he said, "We'll get more information from Bedford and the police station. Maybe your smoking gun is within reach."

"I hope so," I said as our waitress laid my crab risotto—drizzled with olive oil and dotted with grape tomatoes and slivers of basil—in front of me. The delicious smell raised my flagging spirits. Paul's fettuccine with braised rabbit was also generously graced with fresh basil. My mouth watered so much I needed a sip of wine before I drooled all over myself.

The meal was free of talk about the film, but full of moans and groans of gastronomic delight. We talked about his colleagues as well as the other students in the program. Paul asked how Faye's art show had gone, so I had to admit that I hadn't called Meadow yet to ask.

"Oh? Why not? I thought you were crazy for the portrait of Simone?"

"I was. I mean, I am. I love it, it's just that—"

"Embarrassed about our hasty departure?" he asked, looking a little chagrined.

"That's a little bit of it, but I've been, well, things came up this week and I didn't get the chance." *Please don't ask me what came up*, I pleaded.

"So, what came up? You weren't on campus," Paul said.

Oh, nothing. Just a knife in my door and a brief moment when I thought I might be carrying your child. Of course, I couldn't say that. Talk about ruining the moment. I needed a lie. A good one. "Just . . . editing the film," I said. It was lame, but hopefully believable. And not entirely false. I *was* worried about editing the film. A little bit. To keep from fidgeting under his gaze, I drained my wine and held out my glass. "Can you pour me more, please?"

"Sure," he said, watching me carefully.

"Thanks," I said. "Cheers." I raised my glass and took another healthy swig.

When I looked at him, Paul's fingers toyed with his fork as he stared at me with narrowed eyes. *Suspicious.* I'd never really lied to his face before. I'm a horrible liar. I needed a distraction before he could question me more.

I was about to offer Paul the time of his life in the restaurant bathroom, when the hostess came hustling over to our table. Her eyes were bright and her cheeks pink.

"I've got it for you," she said.

My breathing picked up a notch. "What have you got?"

"I asked an old line chef, and he said Greer and her boyfriend were fighting about money. He wanted money for a restaurant. She said no, she couldn't afford another failure, and that's when he slapped her." She practically panted with excitement, her face triumphant.

I felt my own face break into a wide grin. I looked at Paul, gleeful and victorious. "See! I told you it would be money!" I turned back to our hostess and thanked her profusely. She backed away to her station, giving me significant eye contact of solidarity.

"See?" I said. "Now, we just need to find another source to back her up."

"That's a big if," Paul said. "That was, what? Third-hand information? You'd need something in the police report to back that up before we put that line chef on camera."

"Good thing we're going there tomorrow," I said with a smug grin.

I was flying high and wouldn't be daunted.

Chapter
Twenty-One

❦

Excerpt from
The Girl Who Sang a Tune
An Oberlin Hurst Mystery by Greer Larkin

"*D*avid?" *a quavery voice called from the top of the stairs. "David? Where are you? David, I need a drink. David?"*

A woman appeared dressed in a pale pink robe, open over her bra and panties, and pink high heels with feathers at the toes. Her blonde hair was messily piled on her head and her mascara and ruby red lipstick were smeared. Charlotte Crawford was a melting doll of what she used to be.

"Shut up, Charlotte," David said.

"You promised, David. You said if I'm a good girl and stay upstairs, you'd give me another bottle of wine." Charlotte was slurring as she lurched toward the handrail on the stairs.

Oberlin gasped. She was going to fall.

"Don't!" David said, rushing toward the stairs.

"I've been up here such a long time. I've been very good. Please, David. Please?" Charlotte's grasp on the handrail was slipping, and she began to list forward.

David took the stairs two at a time while Oberlin ran to the foot of the stairs, hand to her mouth, trying to keeping her heart from jumping out of her throat. Charlotte was teetering on the edge of the stairs, her feet sliding around in the ridiculous pink heels she was wearing.

"Whoops," she said, her ankles giving out on her.

Oberlin saw it all in slow motion. Her robe fluttered as her body began to spill into the void. Her fingers convulsed and the railing seemed to jump away from her grasp. Her mouth formed a perfect "O" as Charlotte realized she couldn't right herself. Oberlin inhaled, a scream building inside her chest.

Then David was there, his sure hands catching her shoulders, pushing her upright.

"There you go, love," he said, his words coming in gasps.

Oberlin's own breath gushed out in relief. David guided Charlotte back into her room before coming back down.

"Now, where were we?" he said, smiling and relaxed, as if his wife hadn't almost fallen to her death.

"She was drunk," Oberlin accused, brows furrowed.

"Yes, Oberlin, she was drunk. My wife is an alcoholic."

"And you keep her that way," Oberlin said, the horror of Charlotte's condition starting to sink in. *"You keep her drunk and in her room so she'll never know what you're doing."*

"It isn't ideal," he said, *"but it is very convenient."*

Chapter
Twenty-Two

❧

The sky was still dark when I woke. Paul's arm rested on my waist and his cedar and vanilla scent surrounded me. The red clock numbers read five AM. I snuggled into Paul to attempt to get more sleep, but my eyelids continued to stubbornly spring open. I tried for fifteen more minutes before giving it up as a lost cause. Carefully, so as not to wake Paul, I crawled out of the covers and curled up in the chair under the window with my book. The light from the street was just bright enough for me make out the words.

I was well into the sixth chapter when a sleepy voice from the bed asked, "What're you reading?"

"Sorry. I couldn't sleep. I'm reading *The Girl Who Sang a Tune*. It's one of my favorites. It's the second to last book she published," I said, closing the novel and heading back to bed. "You know, it's odd, but there is a character in this book who is basically keeping his wife an alcoholic so he can run her company. It makes me think that, subconsciously, Greer knew what Jonathan was doing to her." My mind flashed to the knife in my door. That also seemed like an awfully familiar scene.

Paul wrapped me back up in his arms as I nestled into his chest. He was still warm from sleep. "Or she wasn't as blind to what was going on as everyone thought. You ready to go and get the footage of the lighthouse?"

I looked out the window. The sky had lightened from black to a dove gray. If we left now we'd get some shots of the dawn over the bay. "Yeah. Let's get dressed and go. Maybe we can be back for the last part of breakfast."

Mrs. Compton was surprised to see us up and out the door so early.

"We want to catch the morning light over at the lighthouse," I said, gesturing to my camera bag.

"Oh, that sounds lovely. But wait." She sailed through a set of saloon doors, sending them flapping. She came back carrying a tray with two croissants and two coffees in to-go cups on it. "Here. You'll need your strength."

"You're a gem, Mrs. Compton," Paul said.

She beamed at him, and in her chocolate chip cookie voice said, "Oh, it's nothing at all. You two run along. Have yourselves a nice morning." Mrs. Compton waved at us until we were out the door.

"She certainly knows how to build a repeat customer base," Paul said.

"Agreed." The croissant was rich and buttery as it melted in my mouth. "I could eat a dozen of these."

"Yeah," Paul said, mouth full. "Let's go get our B-roll footage."

At least once in your life, I recommend watching the sun come up over the ocean. The peaceful calm given off by the rosy light of the sun and the gentle roar of the ocean waves can seep into your being, becoming a part of you. I felt centered. I felt sure I was going to find out what happened to Greer.

The B-roll footage we shot was magnificent. Paired with some classical music, I could sell it as one of those spa ambience videos. Tall, golden-brown grasses lingering from summer waved in the wind. Bare trees, lonely and still, stood between the pine trees ringing the parking lot. The lighthouse towered over the cliff, looking less forlorn than I'd expected.

Of course, there'd been no traces of Greer Larkin. Twenty seasons of wind, rain, snow, and sun obliterated anything we might've found. It's a lonely spot. Secluded. Remote. Paul and I had been there for two hours and not one person had even driven by. Anyone meeting here'd never be seen. And with the cliff being so near, it was the perfect place to dump a body.

I envisioned Greer screaming for help, being chased by her attacker. Her purse hitting the ground, the contents spilling out. I could see Greer running from her car toward the lighthouse or into the thin woods. Did her attacker have a gun? A knife? Or did her murderer come unprepared, grabbing a handy tree branch from one of the pines? Once Greer couldn't fight back her attacker carried—or dragged—her body to the edge of the cliff. The splash muffled by the crashing waves. Her body disappearing beneath the water.

I watched the trees again. Now they looked like they were keeping secrets.

* * *

We sat in Paul's car, one block south of the police station, staring at the front doors. It's a one-story blond brick number that was built in the seventies, complete with the kind of metal lettering schoolchildren love to steal on a dare. The scanty front yard was covered in white rock and short evergreen shrubs that hung around the base of the building like low-lying clouds. No windows in the front, just two large glass doors. I could see just one window on the side of the building from where I sat. It looked tightly closed. This place was a fortress.

I'm insane.

"How do you want to do this?" Paul asked.

"Well," I said, licking my lips. "Since sneaking in doesn't seem to be an option, I thought I'd ask nicely."

Paul chuckled. "You're going to have to do better than that. This is an open case. They don't have to let you see anything. You've got to have a plan. What's your argument?"

"I don't need that much information. Greer may have been on drugs at the time of her disappearance. I only want to see if there were pills in her purse," I said.

"But that's not all you want to see," Paul said. "You also want to see the maître d's statement and find out if there was any other DNA found in the car."

"True, but once I get a foot in the door, I can push it open." I gave Paul a cocky grin.

He grinned back at me. "We'll see."

"This is all about confidence, Paul. If you believe you can do it, then you can."

"You don't lack for confidence, I'll give you that."

I got out of the car, squared my shoulders, and strode purposefully toward the doors, Paul trailing behind me. Let's hope confidence will do the trick.

The sergeant at the front desk was polite, but firm. "I'm sorry, ma'am, but we don't share open case files with the public."

I subtly looked up and around the entry. No cameras. *Interesting.*

"Could I talk to your captain?" I asked. "This is a cold case, so maybe there's some wiggle room, especially for a project that might jog free some new leads." I gave my head a coquettish tilt and batted my amethyst eyes at him. My good looks were about to pay off.

The sergeant, a young guy with buzzed dark brown hair, leaned toward me, his own brown eyes drinking in the sex I exuded. "Well, I guess I could ask. He's going to say no. Besides, no one wants to go into the basement to look for the files. It's dark and there're rats. If he actually says yes, you'll probably have to come back tomorrow."

Being part of the instant gratification generation, I wasn't thrilled about waiting until tomorrow. I was less thrilled about potentially hearing a flat no. In fact, if the captain did say no, the door to the files was shut forever. I'd have to sue for permission to see them, but I didn't have the reputation, money, or time for that process. However, I now knew where those files were. My plan solidified.

I ran the tip of one nail along my lower lip, leaning onto the counter while pressing my breasts up so I had cleavage galore. His eyes dilated and zeroed right onto the girls. "That does sound unpleasant," I said. "I'd really appreciate it, though, if you'd get your captain," I said in the husky voice I reserved for seduction.

"Ye—yes, ma'am," he said. He ducked his head in an awkward bow and weaved around some desks before going through a heavy metal door.

I handed Paul my camera bag and jacket. "Cover for me," I said, jumping over the counter.

"You're going to get caught," he hissed.

"No, I'm not."

Fingers crossed.

I followed the same path the sergeant took through the heavy door, cringing as the hinges squealed, but it was lunch and it looked as if no one was around to pay attention to little old me. No cameras here either. *Small town cops.* I walked into a long white hallway harshly lit with fluorescent bulbs. A big brown door loomed at the end of the hall. Another heavy-looking brown door was to the right of me. I had a fifty-fifty shot at either finding the stairs to the basement or walking in on the sergeant talking to his captain.

I started to do a quick eeny, meeny, miney, moe, but when I got to meeny I heard a *snap-click* of a door accompanied by the murmur of voices from down the hallway.

"Yeep!" I whipped open the door next to me and tried to get through it while simultaneously shutting it behind me, leaving me in pitch black.

Instead of the landing I expected, there were only stairs. I stifled a scream while my legs churned like a duck paddling through water as I tried to find solid ground. I thumped and bumped down half the stairs, quietly cursing, until my legs caught up with my inertia. As soon as I had one foot under me, the handrail magically appeared in my hand. Some primitive part of my brain signaled my hand to close around it and, as a result, my shoulder suddenly jerked backward. My legs flew out from under me again before my butt collided with the hard, slick cement stairs. I winced and breathed out a quiet, but heartfelt "Fuck."

I stood up to take stock of any bodily damage in the darkness. My shoulder felt like it had been pulled out of its socket by a herd of buffalo, my ass was going to have a Texas-sized bruise on it, and my heart was beating so fast it was probably going to explode. But I hadn't been caught, so I was all good.

The stairs were black and the light switch was God knows where, so I brought my cell phone out and turned on the flashlight app. In the dim light, I slowly walked down the small portion of the stairs I hadn't fallen down. The basement was so cavernous I couldn't see the back wall. What I could see were shelves. Lots and lots of shelves, loaded with boxes.

There had to be at least a thousand of them. Surprising for this little town, but I guess they had a whole county to look after too. There were no labels on the ends of the shelves, therefore, no map to where Greer Larkin's file might be.

"Well, like Glinda the Good Witch said, 'It's always best to start at the beginning.' So I guess I'll start here," I said, going down the first aisle to my left.

There didn't seem to be any rhyme or reason to their filing system. A box from 1950 was right next to a box from 2001. A victim named Zelowski was next to one named Amos. I didn't have time for this. Paul could only stall for so long, then he'd have to leave, if he wasn't gone already. I'd have to sneak out of there, maneuvering past a desk sergeant who had nothing better to do than watch for people sneaking around.

I kept searching through the stacks, trying to find a pattern. It wasn't alphabetical or chronological. What was their method of organization? They wouldn't stick things down here willy-nilly. I popped the lid off a box and looked inside. There was a list of contents, with the victim's name, an address, and the investigating officer—Morton Lampe. I opened the box to the right of it and fished out the list of contents. Victim's name, an address, and the investigating officer—Officer Morton Lampe. Same officer. I opened the next one on the right. Morton Lampe had investigated that one, too. The next was under the purview of an Officer James Monroe. *Aha!* They're alphabetized by investigating officer!

Woohoo!

I moved to where I thought the beginning of the alphabet and "Bedford, Hoyt" would be and opened the first box with the year 1999 on it. Greer Larkin. I hooted out loud with joy. I pulled it out to lay it on the floor. Then I pulled out the property record. Greer Larkin, Kilmarnock Lighthouse, Hoyt Bedford. Contents: Hair, 3 strands, dark brown (unk), blood sample (type A).

Dark brown hair, just as Hoyt Bedford said. But unknown? Bedford had confessed that they knew it was Rachel's, so why leave it labeled as unknown? Had they not updated the file? Bedford, and probably the other cops, suspected Rachel had been there—either that night or very recently. Had they left it unchanged because they couldn't prove it? Had Rachel driven down, asked Greer to meet her without Jonathan, and then pushed her off the cliff when Greer refused to leave him? I shuddered at the image of Greer falling to her death.

I took a photo of the list of contents to look at later, then skimmed down to find what I most wanted to know. Purse contents. I took a close-up picture and then skimmed that list. No pills were in the purse. So then why hide the contents? A question for another time. The clock was ticking.

I grabbed the file from the back of the box and spread it across the concrete floor. Quickly, I took pictures of every page—the maître d's statement, photos of the scene, and fingerprint reports. The last thing I saw before I closed the file was Jonathan's statement. A faded yellow sticky note stuck on the top of it: "Claims to have been sleeping at time of disappearance. Ha!" Jonathan was right, the police pegged him as the main suspect right from the start.

I flipped through the pages, trying not to read as I took photos, but when my eye caught on the word "fight," I couldn't help myself.

"She was getting cold feet about the wedding. She said she was feeling depressed and couldn't trust her judgment. I asked if that meant she couldn't trust me, and she said yes. I lost my temper and slapped her. After all I'd done for her, she admits she couldn't see through her depression to just trust me? It hurt me. Deeply. Horribly. It was the worst thing Greer could have said to me."

Weird. The line cook in the restaurant said their fight had been about money. Here Jonathan said they'd fought about the wedding. Plus, Greer was depressed, just as Bethany thought. And then there was the hair that almost proved Rachel was there. I needed time to sort all this out, but I couldn't linger to digest the news. I had to sneak out before someone decided they needed something from the files. Carefully, I boxed everything back up and put it onto the shelf. Then, tiptoeing back up the stairs, I listened at the door. No sound from the hallway, but then again, it was a really thick door.

I was going to have to push the door open a crack and hope for the best.

The fluorescent lights dazzled my eyes as they hummed above me, but I saw the hallway was empty. I turned off the flashlight app on my phone and tucked it into my pocket. Now for the tricky part. I took a deep breath, squatted, and cracked the door to the sergeant's desk open.

I couldn't see anything except the legs of desks from my low position. But on the plus side, no one shouted "Hey!" at seeing the door open by itself. I had to go for it. I squeezed my body through as small an opening as possible. Catching the door with the toe of my shoe, I eased it closed again. On hands and knees, I crawled past an unoccupied desk. As I slowly approached another, I heard a voice that was shockingly close.

"Cletus, did Mrs. MacNamara come by yet to sign her complaint against the Walker boys? She says they stole her mailbox again."

"She sure hasn't," Cletus said.

I put my head on the floor and peered under the desks. There were feet two desks to my left and feet over by the sergeant's desk. I fast-crawled around another desk, hoping to put space between me and those feet to my left.

"Oh, wait," Cletus said. "Here's a note from Mrs. MacNamara right here."

"Well, then bring it to me."

Cletus's feet left the front desk. Crawling at a sprint, I made a break for it. I peeked up, almost crying with relief when I saw they both had their backs to me. Three years of experience jumping subway turnstiles helped me vault back over the sergeant's desk and hustle out the front door with smooth efficiency.

The bell over the door ding-a-linged, but I didn't stick around to see if they turned to look.

Chapter
Twenty-Three

~

"You know, it's weird," I said to Paul when we were back in our room. "If she was depressed, wouldn't there have been other signs? In hindsight, I know she was depressed before, and it stifled her writing. That's why there's a four-year gap between her fifth and sixth books. But she'd just received an award for her fifth book."

"Is that the book you brought along?" Paul said, reaching for one of the glasses of wine we'd liberated from Mrs. Compton's parlor.

"Yes. You know what else is weird? The husband is controlling the wife in that book through her addiction. Rachel told me Jonathan was controlling Greer through her addiction. Is that a coincidence?"

"Maybe Rachel took the situation from the book and made it about Greer. There's no proof in the police file that Greer had an addiction and was being controlled by Jonathan."

"I don't know. That's a weird lie. It's not like Rachel didn't know I was a fan of Greer's books," I said, taking a sip of wine. I thought about Greer's other novels. Her first took place in a boarding school in Switzerland. It was probably like the one Greer herself was sent to when she was twelve. In her second book . . .

"Oh my God," I said, my wine glass spilling out of my hand.

Paul flinched back from the spreading puddle of white wine. "What? You okay?"

"Oh my God! The knife!"

Paul leaped up and ran to the bathroom for a towel. "What knife?"

"The knife in my door. With the note," I said, now up on my feet and pacing around the room.

Paul threw the towel down on the wine. Hands on his hips, he stood looking at me, eyes narrowed. "What. Knife?"

I froze. *Whoops.* Paul didn't know about the knife in my door. In fact, I'd worked hard to keep the whole incident from him. Then my big mouth had to open. I'm an idiot.

Now I had to tell him. "Well," I began. "First, I need you not to freak out."

Paul sat on the bed, his spine rigid and his hands still on his knees. "I will not freak out," he said woodenly. "I will react appropriately to the situation."

That wasn't promising. The vein pulsing in his forehead was ominous. I took a deep breath and decided to plunge right in. "Last Monday when I came home from interviewing Jonathan, I found a note pinned to my door."

"Where does the knife come into this?"

"It was pinned there with a six-inch chef's knife."

A flush started to creep up Paul's neck. His lips clamped down into a thin line as a muscle began to jump along his jaw. But he didn't say anything.

"Nothing has happened since," I said, reassuringly, "so it's okay. It's just a general threat, but—"

"What did the note say?" he said, so low I could barely hear him.

"Um, something like 'Greer is dead. If you want to keep breathing drop it.' But!" I went on before he could interrupt. "The thing is, this happened in Greer's third book. Exactly this. A note made of letters cut from magazines was stuck up on Oberlin Hurst's door with a knife." I held up my arms triumphantly. "See?"

The scene had flashed into my head, along with the images of Greer fighting for her life, as we'd been filming the B-roll footage that morning at the lighthouse. I knew it had felt familiar, and it wasn't because of Hollywood. "This means someone who knew Greer's books was trying to send me a message, but it could be more than the message printed on the paper."

Paul continued to sit like a statue on the edge of the bed. Cords were beginning to stand out from his neck and the muscles in his forearms bulged as he gripped his knees. "No, I don't see. Someone threatened you and you seem . . . happy . . . about it."

"It's brilliant, really. Someone—probably Rachel or Blanche, since it couldn't have been Jonathan—took a scene out of Greer's book as inspiration for threatening me about looking for Greer. Not only that, but Rachel accused Jonathan of controlling Greer with drugs and alcohol. The same thing happens in *The Girl Who Sang a Tune!*" I held up the copy of my book and opened it to the scene I had just read that morning. Thrusting it at Paul I continued, "Someone is taking things out of Greer's books and using them to frame Jonathan. And that someone is Rachel!"

Paul took the book from me and began to read. After a minute he handed the book back to me and very carefully and slowly said, "Let's put aside for a moment that someone threatened to kill you and you chose not to tell me. Do not interrupt me," he said as my mouth opened to explain again. "I am holding onto my temper with both hands as it is. But you think that Rachel is not only the one who threatened you, but has also been getting away with murder for the last twenty years because she set Jonathan up using plot points from Greer Larkin's books?"

"Yes!" I wanted to jump for joy. "It's so clear. I need to get the rest of her novels. Right now. I need to see if there are any other scenes from any of the books that Rachel claims happened in real life. And the suitcase. Just think of what's in the suitcase. Rachel screwed up."

"Why would she give you the very thing that would prove she's guilty?"

"Our whole conversation in the cafe was about winding me up and setting me on Jonathan. She hoped I'd put on blinders to everything else and go after him like a dog on a bone. It almost worked."

"Pear Blossom. Sweetheart. That is insane," Paul said, rising from the bed.

"No, don't you see? Rachel loves her. She wanted Greer to leave Jonathan for her. But she wouldn't, so Rachel started stalking her. Jonathan and Greer got the restraining order, Rachel spread rumors, lured her out to the lighthouse, and then *wham!* She killed Greer in a fit of jealous rage," I said, glowing with triumph.

"How're you going to prove this?" Paul asked, eyes wide and incredulous.

"I'll get it from her in an interview," I said, matter-of-factly.

Paul seemed speechless, then, gathering himself, took a deep breath and bellowed, "There is no way I'm letting you go anywhere *near* that woman! She *threatened to kill you*! There's no way she is going to admit to *any* of what you've just said.

She's been successfully *getting away with murder* for twenty years! No. I won't allow it."

My mouth hung open. I'd never seen Paul like this before. His face was a dark, ugly red, and spittle was flying from his mouth. Plus, he'd never yelled at me before. Or forbidden me to do anything I wanted to do.

Well, this wasn't going to stand. I narrowed my eyes and clenched my fists. "Excuse me? You won't allow it? I don't think you have a say in this. This is *my* film and *my* graduation—my career. I am going to interview her again, and I'm going to make her sing like a bird. You didn't see her when she gave me the suitcase. She *wants* to tell me."

"Wants to tell you? Ha!" He grabbed my shoulders and gave me a little shake. "Wake up. She's a murderer who's gotten away with it. You think she's going to tell you and willingly go to jail? No. What she's going to do is throw you into the East River with a pair of cement shoes."

"You don't know that," I bellowed back, struggling as his fingers gripped my shoulders. "You've never met her."

"I don't have to meet her," Paul shot back. He was breathing hard and shaking like a volcano about to erupt. He dipped his head and took several deep breaths. When he looked up, his sapphire blue eyes were glittering with emotion. I didn't know this Paul. Paul was always so calm, so in control of his emotions. Now he looked like a man burning from the inside. "Pear Blossom, I can't let anything happen to you. I wouldn't survive it."

"Nothing's going to happen to me. You'll be there," I said, placing my hands on his chest and sinking into him.

His hands eased from my shoulders and wrapped around my body. The muscles in his biceps were rigid. Lips touched the top of my head in a reverent kiss. "When I approved this topic, I didn't think it'd mean death threats and stealing from police stations. I thought it meant online research and talking to lawyers. I didn't think you'd actually try to solve the case."

"Do you regret it?" I asked, snuggling deeper against his chest. His heart was thudding against my cheek. I breathed in his scent and kissed the spot where his heart was threatening to break through.

He sighed, kissing the top of my head again. "Yes and no. You're as happy as I've ever seen you. It's electrifying. You're even tolerating Dave Zukko, which I didn't think possible. But I don't like that I have to worry about you. Or wonder if you've gotten yourself in too deep."

"I'm not in too deep." Even to me I sounded like a sulky teenager.

"I'm only wondering," he said, removing one hand from my back and using it to tip my chin up to meet his gaze. There was love there, and longing, and desire.

I stood on tiptoes and, with butterfly pressure, lightly brushed my lips to his. He let out a small, wretched sigh and increased the pressure. Our mouths fixed themselves together as Paul's arms clamped around me to lift my feet from the floor. Soon the room was awhirl with clothes as our bodies made promises to each other that I hoped our hearts would keep.

* * *

The world is a magical place when you are in the arms of the person you love. The morning sun kissed my naked body awake just enough for me to register a contented blissful feeling. I wanted to be in this moment forever.

Then my mind turned to Greer Larkin. How would she have told my story? Would I have been the villain? The ruthless mistress trying to steal another woman's husband? Or would I have been the hero? A woman questing to find the truth about a mythological being while wrestling with the costs of keeping the man she loves?

Or would I simply be fodder for the cannon?

How would Greer see the pattern of evidence I'd found? The connections to her books were undeniable. One was a coincidence. Two was the start of a pattern. Now that I'd confirmed two, I'd look through that suitcase of notes for more. Rachel must've made a mistake in that pile of papers.

The money bothered me more than I cared to admit, however. Rachel couldn't have put the money into that offshore account. Uncle Morty never mentioned any woman other than Greer. Only Greer or Blanche had the signature power to do that. Or did Jonathan forge Greer's signature? Then there was Uncle Morty and the trust. I hadn't heard back from Will yet. It was possible Alzheimer's had eaten that information out of Uncle Morty's brain, so we'd never know to whom that trust was about to be signed over.

If Jonathan had been embezzling from her, then what? He couldn't have been the one who threatened me. No way he'd have beaten me home from that interview to stick the knife in the door. In fact, he seemed overjoyed to tell me all about his relationship with Greer. But there's something there, something in what he wasn't saying that bothered me. Shouldn't he have brought up the money? Surely he must have known that question was coming. Everyone knew about it. I'd had to dig to get him to talk. As an innocent man, wouldn't there have been an innocent explanation for all the money showing up in that account?

I remembered how I'd vomited in his bathroom. The majority of the nausea thankfully passed in just one day. The remaining stomach issues could be chalked up to anxiety after finding a knife jammed into my door. And, as I found out after five agonizing minutes, none of it was caused by pregnancy. I pushed my suspicions aside; I probably hadn't eaten enough lunch. But I'd been feeling fine before I'd had that cup of coffee. I frowned as the suspicions bubbled up inside me.

Next to me, Paul stirred in his sleep. An arm snaked over my body, drawing me closer to him. I brought his hand up to my lips to kiss his fingers. It twitched and then moved to my cheek, where his thumb gently caressed my jawline.

"You awake?" he asked, his voice heavy with sleep.

"It seems that way. Just thinking, though. You can go back to sleep," I said.

"What time is it?"

"A little after seven," I said, turning to face him.

"No, I'm up," he said, stretching his body.

I walked my fingers up his well-muscled chest. When they got to his mouth, he playfully snatched them before kissing them and laying them on top of his heart, his hand resting over the top. "Morning, my Pear Blossom," he said, smiling contentedly.

"Morning. We need to find Mr. Bedford today."

"Any ideas on where to look?"

"Well, I know he loves to fish. We could stake out every fishing hole in the county."

A rich chuckle rumbled in Paul's chest. "That's going to take a few days. Are you trying to extend our research holiday?"

"That's only a bonus. It's imperative I make contact with a very necessary element of this documentary," I said, leaning forward to give him a slow kiss.

"As much as I'd love to have more than a few days with you, the deadline clock is ticking. You found his phone number through the library. Maybe you can do a little more internet searching."

"Police officers tend to keep their addresses on the downlow. We actually might have to ask around and drive to the most likely fishing spots."

"Well, any day with you is a good day," Paul said, kissing my fingers.

"Aw. You're the sweetest," I said, giving him a noisy kiss on the cheek.

He started laughing. "Do you feel like breakfast? Or . . . some other activity?" He started to stroke my hand on his chest, while his other hand foraged into different territory.

"Oh, I always like a little exercise before breakfast," I said, my lady parts starting to light up like a Las Vegas casino.

"Wonderful."

Even though we'd showered, I still felt like Mrs. Compton could tell that we'd just had sex. Her smile seemed a little too knowing, her demeanor a little too warm. It was like having your grandmother hear you. Fighting to keep my blushing to a minimum, I dug into another slice of quiche.

When I finally pushed back from the table, I was full to bursting. I hoped Officer Bedford wouldn't chase us off his property with a shotgun. I wouldn't be able to run.

"What're you two up to today? More pictures?" Mrs. Compton asked.

"We're going to see police Officer Bedford to ask him about his experiences in law enforcement," I said.

"Hoyt Bedford?" she asked.

"Yeah," Paul said. "You know him?"

"I do," she said.

"You wouldn't happen to know where he lives, would you?" Paul asked.

"Or where he fishes?" I added.

Mrs. Compton fidgeted with the coffee pot for a couple of seconds, then abruptly went back to the kitchen.

Paul and I looked at each other. His brow was puckered in confusion. My eyebrows were residing around my hairline and my eyes were wide with curiosity. She obviously knew Bedford, and the mere mention of his name had sent her running into the kitchen.

Then the saloon doors to the kitchen swung open again, allowing Mrs. Compton to come back into the dining room. In her hands was a large plastic container steamed up with something hot. "Here," she said, thrusting the container at me. "If you want to talk to Hoyt Bedford, then you're going to need these."

I lifted the lid and was hit with the sinfully delicious smell of blueberries and sugar. "Hoyt Bedford can't resist my blueberry muffins. Those'll get you in the door," she said.

"Thanks," I said, a little bit confused, but entirely grateful. "How do you know this will work?"

"We used to be married. He said these muffins were his favorite reason for proposing to me," she said.

"Oh!" I said. My voice was squeaky and way too loud. "That's . . . nice." He'd divorced a woman like that? More likely she divorced him. She's the kindest woman ever. What was he like if the nicest woman on the planet couldn't live with him?

"Thanks for the muffins," Paul said, as if he'd always known sweet Mrs. Compton had been married to a crusty, retired police officer. He took the container from me and said, "We should get going while they're still warm."

"Sure thing!" I said, leaping from the chair, my voice still too loud and too bright.

I grabbed Paul's hand and started dragging him toward our room. Paul was chuckling as I hurriedly shouldered my bags. "Fine, laugh, but I'm not thrilled about talking to a guy we need to bribe with warm muffins made by his ex-wife. And if they need to be warm, then we're leaving right now," I said as I pushed him out of the room.

We were almost out the front door of the inn when Mrs. Compton called, "You should start with his fishing spot off Pohick Road. The turn is just after Backlick."

God bless Virginia, and her odd road names.

Paul saluted her and we programmed the GPS to the inter-section of Backlick and Pohick Roads. Highways turned into gravel roads, which turned into a bumpy dirt lane cutting through a wood. Tall, dried grasses brushed the sides of the car and leafless trees towered over us. The lane widened to a largish spot in the woods where a red truck, pockmarked with rust, was parked. We pulled up next to the truck, but turned around so the nose of our car was pointed toward the dirt trail in case we needed to beat a hasty retreat.

The woods were silent, the birds still on their tropical vaca-tions. It felt lonely, but familiar. The woods that surrounded the commune where I grew up would still be coated with snow. This place was brown and empty. And cold. Why on earth anyone would be fishing out here in the winter was beyond me. I walked over to the truck. It was unlocked, which I found trusting for an ex-police officer. "Over here," Paul said, his voice loud in the stillness. He pointed to a crease in the dead grass. As someone who'd grown up running wild and free in the woods, I recognized it as a trail.

"I'll go first," I said. I hated walking behind people on a trail. I wanted to see what was coming at me, not the back of someone's head.

The trail sloped steeply down with tree roots crisscrossing the path, creating a natural staircase down to the river. Below, a lone man in a red plaid hat stood with his eyes on the water. One hand held his pole, the other was tucked into his tan Carhartt coat. When we were close enough, I called out a hello.

"I assume you're June Masterson," he said, his voice richer than it had been on the phone.

"Yes, sir," I said, surprised at how small he was. I'd pictured Mrs. Compton with a burly mountain of a man. Hoyt Bedford was compact and wiry. His face and hands were windburned into a permanent reddish brown color. He hadn't even looked at me yet, and I already knew he was disdainful of my efforts to find him. "I'm hoping you have a moment to talk," I said.

"Talk is cheap, said the poet," he said, his eyes never leaving the tip of his pole.

Lord, it was cold! There was a light wind off the water that drove the chill into my skin. I hugged my coat tighter around myself. My breath billowed out as I spoke.

"I'm also hoping you'd consent to being filmed for my documentary."

"I don't think I'll be doing that," Bedford said, adjusting his line.

"I'd appreciate it if you would," I said.

He snorted. "I'll bet."

"Mrs. Compton sent some blueberry muffins. Still warm," Paul piped up.

That caught his attention. He turned away from his fishing pole to look at us for the first time. Hoyt Bedford looked more like a hawk than a man. He had a large, hooked nose and small, shrewd eyes. I flinched as they assessed me. "Blueberry muffins, huh? Well, she must like you to have given you those," he said.

"She sent them for you," I said.

"Huh," he said with a grunt. "I guess I could take a break." Mr. Bedford propped his pole up against a log before coming over to take the container. He opened the lid and inhaled the delicious scent. Steam from the still-warm muffins made puffy clouds as it hit the cold air. "Almost makes me wish we hadn't divorced."

"Why did you divorce?" I asked.

"She wanted me to stop being a cop and start being an innkeeper. I wasn't about to do that. For one, I hate people. For two, I hate people," he said as he sank his teeth into a springy muffin. His eyes rolled back into his head and he groaned so loud it was indecent. "God. Almost makes me reconsider."

"Can we set up our video equipment, Mr. Bedford?" I asked.

"For filming. Sure. I suppose that would be fine," Mr. Bedford said. "She sent six muffins! She misses me."

I gave Paul a nod, but he was already securing the camera to the tripod. He gave me a wink. I winked back and turned to Mr. Bedford, who was deep into his second muffin. "Mr. Bedford, can you introduce yourself for the camera?"

He nodded and swallowed his mouthful of muffin. "Officer Hoyt Bedford, formerly of the Northumberland County Sheriff's Office. I was the lead investigator in the disappearance of Greer Larkin."

* * *

"The call came in at four thirteen AM on August 24, 1999. The park ranger in charge reported a red Fiat Spider convertible, door open, with blood on the seat. A lot of blood."

"How much blood?" I asked.

"At least a couple of pints," he said. "We're not that large of a department, so I was the first on the scene. The ranger assured me that everything was just as he found it. He even left the door of the car open. A purse, later identified by her mother as Greer's, was found on the ground with the contents strewn over the ground in front of the open door. There were other signs of a struggle. The ground had been disturbed along the bank of the cliff, although no clear footprints were recovered. The keys to the car were found in the ignition." He'd recited this litany like he'd done it hundreds of times, even though I doubted he'd been interviewed by anyone in fifteen years. His captain had taken all the glory, which seemed to suit the man in front of me just fine. But he wasn't as distant from this crime as he liked people to think.

"Mr. Bedford, we know that a DNA test conducted in 2015 confirmed it was Greer Larkin's blood. But hairs were also found at the scene that didn't match Greer. What can you tell us about those?"

"How do you know about that?" he said.

I simply smiled at him. If he didn't remember telling me, then I wasn't going to remind him. Plus, sometimes not saying anything is a great way to get someone else to talk.

After a moment he went on. "There were some hairs found in the car. At first we suspected Rachel Baumgartner, Greer's best friend. She had brown hair of the right length, but it was established that they hadn't had contact in over a year. There was no root to the hair and therefore no DNA to test, so who left them remains unknown. However," he added, "it's important to note that everything we found at the scene is being kept in a secure storage facility in case technology improves."

Not that secure, I thought. "Was there any other reason to suspect Rachel?"

He squinted. "You mean besides the restraining order and photographic evidence that Rachel and Greer could be violent toward one another?"

Asked and answered.

"Mr. Bedford, can you tell us how your suspicions landed on Jonathan Vanderpoole?" I asked.

"We always look at a person's spouse or partner first. When a woman is murdered, one-third of the time it's committed by their spouse or partner. Now, we don't know for sure she was murdered. We never found a body, and there wasn't enough blood at the scene to assume death."

"What does that mean, 'enough blood'?"

"It means there was maybe about a thousand milliliters at the scene—about two pints. There are about eight to twelve pints in the human body. She could've survived losing two pints of blood. Heck, people donate a pint of blood to the Red Cross on a regular basis, and they only need a cookie and some juice to put them back on their feet again," Mr. Bedford said.

"So she could've walked away?"

He nodded. "She would've been weak, maybe a little dizzy, but Greer could have walked away."

"Yet you were looking at Jonathan Vanderpoole for murder. Why?" I asked, genuinely curious.

"There was something . . . careful about the scene. Things, like the purse, seemed placed. Usually, that's the sign of a premeditated murder, not a murder of passion. We know Greer and Jonathan had a fight and he slapped her. Well, maybe that was the last straw. Maybe she was going home to pack a bag and leave him. But he catches her and kills her. Then he waits until it's dark, plants the car, dumps the body into the water, and walks home."

"It's over three miles from the Kilmarnock Lighthouse to their home. You think he walked?" Jonathan didn't strike me as a walker, or someone who'd put in that kind of effort and planning.

But Hoyt was nodding, "I do. In my interviews with Jonathan Vanderpoole he was always calm, collected. He never cried. Plus, he and his lawyer had an answer for everything. Look at him. He has a meticulous nature. He thinks about the big picture and can also scan down to the minutiae. That is a rare gift."

"You think Jonathan Vanderpoole is gifted?" I asked.

"In crafting lies, yes," Bedford said. "A person telling the truth is going to sweat a little. They're going to be desperate to be believed. Mr. Vanderpoole didn't seem to care if I believed him or not."

"What about when you discovered the offshore bank account? Did he care then?" I said.

Hoyt Bedford's face broke into a smile, creasing his weather-beaten face into deep crevices. "He did. He did most definitely care then. Got a little angry even. He insisted he knew nothing about that money and that he was being set up. Called me a stupid, hick cop of a podunk town who wouldn't know my ass from a hole in the ground." He chuckled to himself and shook his head. "Real poetic."

"So he thinks he was, or is, being set up by someone?" I asked.

"He does. But that's the thing with narcissists; they're never to blame. They're special. They need to be admired and appreciated for their specialness. But it also means that they can be paranoid and have trouble taking responsibility for their actions. They're the victims in every scenario," Mr. Bedford said.

"You believe Jonathan to be a narcissist?" I tried to keep the skepticism out of my voice, but wasn't entirely successful.

"Yes. He's pretty textbook, actually. Watch his statements to the press. He's always the victim. This is something being done to him on purpose. He's not asking about Greer or pleading for her safe return, unless it's in conjunction with what it's doing to his emotional state."

I mentally flipped through his statements to me. He did usually talk about how horrible it was for him. He hardly mentioned Greer. This wasn't good; in fact, it kind of scared me. "Do you think Jonathan Vanderpoole is dangerous?' I said, forcing my voice to be louder than a whisper.

"If he or the way he views himself—his importance, his specialness—are threatened? Absolutely," Hoyt said. "And if Greer Larkin was set to leave him? He would be very dangerous indeed."

Chapter
Twenty-Four

~

We drove out of the woods in silence.

Jonathan's a narcissist. Why hadn't I seen it? Isn't it supposed to be easy to spot someone who's only talking about themselves? Not according to Hoyt Bedford. He'd said it to make me feel better about myself. Wrong.

If Greer had threatened to leave Jonathan, if she'd threatened to throw him from a wealthy, privileged lifestyle, back into the life of a failed nightclub owner, would that be enough to push him to violence? Bedford certainly thought so.

I tried to imagine living with someone who made everything about them, someone who was self-centered, materialistic, and greedy. It sounded exhausting. It sounded tedious. It'd make me want to have a drink.

Thinking about a cool glass of wine got me pondering Mr. Bedford's answer to the last question I'd asked: "There are people who believe Jonathan controlled Greer through drug and alcohol addiction. What do you think of that theory?"

"I believe I've heard from those people." He'd smiled again, shaking his head. "I can't comment directly, but what I will say is this—it never surprises me what desperate people will do."

The maître d' of Battaglia's said they hadn't been fighting about money or another woman; they'd fought about the wedding. I thought about how the fight ended with Greer driving off after Jonathan slapped her.

How desperate had Jonathan been in that moment?

What else in Greer's books was true? If Rachel was being honest, Greer had told the world all about Jonathan controlling her with drugs in *The Girl Who Sang a Tune*. In her third book, Oberlin Hurst is seduced by an older man. Was Greer telling us how Jonathan wooed her?

But what if Rachel was lying? What if she was the one Greer was talking about in her books? And what about Blanche? There was more than one abusive mother featured in Greer's novels. Both of them had been pleading with me to believe Jonathan was the bad guy. Was that all a smoke screen to keep them from being suspects?

I needed to reread Greer's books. All of them. Immediately.

As we approached civilization, my phone began beeping at me. In this age of texts and emails, no one ever called me. Yet I'd six missed calls—two from Meadow, two from Blanche, and the others from numbers I didn't recognize.

"That's weird," I said, frowning at my phone.

Paul glanced over at me. "What's weird?"

I tapped on the voice mail button. "I have a ton of messages. Do you have any?"

Paul shook his head. "Nothing's beeping. I can pull over if you want me to check."

All these messages and none of them were from Bethany. As soon as I got back to New York I'd camp outside her office door. Bringing the phone up to my ear, I said, "No, I'll see what Meadow says."

"June? You okay? Call me."

Short and sweet. That's Meadow, but her voice sounded worried. Blanche had left a similar message.

My second message was from Will. "Hey there. So I tried to talk to Uncle Morty, but when I brought up Greer Larkin and the trust, he'd no idea who I was talking about. Sorry, but I don't think he's going to be of any more help."

Well, damn. That was a kick in the teeth. I didn't realize how much I'd been counting on Uncle Morty. Stupid Alzheimer's. What a wretched disease. I'd have to settle for using the little bit of footage I'd gotten and look elsewhere for additional evidence against Blanche, Rachel, or Jonathan. My shoulders sank as I deleted Will's message and went on to the next one.

"Ms. Masterson, I don't know if you've heard the news, but I'm assuming you have. You need to call me so we can move forward with the case against Jonathan. You will call me as soon as you get this message." Blanche's command was unmistakable. She didn't sound worried, she sounded angry. Furious even. I sucked on my lower lip in confusion and worry.

"Everything okay?" Paul said, glancing over again.

"I'm not sure. Meadow and Blanche want me to call them. Blanche wants to move forward on the case against Jonathan and has instructed me to call immediately. She said there's news." I rubbed my knotted brow, studying Blanche's number. The other messages were exactly the same: call both of them immediately.

"What're you going to do?"

"Call Blanche," I said. I clicked on her number and pressed the phone to my ear.

The phone didn't even ring; it went from silence to Blanche's agitated voice. "Thank God. We thought he might've gotten you, too."

"He who? Who'd get me?" Blanche wasn't making sense. "Blanche, are you okay?"

"No, I'm not okay," she yelled, her refined façade shattering. "That monster killed Rachel!"

"Rachel? What do you mean? Who killed Rachel?" Then it hit me. Blanche was telling me Rachel was dead. But that couldn't be right.

"Who do you think I mean? Jonathan, obviously," she said, exasperated at my slowness.

The words were going into my ears, but they weren't making sense. Jonathan killed Rachel. How could that happen? Jonathan didn't like her, but didn't it take a special kind of loathing to want to take another person's life? "How do you know Jonathan was the killer? There were witnesses? The police caught him? They actually caught him and he confessed?" I asked, my brain foggy. Was I talking out loud? My vision was fuzzy around the edges.

"No, of course not. They're incompetent idiots. They think Rachel was killed in a hit-and-run. Ribs broken, legs broken, face—" Blanche's voice broke. She gathered herself and with a newfound calm said, "We all know Jonathan hated Rachel. Rachel called him two days ago and told him you're going to finally prove that he killed Greer. It was stupid of her to provoke him. But the police say he has an alibi." She snorted in derision that the police would believe such an obvious lie. "You need to be careful. He might come after you, too."

He might come after me? "But I haven't found any evidence that proves he's guilty of anything. There's nothing that says he killed Rachel or Greer," I said.

"Of course he did it. He did all of it." Blanche said, incredulous. I'm sure if we'd been face-to-face she'd have shaken me.

But she didn't know I'd been threatened too—and Jonathan hadn't done it. "There's someone else out there besides Jonathan. I was threatened too. When I got home from interviewing Jonathan, I found a threat knifed to my door. There's no way he could've gotten there before me. There's someone else out there who wants everyone to forget about Greer," I said. I didn't tell her I'd thought that person had been Rachel. It seemed indecent to suspect her now.

Blanche was quiet for a long moment. "Come and see me."

"I will as soon as I get back," I said.

"Where are you?"

"I'm in Virginia. I'll be back tomorrow. Probably late in the afternoon."

"I'll be busy tomorrow. The memorial is the day after that. We can talk there. I'll have Gerald send you the information," Blanche said.

The line went dead.

I looked up to find that Paul had pulled over onto the side of the road. He was staring at me, eyes wide in horror. "Rachel . . . *died*?"

A wave of dizziness rolled over me. I took a long, shaky breath. "Yeah. She was killed. Blanche said the cops called it a hit-and-run, but she thinks Jonathan did it. She thinks Rachel goaded him about the documentary and that he, uh, killed her for it." My voice was tremulous and soft.

"Oh my God," Paul said. "That's it. You're off this project. That is final."

I was already shaking my head as he spoke. I couldn't leave this project. I had to find out who wanted me to stop searching for the truth so badly—bad enough to kill. "Wait just a minute," I said, trying to beat down the urge to heave up Mrs. Compton's croissants and coffee at any moment. "I have almost everything I need to finish this. I don't have to interview Jonathan again. Most of what's left is voice-overs and editing. I can switch to interviewing cops and lawyers." Paul stared straight ahead, his hands gripping the wheel so hard I thought he was going to rip it off. "You can't make me change topics again. I won't graduate if you do."

"Is that so bad? You'd graduate a semester late, but you'd still be alive. You'd still be with me." His face was white and his eyes were pleading. "You heard Hoyt Bedford. Jonathan's a narcissist. There's no telling what he'd do if he felt threatened."

A leaden feeling that was a combination of dread, sadness, and guilt settled in my stomach. While I felt bad for Paul, and loved that he cared about me so much, I had to finish the movie. If Jonathan did it, then I needed to prove it to everyone. I couldn't let Rachel be dead for nothing.

I rested my hand on his arm. "The police aren't even sure this was Jonathan. It could have been anyone." I gave a mirthless laugh and said, "It could've been Blanche in her giant Rolls Royce, and she's framing Jonathan. She hates him. She'd do anything to get him thrown in jail."

"Don't even joke about that," Paul said, his voice void of emotion.

That's true. But I needed to finish this movie. I was too close to stop now.

"Let me finish. *Please.* I promise I'll be safe and careful."

His jaw was tight. He refused to look at me, but he nodded. I let out a breath. Signaling, we pulled back onto the highway and drove the rest of the way to the inn.

We made love that night, slowly and tenderly, clinging to each other like two orphans lost in a storm.

* * *

As we drove back to New York, the weight of our roles and duties settled back onto our shoulders. I owed Meadow a call. I couldn't bear to talk about Rachel, and if she had happy news I didn't want to crush her joy. It'd be better if I talked to her later. Knowing Paul would drop me off at my apartment, only to then drive back into his other life, made me melancholy. Paul tried to keep the light tone we'd had during the trip, but the closer we got, the harder it became. He, too, became moody and silent.

The lights of New York cheerfully greeted us, warm and welcoming. I'd always loved the New York skyline at night. There's something majestic in how the lights look like galaxies of stars living right on top of the earth. Usually, seeing the lights of New York emerge over the horizon made me feel relieved to be home, but today I felt dread.

At my building, Paul gave me the deep, passionate kiss of lovers who don't know when they'll next see each other. He'd told me he couldn't go with me to Rachel's memorial service. I hadn't even asked. I'd already known he'd have to stay at Martha's beck and call for a few days.

It was late. I thought about letting Mrs. Bukowski know I was home as I passed by her door, but most people in my building were already asleep. My door was pristine, untouched by knives or threatening notes. Still, I was glad that I'd left the suitcase full of journals with Mrs. Bukowski. I'd pick it up after the memorial service to start comparing the journals to the scenes in Greer's books again.

I hadn't felt like eating much on the trip north, but now I was ravenous. My refrigerator contained moldy cheese and two beers. I had a couple of packets of oatmeal in my cupboard, but I didn't feel like oatmeal. I felt like dumplings and noodles from Chen Yu—comfort food loaded with fat and MSG. I put in my order for pan-fried pork dumplings and beef lo mein, then downloaded the pictures I'd taken at the police station onto my computer.

The hair the police found bothered me. The analysis said it was human, untreated and naturally brown, and approximately eight inches in length, with no root for DNA analysis. They'd compared it to hair from Greer's brush as her hair was the right color, but it wasn't a match. The cuticle was thicker and the thickness of the strand was a bigger diameter, too. Too long and too light to be Jonathan's. Blanche's hair was blonde and white. Rachel's hair was the right color and the right length, but she hadn't seen Greer in over a year. I knew that was a lie, though. But let's say Rachel hadn't seen Greer in six months. Could a hair still be there from six months ago? Or had they seen each other more recently? Had Rachel been in Virginia? Or was there an unknown person walking around out there? There was Greer's agent, Bethany, but she was blonde. Plus, there's no way she'd compromise her meal ticket. She's barely willing to be in the film, lest Blanche fire her.

But now Rachel was dead. So even if it was her hair in the car, it didn't matter now. Did it? Could Rachel have killed Greer only to have someone kill Rachel in return?

Was this revenge?

This new angle appealed to me. What if, as I was digging around, I'd uncovered some kind of clue, but I didn't know it was a clue at the time. I needed to review everything—starting with Greer's books. My food arrived in time to bolster my flagging energy levels.

When I dropped off to sleep, Oberlin Hurst escorted me through long hallways in old stone castles, telling me about the time she lost her dog Buttons and ended up finding a body.

Chapter
Twenty-Five

❧

I'd barely fallen asleep when Gerald called to inform me of the memorial arrangements for Rachel. Groggy, I listened as he relayed that visitation would start at four in the afternoon and run until around eight. Somewhere in there, he told me the details of the service—a kind of shiva-slash-Methodist funeral to represent her two faiths. I promptly fell back to sleep when Gerald hung up.

When I woke up again, a book was next to me in the bed, the TV was still on, and papers were scattered across the floor. I looked at the bare spot on my coffee table where the suitcase lived, remembering I hadn't retrieved it yet. It was time to reclaim my treasure trove of clues. The sun told me Mrs. Bukowski should be up, no matter how much gin she'd had the night before.

Pulling on a robe to hide my holey T-shirt and too-short soccer shorts, I knocked on Mrs. Bukowski's door. My knocks went unanswered. She'd probably gone to buy more booze. My fingers itched to get hold of those papers. I would've loved to jimmy the lock and take back the suitcase, but there were rumors Mrs. B's son had ties to the Russian mob. I wasn't willing to take the chance that a complaint from his mother would send the son to my door for a "chat." I'd have to come back later. Maybe I'd see her on my way out to the memorial service. In the meantime, I logged onto the fan site to see what people knew about Rachel's death and what theories I could add to my own list.

Sure enough, the top posting was "RIP Rachel Baumgartner."

Showgirl: *From the NYT: Best Friend of Greer Larkin Slain in Tribeca Alley*

Rachel Baumgartner, longtime friend and sometime foe of famous author Greer Larkin, was killed in a hit-and-run accident in her tony Tribeca neighborhood. Officials say she was on her way home from watching a film with friends when she was struck from behind and killed by one of New York's famous yellow taxicabs. Witnesses say the driver, a male of undetermined age and ethnicity, sped off. Witnesses captured the event on video. The cab was later discovered abandoned and burned outside Trenton, New Jersey. Ms. Baumgartner was pronounced dead at the scene.

Ms. Larkin, the wunderkind mystery novelist who disappeared under suspicious circumstances in 1999, befriended Ms. Baumgartner when they met as teenagers in the offices of the Barry Allen Literary Agency. Ms. Baumgartner's father, Daniel Baumgartner, worked as a top agent alongside Greer's agent, Barry Allen, and then, later, with Mr. Allen's daughter Bethany Allen upon her father's death. The two had been inseparable until Ms. Larkin, then aged seventeen, met Jonathan Vanderpoole, who became the love of her life and, some say, the reason for her disappearance.

Police refused to comment on the possibility of any connection between the two incidents, saying, "The fact that Ms. Baumgartner has suffered this unfortunate accident while approaching the anniversary of Greer Larkin's disappearance is purely coincidence. There is no evidence connecting the two in any way."

Ms. Baumgartner, who never married, leaves behind her father and mother, Daniel and Julia (née Davies) Baumgartner. A private memorial service will be held.

Swiss Miss: That is so sad. RIP Rachel.

Buttons: This is the worst! I feel so bad for her family. The taxi drivers in New York have to be better monitored with background checks.

<3Greer4ever: Such a horrible accident. :-(

Vixen42: I can't believe they think this was an accident. Taxi drivers don't just hit people and speed off. @Buttons is right—they have GPS and those cabs are registered. The police will be able to find out who did this.

OHurst: They barely said anything about Rachel in the article. It's mostly about Greer. What about the fact that Rachel's a person? With a family of her own? They didn't tell you that she was funny and smart and loyal. She wasn't famous, so the newspapers don't care about all that.

Champ624: They don't care about famous people, either. They want to sell papers. RIP Rachel.

QueenB: Rachel was a nobody, in reality. Another cog in the wheel of the publishing industry. She was approaching the anniversary of her best friend's disappearance/death. Is it possible she jumped out in front of the cab?

<3Greer4ever: @QueenB: That actually makes some sense. I hadn't thought about it that way.

Vixen42: You think she committed suicide? That's ridiculous. No one waits twenty years to end their life because their best friend died.

QueenB: You don't know what was going through her mind. It's a possibility. I'm entitled to theorize.

Vixen42: That's a harmful and insensitive theory. You should delete your post.

WBJ: I agree with @Vixen42. That's insensitive to suggest she killed herself.

QueenB: Lord. @Vixen42, you have a fan.

<3Greer4ever: Insensitive or not, it's a theory and she has the right to speak it. Last I checked the First Amendment was still in the Constitution.

OHurst: If we're posting random theories, I have one—It could just as easily have been murder. There's a film being made. Dirt's getting dug up from the depths. Someone's got a motive for keeping Rachel quiet. The most likely suspect is Jonathan. So I wonder if the police are going to visit him? I hope it's early, so they wake him up.

Bobbie7: So there really is a movie? Starting new thread right now!

Fuck. Now the cat was well and truly out of the bag. I clicked back to the main forum. Ugh. Bobbie7's new thread "GREER LARKIN MOVIE!!!" had four hundred comments and was growing.

I slammed my computer shut, then quickly opened it back up and pulled up the forum again. Was I mentioned? Did people know that PricklyPear was the one dredging up all the dirt? I searched for an hour and couldn't find a single mention. So how did OHurst know a movie was being made? Was someone else making a movie too? Not out of the realm of possibility. The twentieth anniversary of Greer Larkin's disappearance is a big date for a lot of people. Other documentary filmmakers or news people were bound to be putting together stories.

My eyes flicked through the news story Showgirl had posted. A private memorial service was being held. Rachel's dead, probably murdered. If she was murdered, then it was my fault. I'd gotten a warning to stay out of it, but I'd ignored it. I'd more than ignored it. I'd willfully plunged in and dug up more information. I didn't know what to do. Should I keep investigating? Was Blanche next? Or was Blanche the murderer? Nothing made sense anymore.

Cold guilt sank into my bones. I shivered. I needed to talk to someone. I needed my best friend.

Meadow picked up on the second ring.

"I THOUGHT YOU WERE DEAD IN A DITCH AND YOUR MOTHER HAS BEEN CALLING ME BECAUSE YOU REFUSE TO GIVE HER YOUR NUMBER AND I CAN'T TAKE THIS ANYMORE!"

I winced. She was pissed and she was loud.

"I'm really, really sorry, Meadow. I'm fine. I was in Virginia with Paul when it happened," I said. "But, Meadow. I think I've made a horrible mistake. What if this is all my fault?" My voice broke as a sob crawled up my throat.

"Oh, honey," Meadow said, her voice growing soft and sympathetic. "What happened to Rachel isn't your fault. It's the fault of some deranged lunatic. You didn't make anyone run her over with a car."

"So, it wasn't an accident?" I said, my voice breaking.

"No, sweetie," Meadow said, gently. "I talked to one of my police contacts for you. It's officially a homicide. There were, uh, other injuries inconsistent with being hit by a car. It's likely her, um, injuries happened elsewhere and she was shoved out of the car. They're keeping it quiet."

"I feel awful." My eyes grew hot with tears. Rachel was murdered. There's a murderer out there who'd killed Rachel and who'd probably killed Greer, if—and I felt guilty even thinking it—Rachel hadn't killed Greer herself. The police were keeping it quiet. You know who they do things like that for? Rich people like Blanche Larkin.

"I know. I'm sure your college will give you an extension when you tell them why you have to switch your film topic again."

I swallowed hard. I'd just had this argument with Paul. I wasn't ready to have it with Meadow, but I knew I couldn't let her think I was actually going to stop searching for the truth. "I'm not switching. How could I switch topics now?"

"Someone died," Meadow said, incredulous.

"Yes, but like you said, it wasn't my fault."

"Pear!" Scandalized shock dripped from her voice.

"Meadow," I tried to sound matter-of-fact. "I owe it to Rachel to find out what happened. She wanted me to prove Jonathan killed Greer. Even if that wasn't the truth, I've got to see this through. I have to find the *real* truth. It's—it's my fault she's dead. I can't just let her be dead and not seek justice for her. I'm the only one who knows this might be connected to Greer."

Meadow was quiet. I didn't know what to say that would convince her I was right. I tried anyway.

"Look. I have a lot of information to go through. Between the suitcase Rachel gave me and the police case files, there're bound to be more clues to who could've killed Greer."

"Police case files? I thought those were closed."

Uh. Oh.

"Well, I . . . uh . . . I happened to get the files from the sheriff's office," I said.

Meadow started making weird choking sounds.

"You okay, Meadow?" I asked, hoping someone was there to slap her on the back.

"You *stole* the files? You STOLE them?" she said, getting louder. "You broke into a police station AND STOLE THEIR FILES?" Meadow was shrieking so loudly I probably could've heard her without the phone.

"Meadow, I—"

"THAT IS AGAINST THE LAW, PEAR! AGAINST THE LAW!" She was breathing hard, and then she gasped. "Oh my God! I'm a *lawyer*! I can't hear this. I DID NOT CALL YOU!"

Then the phone went dead.

I flopped down on the bed. Meadow was well and truly pissed. Yes, I'd broken the law. Kind of. She didn't understand. I needed to know if there'd been pills in Greer's purse. It would've proved Rachel's story about why Jonathan killed Greer.

Plus, she never let me explain that I didn't physically *take* the files. I took pictures.

Yeah, that still wasn't good. Meadow was right—stealing was wrong. But didn't the ends justify the means? I needed to find out what happened to Greer. Now more than ever. Sure, this started out as a lark, the fulfillment of a childhood obsession. Now finding out what happened to Greer could help find whoever killed Rachel. I owed her that.

*   *   *

Mrs. Bukowski was still out when I visited her apartment again. Jesus, woman, get home already. Was there bingo at the church or something? My impatience had me reconsidering my decision not to break into her apartment. A little voice said, *Don't mess with the Russian mob, June.* Grr. Fine. I'd wait a little longer to get the suitcase back. It wasn't like it was going to do me any good this evening while I'm at the Simon-Hamilton Funeral Home for visitation.

About 2:10 PM, I realized I didn't own anything black that wasn't a concert T-shirt or leather. This was a problem. I couldn't show up to a richie-rich memorial service in a Black Sabbath T-shirt. I looked at the heap of shoes in my closet. If I'm going to buy a new dress, I'd need new shoes, too.

Two hours later I'd found a black dress at the Goodwill and a pair of black Sam & Libby heels. The whole ensemble was less than fifteen bucks. The dress wasn't even that bad. It was a sleeveless H&M shift dress with a jeweled neckline and a skirt that hit about two inches above my knee. I knew it was a jeweled neckline because it said so on the tag. I decided to compromise on formality by wearing my leather jacket, my other jacket being nowhere near nice, or clean, enough for bereavement. I did have black hose on, so that was at least something.

Because I looked so nice, I decided to take a cab to Simon-Hamilton, which was over in Brooklyn, close to where Rachel's parents lived. The line of cars stretched around the block. My taxi edged past them and dropped me off at the corner just past the funeral home.

The Simon-Hamilton Funeral Home is a huge monolithic brick bunker with Greek columns carved out of some kind of pale stone in the front. A cross and a Star of David flanked their name printed in black and gold across the top of the building.

Attendants ushered the crowd toward the Memorial Room in the left wing of the building. At least a hundred people were there. Maybe more. A small woman with inky black hair was seated on a couch next to a picture of Rachel. She clutched a white handkerchief in one hand. Her other hand was being held by a barrel-chested man with a yarmulke on his head seated next to her. Those had to be Rachel's parents. Rachel's dad, Daniel, must've been very popular in the publishing business. The line to condole with them stretched around the room. I got in line. I wanted to tell them how sorry I was. How responsible I felt. Even if Rachel's mom slapped me and yelled at me, I had to do it.

There wasn't a coffin. I assumed the coroner hadn't released the body yet. The funeral service wasn't until Thursday. I wasn't familiar with Jewish funerals, or funerals in general. This was my first one, so I didn't know what to expect.

Suddenly, a man appeared at my elbow, touching my arm ever so lightly. I nearly jumped out of my skin, but caught the scream in my throat when I saw it was Gerald.

"Ma'am," Gerald said, "Ms. Larkin would like you to join her."

He gestured to Blanche, seated on a pink loveseat at the edge of the room past where the Baumgartners sat receiving people's sympathy. She sat, ramrod straight, chin up, hands folded over the black leather clutch purse in her lap. She was dressed in a black suit with a pencil skirt that showed the world she still had the legs of a twenty-year-old ballerina. Her haughty blue eyes met my wary amethyst ones. "Well," she seemed to say, "are you coming over here or not?"

I felt like I was about to be yelled at by the principal, but, heart hammering, I went anyway. Blanche held my eyes all the way across the room, pulling me in like a tractor beam. Unsettling, which I'm sure was the point. Blanche didn't even have to pat the seat next to her. She simply glanced down at it before locking her eyes back on mine. I sat down gingerly, bracing myself for whatever Blanche was about to throw at me.

"Here to give the Baumgartners your sympathy?" she asked in her whiskey voice.

"Yes, and because you told me to be here," I reminded her.

Blanche nodded. "Well, let me tell you something first. They don't want your sympathy. Look at them. They're miserable. They aren't going to remember a single person who came through that line. I don't remember a single person who came to my father's funeral."

"You didn't have a memorial for Greer," I said.

Blanche gestured to the couch where Rachel's parents sat. "Can you blame me?"

Rachel's parents looked dazed, like they were in some kind of bad dream, waiting to wake up. Person after person walked by them, murmuring things like "sorry for your loss" or "I'm praying for you," but the Baumgartners didn't seem to notice. Mrs. Baumgartner continued to study her handkerchief.

"What do you think happened?"

Blanche scoffed. "Happened? Rachel was obviously murdered. Someone believed she was going to tell you the truth, and it scared them. It'd expose them. When guilty people panic, the innocent are the ones who suffer."

"Do they blame me?" I whispered.

"Nobody blames you. We all know it was Jonathan, except, perhaps, for the police. Jonathan's worried you know too much. It's those papers Rachel gave you. He's worried there's something in there that could convince a jury he did it. He's worried enough to kill," Blanche said, her icy blue eyes now on the Baumgartners.

I blinked in surprise. "How do you know about the papers she gave me?"

"She called me to ask for my blessing. I didn't give it, but Rachel never did like to listen to her elders," Blanche said, a wry smile playing at the corners of her mouth.

Bile rose in my throat. Rachel had taunted Jonathan about handing me evidence against him. And he knew I had them because I'd stupidly told him where they were right before I barfed my guts out. I'd have to be very careful. "So you think Jonathan's going to come after these papers? He's going to come for me?"

She turned to me with a guarded expression. "I don't know. I'd say probably not if he killed Rachel first. Although she might have told Jonathan she gave that suitcase to you . . . at the end. I don't think so, though. Rachel was tough as nails and loyal to a fault."

Blanche's mask slipped a little, revealing her heartache. Her daughter was missing and now her daughter's best friend had been killed. She put up a good front of being a strong battle-ax of a woman, but inside she was despondent and grieving.

Tonight I'd get those notes from Mrs. Bukowski and stay up until I'd uncovered whatever truth they contained.

Blanche broke into my thoughts. "You haven't shown me the tapes yet. I'll have Gerald send the car for you tomorrow. You can either bring them or send a copy with Potter, my driver. I'll need Greer's journals as well."

Her aura pulled me up with her as she started to rise from the loveseat.

"The journals?" I said, alarmed. "Why do you need those?"

"You were never meant to have them. Rachel made a stupid mistake giving those to you," Blanche said. "I expect them to be given to Potter along with the video you promised."

"But I need those. They're going to be part of the film!"

"You do *not* need them and they will absolutely *not* be part of this documentary," Blanche said with finality, as she smoothed imaginary wrinkles from her skirt.

Blanche's tone set off alarm bells in my head. Is Blanche lying to me? Is she nervous about what I might find while digging through those papers? Blanche seemed angry Rachel gave them to me. Was her appearance here an elaborate show? Well, she wasn't getting her psychopath hands on them. I shifted away from Blanche. "I'll make you a copy of the videos. But the notes stay with me. What time will you send Potter?"

"Eleven. I have a facial at nine. And, June, you *will* hand those notes over. Or you can expect to hear from my lawyers. Or worse."

The threat hung in the air. I wasn't about to be the first to blink. I was going to expose her. Then her eyes peered over my shoulder and narrowed. The lines forming around her mouth as it tightened told me the interruption wasn't welcome.

Uh oh. I slowly turned my head to see the unlucky person was Bethany Allen, Greer's agent.

"Bethany's here? She and Rachel were friends?" I asked.

"More like respected foes. Although Rachel's relationship with Bethany may have been more cordial than my own." Her mouth spread into a brittle smile. "Bethany," she said. "Good of you to come."

Bethany's own smile was shark-like, her wide eyes glittering with joyful malice. "Mrs. Larkin. I see you decided to descend from your tower and come over the bridge to Brooklyn."

"And I see you decided to come out from under it," Blanche said, overarticulating each syllable.

Bethany's smile hardened, but her eyes continued to sparkle, like a player who's finally met some real competition, and is going to enjoy what comes next. "Glad to see you're here for Rachel's parents. This is what it looks like when people grieve. Normal people don't hold court."

"What would you know about the emotions of normal people? 'Money' isn't an emotion and greed isn't a virtue. Speaking of money, have you found a follow up to the hit book *All That Hops*?" Blanche said with vicious innocence.

The enjoyment snuffed out of Bethany's eyes as her smile expanded into bared teeth. "Bitch," she spat.

"Your creativity continues to disappoint." Blanche turned to me and said, "Tomorrow," before cutting the line to give the Baumgartners her hand and her own version of "I'm sorry." Then she signaled Gerald and glided out the door like a queen.

I felt like a survivor in a King Kong movie—nervous, relieved, and exhausted.

"I'd be careful, if I were you," Bethany said, also watching Blanche's exit.

"Careful? What do you mean?" I said, feigning innocence. I knew what she meant. Blanche Larkin was a dangerous woman and I was about to cross her. But I didn't know who I could trust right now, and I'd learned from *The Book of Deuteronomy* that when you don't know who to trust, you keep your mouth shut.

"Blanche Larkin cares only about Blanche Larkin. She loved Greer because of Greer's success. When Greer showed signs of writer's block or had a hard day of writing, Blanche would lock Greer in her room until 'inspiration struck.' Greer wrote about it in her second book."

Bethany had my full attention. I was about to get confirmation of my theory. "She did?" I said. *Stay calm. Giddy dancing is not appropriate at funerals.*

"Yeah. That girl, Margo, in *When She Was Seventeen*? Her mom locked her in her room to practice her violin." Bethany snorted. "Blanche didn't like that part too much. She wanted me to edit it out. Greer insisted it stay, so," Bethany shrugged, "it stayed."

"Were there any other scenes that came from real life?"

Bethany shrugged again. "I'm sure there were some. Mostly they were little things that were never central to the plot. You had to know Greer to find them. Hardly anyone really knew Greer."

"Imagine having a life worthy of being the basis for thrillers. I bet if I read through her books again, knowing she wrote about herself, I'd learn a lot about the person underneath the prose. I feel kind of sorry for her."

"Yeah," Bethany said with a sigh. "Everyone did."

"Except someone didn't," I said.

Bethany turned away from me then. "Good luck finding out who. Everyone believes Greer's such a saint. But there are a few people who know better. Jonathan had his hands full."

I hadn't been able to interview Bethany yet and I still had questions about how's Greer's disappearance had hurt Bethany's livelihood. Turning on my phone voice recorder I asked, "Are you saying Greer wasn't a saint?"

"She was extremely temperamental. She wouldn't take edits. Deadlines meant nothing to her. She hated book signings. She was moody and drunk most of the time. I'd say she was far from being a saint."

Yikes. "Yeah. That doesn't sound like saint-like behavior."

"If it hadn't been for Jonathan, her last three books wouldn't have made it to the publisher. I don't know how he did it and I don't care, but he managed to get Greer to actually produce novels. Instead of slinging mud, her fans should be bowing to him."

"Are you and Jonathan close?"

"Not really. Greer was my client and I knew him as her partner. We don't socialize."

That seemed odd. If I were accused of murdering my fiancée and their agent was the one person in the whole world who thought I was innocent, I'd be making that person my new best friend.

I'd been about to ask another question when Bethany's eyes slid down to my phone. Her face went an angry pink as she registered my recording app was open.

As she slid her narrowed eyes away from my phone I asked, "How's the publishing business been?"

She shot me a cold, appraising look. "It's fine." I could have chilled a drink with the ice in her voice. "Why?"

"Just wondering," I said.

She paused, then said, "Do you read a lot of books, June?"

I shrugged. "I did when I was a kid. I'm not much of a reader now." *Now that I have a choice and can watch TV whenever I want instead of having Dickens shoved down my throat.*

"Well, then you have your answer."

Before I could pin her down on a date for an interview, Bethany walked away. I was left feeling a little bewildered about our conversation and anxious to get back to that suitcase full of notes.

Chapter
Twenty-Six

❧

I took the subway home. Cabs are expensive, and I didn't have to look nice for anyone else. Plus the trip to my apartment would give me time to think.

The best way to describe the scene between Bethany and Blanche was frosty. No love lost between the two of them, that's for sure. The animosity was there long before Greer disappeared. Probably stemming from how Blanche controlled Greer and her career with an iron fist. Bethany thought Greer had committed suicide. Did she blame Blanche for causing Greer's depression and anxiety? Did she think Blanche drove her to her death? That Blanche was somehow to blame?

One thing was clear—Bethany's business had suffered since Greer disappeared. She wasn't attracting clients, and the ones she did sign sucked. Was Bethany a bad agent? Or was Blanche torpedoing her just like she'd poisoned her friends against Jonathan?

I heaved a sigh of frustration. I wasn't getting anywhere, and my phone had been annoyingly silent. Paul was on lockdown with his wife, while I was trying to keep Meadow from being disbarred. That meant I had no one to talk to. Still, I sent Paul a text with a picture of me in my cute little black dress. He sent back a text with three flame emojis. That gave me hope I'd get to see him in a couple of days instead of the whole week I'd feared it would take to keep Martha from getting suspicious.

I actually felt bad for her. I'd never felt bad for Martha before. I didn't know much about her, and preferred to keep it that way. But I knew she was a good lawyer. I knew that Paul felt he had to stay with her. I knew she loved him. She probably loved him like I loved him. I knew that her heart would break just like mine would if he ever decided to leave.

But did he love *her*?

Did he love *me*?

Who did he love more?

I was in a melancholy funk from the funeral. I was about to cross Blanche, which was incredibly stupid given her wealth and affluence, and the fact she was now my top suspect in not one, but two deaths. And thinking about Paul, his wife, and me, had me confused and upset. Love was crazy-making.

That was my last coherent thought as I tried to put my key in the lock, only to find my door already partially open. I pushed the door the rest of the way open on creaking hinges to find my apartment had been ripped apart. Every drawer open. Papers scattered across the floor. My bed had been flipped over and the sheets lay in a heap. My couch had been flipped on its back. One side of a curtain rod had been pulled down so that it hung askew.

I ran for my laptop. It was open with the screen smashed into a spiderweb. Someone had punched or stomped on it. I hit a key and it sprang to life. I let out a sigh of relief. My project wasn't destroyed, thank God.

At first glance, it didn't look like anything had been taken. Should I call the police? I couldn't think. I had to clean this mess up. If the mess was gone, then it never happened, right?

I was walking through the kitchen, shutting drawers and cupboard doors, when I saw it. Scratched into the countertop were the words "I'll be back."

My throat closed and bells started clanging in my head. Someone had been looking for something and they hadn't found it. It had to be the suitcase. They didn't find it because Mrs. Bukowski had it. My world swirled in front of my eyes.

They'd be back.

I fumbled for my phone. With shaking fingers I tried to unlock it, but it refused. When I tried to type in my passcode, I dropped the phone. Picking it up, I took a deep breath to calm my racing heart and weak hands. Then I dialed Paul.

It took several rings before he answered. "Hello," he said in a hushed voice.

"Hi," I said, my voice as shaky as my hands.

"What's wrong?" he asked, still whispering.

"My apartment got broken into. They ripped everything apart. All my papers are on the floor and," I swallowed down a sob, "they broke stuff."

"Are you okay?" Paul asked, a little louder.

"I'm okay. Kind of. They scratched a note into my counter top. They said they'd be back. They're searching for something. I—I'm scared. Can you come and stay with me?" I'd never asked Paul for his emotional support before. I'd never needed it. I'm the fun-time girl where there are never any complications. But I really needed him now. I was vulnerable and alone and very, *very* scared.

"Shit. I can't. I'm at a work dinner with Martha."

"Pu—pu—please?" Tears started to fall down my cheeks, gathering under my chin.

"Sweetie, I can't. I'm sorry."

"But I need you," I said.

"You need to call the police. Stay at a hotel. Let me know which one you're at, and I'll pay for the room. I'm so, so sorry, but I just can't be there right now. I have to be with Martha," Paul said, asking for understanding.

I knew it was pointless to keep asking. I'd already stooped to begging and he'd said no. Plus, he'd told me to stay in a hotel. He'd come up with a solution, so, to him, the problem of my terror was solved.

"Okay," I said. "I'll call you."

"Text, okay? I don't want to have to excuse myself from the table to go outside again."

"Okay. Text." I said, numbness creeping out from the center of my body and into my limbs.

"Great. Call the police. And, honey? I love you. I'm sorry I can't be there."

"Sure," I said before hitting the red button, ending the call.

He couldn't come. Devastated, I started sobbing. He could never come when I needed. I knew that, which is why I never asked. But I needed somebody to be here for me.

Rule Number Ten: The mistress will always be second.

Well, fuck Paul. I'll save myself.

First I needed that suitcase, because whoever had torn apart my apartment had been looking for those papers. That case must contain some hard evidence that would prove who killed Greer Larkin. Evidence I was going to need not only to help my movie leave Dave's in the dust, but also keep me alive.

My fingertips began to tingle and my knees shook. I had to get out of here. I shoved my broken laptop into my shoulder bag, then I took the weekend bag I hadn't unpacked from my trip to Virginia, threw in new underwear and a pair of Chucks. I attempted to lock my door, but the frame was too splintered. I would just have to leave it.

I knocked on Mrs. B's door. "Mrs. Bukowski? It's June. I need you."

No answer. Had Mrs. B tried to stop the thieves and ended up getting hurt? It was hard to believe anything could take that old battle-ax down. I pounded on her door. "Mrs. B! Open up!" Still no answer.

I was going to have to break in. Sure, her son might be in the Russian mob and he'd want to kill me for breaking down his mom's door, but he was going to have to get in line. I had to get that case before it fell into the wrong hands.

Running back to my apartment I grabbed a butter knife and a screwdriver. Using them together I managed to slip the lock open. Tiptoeing in, the overwhelming smell of gin hit me like a Mack truck. I gasped and a cough lodged in my throat. This woman must have 120 proof blood. I was relieved to see Mrs. Bukowski was nowhere in the apartment. The case, however, was right in the corner by her umbrella stand.

Without hesitation, I snatched up the case and bolted.

*　*　*

One thing I will say for New York, you can always catch a cab.

I didn't want to chance running into whoever it was that ransacked my apartment on the street, but I still had to walk two blocks to a well-lit section of the neighborhood where I knew cabs would be plentiful at this time of night. I was still shaky, and my heart was beating through my chest. I nearly passed out when a cat jumped out of a trashcan in front of me.

First Rachel had been killed, and now my apartment had been broken into and searched. Worse, they promised to be back. I had to get out of New York. But I needed a car.

I ended up on Meadow's doorstep by nine. She and Faye were waiting for me at the front of her townhouse. Meadow helped me out of the cab while Faye threw the driver some money. She took in my black dress and big-girl heels and brought me inside. As she gave me a glass of wine, she asked, "What happened?"

That's when I burst into tears.

Through hiccups and crying jags, I told her everything— the knife in my door, suspecting Blanche of Rachel's murder, and then coming home to find my apartment torn apart.

"What were they looking for?" Meadow asked.

"This suitcase full of journals that Rachel gave me, I think. They belonged to Greer. They probably have evidence in there as to who killed her," I said.

"And you didn't immediately give them to the police?" she said, exasperation creeping into her voice.

"Meadow, I don't know for sure they're evidence. They could just be artifacts. I haven't even looked through them properly," I said, stung.

"They didn't find them?"

"I'd left them with my neighbor across the hall. I'd given them to her for safekeeping while I was in Virginia. I didn't want them in my apartment while I was gone," I said.

Meadow closed her eyes and took a deep yoga breath. "So you expected something like this might happen. Pear, I—"

"Now, Meadow, don't lecture," Faye said. She took my empty glass into the kitchen. "Let's get you more wine."

"Thanks, Faye," I said. "Meadow, I can't stay in my apartment. I couldn't even lock my door. They can get in."

"Who is they?" Meadow said.

"I think it's Blanche. I think one of her 'people' broke in. She has 'people,' did you know?" I said, my voice rising, "She knows I have the journals. She was mad Rachel gave them to me. She didn't want me to have them. In fact, she demanded I give them to her, but I refused."

"We should call the police! Let's go back to your apartment and wait for them."

My laugh had a ring of hysteria in it. "Blanche Larkin is one of the richest women in New York. You're a lawyer. You know that rich people are above the law. If I called the police they wouldn't do anything." I seized her hands. "She's going to find me! I have to get out of here!"

"But you're safe here with us," Meadow said, moving her hands so that mine were now inside hers. "Nothing's going to happen here."

Faye came in with my wine. "She's right. We're perfectly safe here."

But I was already shaking my head. "No, I have to get out of town where she can't find me. What if she's the person who also plunged a knife into my door? She was always controlling of Greer, and, when she lost control, she punished Greer. She is punishing me! She might've had Rachel killed!" Tears cascaded down my cheeks, and I was shaking again. "In Virginia, when she told me what happened, she knew about Rachel's injuries. The police were keeping that information quiet. How did she know about Rachel's injuries if she wasn't there?"

"Okay," Meadow said, her voice rising an octave in alarm. "I'll get you out of town if that will make you feel better. But I'm also calling the police. We have to have them look over your apartment and report this."

"Thank you," I said, now crying with gratitude. She could call the police all she wanted. I was getting the fuck out of town.

Faye picked up my overnight bag and maneuvered both it and me into their bedroom. "Change your clothes into something more comfortable. Meadow and I will take care of everything." I gave Faye a long hug. "Thanks, Faye. You're pretty cool."

"You're pretty cool, too. Now, get changed." She left, shutting the door behind her.

I looked around the room. Faye's presence in Meadow's apartment was now unmistakable. I suspected that she'd moved in. A gorgeous painting filled one wall with abstract shapes in soothing colors: purples, pinks, blues, with a hint of yellow light at the bottom. I think it was a sunrise. Or a sunset? As I looked at the peaceful colors, my chest began to unknot and my breathing slowed. I felt tired and wrung out.

Slipping out of my simple shift dress felt like I was trying to remove a lead vest from my body. My movements were slow and clumsy. I sighed audibly with relief when I slipped back into my jeans, Nirvana T-shirt, and purple Chucks. I went into their bathroom to splash some water on my face, rinsing away my salty tears and panic sweat.

Meadow and Faye had their heads bent together when I came out of their bedroom. Faye stood, handing me a glass filled to the top with a golden liquid. "Here. I poured you some wine."

"Thanks, Faye," we both said.

"She's a keeper," I mouthed to Meadow.

Meadow flushed with joy. "I know," she mouthed back.

Meadow and Faye sat down across from me as I took a gulp of wine. "Faye is going to go to your apartment to deal with the police."

"What if whoever threatened me comes back before the police get there? No. I don't want anything to happen to Faye. I'll call my super."

I went into the bedroom to make the call. After telling my super what vengeful strangers had done to my apartment, I called Mrs. Bukowski. I could smell the gin over the phone. She'd been in the bedroom when I'd broken in.

"Don't worry, dear. I'll take care of everything."

"Please don't mention the suitcase to the police."

"No problem. I'm Russian. We can keep secrets."

Chapter
Twenty-Seven

~

Excerpt from
The Book of Deuteronomy
An Oberlin Hurst Mystery by Greer Larkin

Oberlin knew Eric MacMillan had killed his wife. She also knew his mistress, Claudine, had helped. She just couldn't prove it.

Yet.

At first it had seemed like bad luck when Ruth MacMillan's car had careened out of control and collided with a tree. But something nagged at Oberlin, so she'd pestered Constable Parks until he'd finally broken down and given Oberlin an envelope stuffed with crime scene photos.

Ruth was draped over the steering wheel, her head resting on the top, while her arms, hands palms up, lay on her lap. Blood dripped down her cheek from her hairline, but otherwise there wasn't much blood. Oberlin thought there'd be more. There wasn't even blood on the steering wheel, which was odd, in her limited opinion.

The gash was high on Ruth's head, but shouldn't it be closer to where her head rested on the steering wheel? Constable Parks said her head had rolled, but shouldn't there be at least some blood on the wheel?

It didn't seem right.

Another thing that nagged at Oberlin was Ruth's seat—it was very far back. Ruth wasn't a big woman. When Oberlin met her at a church fete giving out slices of cake, Ruth seemed like a frightened bird— small and fragile. Oberlin looked at Ruth's hands, her fingers curled like they were offering up another slice of cake. They seemed awfully far away from the wheel.

Then Oberlin looked at Ruth's legs. Her left leg was fully extended, reaching out for the clutch.

And it was at least six inches away from the pedals.

No way Ruth MacMillan had been driving that car when it collided with that tree.

This wasn't an accident.

Chapter
Twenty-Eight

⁓

When I came out of the bedroom, Meadow was hanging up from her own phone call. "Who was that?" I asked.

"The people we're going to stay with. Get into the car," she said. She kissed Faye goodbye and started driving.

Gin fumes wafted up from the suitcase in the backseat as we sped through the city streets on the way to the interstate. I wasn't paying attention to exactly where we were heading, I only cared that it was *away*. But when Meadow merged onto Interstate-87, I figured out where she was taking me.

And I wasn't happy about it.

"Are you sure you didn't break into my apartment so that you'd get me back there?" I said.

"Yes," Meadow said. "This's the safest place I could think of. You never tell people where you came from, so who's going to know you're going back home?"

"Paul knows where I grew up."

"But do your friends?"

I snorted. "What friends? Like I can make friends."

"I have friends. You could have friends."

"And how would I do that? I never learned how. You at least got to learn how to function in society when you were young, going away from the commune for things like shopping and haircuts. I didn't have my hair cut by a professional until I went to college. I barely knew how to buy clothes. I kept buying things, trying them on at home, and then taking them back when they didn't fit. I didn't know changing rooms existed. I felt like an idiot."

Meadow sighed. "I know. I'm sorry about all that. I think you need to talk to your parents. I'm sure they had their reasons."

"I know their reasons. They're banana-pants recluses hiding from an evil world on a commune in the middle of nowhere."

"I mean . . . well, I hope you talk to them. You can stay with my parents if you don't want to be in your house. But this is going to be the safest place for you."

Meadow's hands fidgeted on the wheel and she was chewing on her lip. I could feel the waves of stress rippling off her. She knew this wasn't a good idea and yet she was forcing me right back to the place I'd spent most of my childhood trying to escape. I knew she wanted my resistance to crumple and for me to forgive my parents.

Well, that wasn't going to happen.

I crossed my hands tightly across my chest. "Fine," I said. I knew I sounded like a sulky teenager, but I couldn't help it. When I'd left six years ago, I'd vowed I'd never set foot in that yard ever again. I remembered hoisting my backpack onto one shoulder and lifting my overstuffed duffel bag up onto the other, refusing to look backward as the sounds of my mother crying drifted to me on the breeze. I was eighteen and there was nothing they could do to stop me from finally living my life out in the big, wide world.

Now here I was, driving through the young woods and down the long, narrow lane that opened onto a gravel and dirt yard flanked by two white farm houses and a big, red barn.

The first thing I noticed when we drove into the yard was the paint peeling off one of the columns on my parents' front porch. When I left, the porch had been pristine, freshly painted by my father just the month before. The barn was still a large, red monstrosity, weathered by seasons of pounding sun and caressing snow. The scent of hay caught me by surprise, transporting me back to torturous summers of sweat dripping into my bra while stacking hay bales in that hot box. It should've counted as a violation of the Geneva Convention.

Snow ringed the courtyard and sloped into the woods, covering the bushes and rocks that I knew were there, like a white fluffy blanket. A big pile of snow loomed to the right side of the driveway, pushed there by Uncle Chuck's front-loader tractor. It looked like Christmas might arrive tomorrow rather than having been and gone over a month ago. Spring was being too shy for my liking.

Meadow parked in front of her parents' house. "You can still stay with us. If you really want to."

I gave a stiff nod, but I knew I'd have to see my own parents. Rosie and David Masterson would demand it. There wasn't much they took lying down. I was still shocked they'd let me just walk away from them. Maybe this time they wouldn't. Maybe that was why my hands were clenched into sweaty fists.

* * *

Any hope that my arrival might go under the radar was in vain. The engine had just cut off when the doors to both houses flew open and the adults ran into the yard. My parents stood for a moment like they couldn't believe their eyes. It'd been six years since I'd seen them. A little more gray shot through Mom's brown tresses, and the lines around her mouth were deeper. My dad's blond hair looked recently cut, exposing more lines around his green eyes. Aunt Bev and Uncle Chuck looked the same. Maybe a little bit of age was creeping around the edges, but you had to squint to see it.

Mom ran to me, her arms reaching out to fold me into her like when I was ten. But as she took in my stony face with my arms remaining rigidly at my sides, she slowed and her own arms drifted down as uncertain hurt filled her eyes.

"Pear Blossom. It's good to see you home," my dad said, his voice deep and reassuring. He placed his hand on Mom's shoulder. Her eyes were overflowing with tears, a silent plea on her face for me to reach out and touch her.

Her pleas dented my armor. I hated seeing her so sad. Broken. I'd done this to her. As a child there was nowhere I'd rather be than in her arms. But she'd kept me out here in the middle of nowhere, trapped in this wooded jail for eighteen years. They both had. Without showing any remorse whatsoever. Now here she was, crying like she was glad to see me and not plotting how to keep me here.

Well, I was keeping the life I'd spent the last six years building. Beginning with my name. "It's June now. Call me June." My voice sounded robotic, hollow.

My parents looked at each other, then back at me. "Okay, then." My mother's clear, tinkling soprano was full of uncertainty. "June. It's a nice name. Isn't it nice, David?"

"A lovely name," he said. Now he was starting to tear up. A momentary pang of guilt hit me in the stomach, but, I reminded myself, they'd brought this upon themselves.

I turned to Uncle Chuck and Aunt Bev, who'd stood silently watching my reunion with my parents. "I'm going inside to Meadow's room. If she wants, she can explain things to you." I kept my voice from shaking by digging my fingernails into the palm of my hand. Without looking back, I picked up my overnight bag and the purple suitcase, walked past Uncle Chuck and Aunt Bev, and entered their house.

Meadow told them everything. I know because I watched from her bedroom window. I saw as the horror filled my parents' faces. My mother's hand flew to her mouth as she looked to my father for his strength and steadiness, just as she always had. He responded by wrapping his arms around her to pull her close. Uncle Chuck and Aunt Bev turned white as ghosts. They crossed to their friends to put their hands on them in solidarity, as if I was their daughter too.

I wanted to feel bad. I think part of me did. Or it could've been guilt bubbling away in my chest. I knew I was being cruel, and I tried not to care. I wasn't sure I was succeeding. They're my parents, after all. I'd spent the first half of my life thinking they were perfect. Hating them was a new habit.

But I couldn't forgive them for keeping me prisoner. For forbidding me from going to school. For keeping me in ignorance about the larger world. For preventing me from seeking out my dreams.

Meadow and Sage got to see the world. They were encouraged to follow their ambitions. Why did our parents show them the world and leave me in the dark? What was wrong with me that I had to be excluded? Meadow and Sage always came back from town with incredible stories. A checker in the grocery store gave them suckers. A toy horse you could ride outside of the pharmacy bucked and jumped when you put in a quarter. On Main Street there's whole stores full of nothing but cookies, cakes, and donuts. It sounded glorious.

The envy ate away at me. At first I only asked why I couldn't go. Then I whined and pleaded to be taken along. When that didn't work, I demanded. Meadow, a born lawyer, used to argue for me. I'd watch them from my window and hope that this time my parents would see reason. After they said no for the thousandth time, I started to sneak out with Meadow.

Now I'm back, staring out of a window as they discussed my life. Just like when I was fifteen.

This sucked.

Just as I started heaving some epic sighs, my parents nodded and turned to go back into their house. My dad wrapped his thick arm around my mom's narrow, hunched shoulders.

Walking away, she looked thinner than I remembered, more fragile. The cardigan she wore enveloped her stooped shoulders. My dad was tall. At five foot, eleven inches, he'd been handily taller than Mom. Now he towered over her. He opened the door for her as she looked back at Uncle Chuck and Aunt Bev's house. I ducked out of sight to hide on Meadow's bedroom floor.

Meadow's room was just like it'd been when she was sixteen. The walls were cream and her bedspread was white, printed with tiny sprigs of lavender. A grass green shag rug covered wide planked pine floors. I shivered, pulling my jacket tighter around me. It was chilly. The heat registers in Meadow's seldom-used bedroom were closed to save energy. I was looking for a sweater in my bag when the door opened.

"Meadow, I'll be down in a minute," I said to her. "I'm looking for a sweater."

"Mom wants to see you," she said, her voice cool. "Now."

Uh oh. My annoyance at seeing my parents made me forget to be scared. The fear I'd felt about Blanche sending her goons after me had melted away the farther we'd gotten from the city. But Meadow's cold, low voice kicked my fight or flight response back on. It was the same tone she'd had every time we'd gotten into trouble. Aunt Bev and Uncle Chuck didn't play. Elephants started to stomp around in my midsection. I wanted to dive out the window, but instead I followed Meadow downstairs to the kitchen.

They were seated at the maple kitchen table my dad made for them. Nicked and dinged from over a decade of loving use, it was still red-gold and glossy from waxing. I remembered when my dad made it. I'd helped to clamp the boards together and sand it smooth.

Steaming cups of tea now sat on the table. I sat down in front of one. It felt awkward to be sitting here. After all, I'd cut them out of my life too. "Hello, Pear—I mean, June." Aunt Bev greeted me with cautious warmth. "You're looking well."

"Thanks," I said, my shoulders tensing. I wasn't sure where this was going to go, but it wasn't going to be smooth.

"Meadow tells us that you're in a bit of trouble," Aunt Bev said.

I shot Meadow a dirty look. "I'm not in trouble, per se. I just had a scare and Meadow brought me here." Was I downplaying the seriousness of the break-in? Absolutely. I wasn't about to let them think running home was my idea. This was Meadow's fault.

Aunt Bev nodded while Uncle Chuck played with his mug of tea. Meadow looked down at her folded hands, avoiding the blame I'd tried to lay at her feet. "That's fine. Whatever the reason you're home, we're glad to have you."

"Thanks," I said again, eager to cut off the flow of conversation.

Aunt Bev gave a sharp nod, lifting her blue eyes to meet mine. "But if you're going to stay here, you need to go over and talk to your parents."

"But Aunt Bev!" I exclaimed. "Meadow said—"

"No," she said, banging the table with her open palm and standing up. Meadow and I jumped in our seats. Aunt Bev loomed over me, her oval face flushed. "You *will* listen to me. My best friend in the whole world is over in that house slowly dying because her only child left her and refuses to talk to her. We love you, Pear Blossom Jubilee Masterson. Were we over-protective of you? Yes. But we had *reasons*. Reasons we couldn't tell you at the time. But now we can, so you owe it to your mother and father to go over there and listen to them. And you *will* listen to them. You'll sit there, quietly, and you'll hear them out, because you have no idea what this is doing to all of us." She lifted her arm, pointing toward my parent's house, stabbing the air with her long index finger as she made her point. "Now, get over there before I have your Uncle Chuck carry you there."

Suddenly I was six years old again, being lectured about not letting the goats into the garden just because they looked like they wanted a salad.

Meadow wasn't looking at me. Her eyes were burning holes in her cup while a muscle in her jaw jumped. Uncle Chuck wasn't looking at me either. He was watching Aunt Bev. Probably waiting to see if she was going to have a heart attack or lunge for me to drag me over to my parents' house herself.

There were many other things that I'd rather have done at that moment. Like get a pap smear or a Brazilian wax. *Damn you, Meadow. I knew this would happen.* But Aunt Bev wasn't going to let me talk my way out of this. Her eyes told me it was her way or the highway.

But talking to my parents wasn't as easy as just walking over there and knocking on the door.

* * *

My fist hovered over my parents' front door. I looked back to see Aunt Bev and Uncle Chuck in the middle of the courtyard. Aunt Bev waved her arms at me in the universal gesture for "go on and knock before I make you knock." I grimaced at her, but before I could bring my hand down onto the wood, the door flew open.

"Pear Blossom!" my mother squealed with joy. "David. It's Pear Blossom."

"June," I muttered, but I was already clenched in a rib-cracking hug. My mom looked frail, but she was as strong as an ox.

Mom waved to Aunt Bev before shutting the door behind me.

Trapped like a rat.

"I—I like your shoes," Mom said, pointing at my Chucks. "I used to have a pair just like them. Actually," she laughed, "I had about ten pairs in all different colors."

I gave her a suspicious glare. The woman who'd limited my own shoe wardrobe to one measly pair a year used to have ten pairs of Chuck Taylor Converse All-Stars? In all different colors? Was she trying to bond with me through shoes? I don't think so.

I looked around my former prison. It hadn't changed, which was depressing. There were the same brown couches and chairs draped with brightly tie-dyed scarves and crocheted blankets. A faded Persian rug lay on the floor in front of the fireplace, which held a joyful fire. There, in front of the fire, was—

"Wilfred!" I exclaimed.

I ran to my beloved German shepherd. He was seventeen this year, which is extremely old for a German shepherd. I knew he hadn't died, because Meadow would've told me, but when he hadn't come out of the house, I'd been afraid to ask about him. Wilfred lifted his big, shaggy head and gave a few happy thumps of his tail.

"He's pretty weak," Dad said. "We don't expect him to make it much longer."

"He was always such a good dog. Weren't you, Wilfred? Who's a good dog?" I crooned as I scratched his ears and rubbed his cheeks. He gave a happy whine as he pulled himself to his feet.

"He missed you," my mother said.

"I missed you, too, boy," I told him as he licked my face with his big, pink tongue.

"We missed you too," my mother said, tentatively. I could feel her hand reaching out to me. My back stiffened against the vibrations of need and hope I felt. Wilfred gave me another lick.

I needed to get this over with before my mother started crying again. "Aunt Bev told me to listen to you. So, start talking," I said, my voice dripping with icicles.

"Hey!" Dad shouted, making Wilfred and me jump. "You watch your tone, young lady. That's your mother. Whatever you think we did to you, however you think we ruined your life, you don't get to talk to her that way."

David Masterson never shouted. Ever. It hit me like a slap in the face. My body jerked back, bringing my chin up to look at him. He stood over me, his face red and his breathing hard. Hot shame arced through my chest. I dropped my eyes back down to Wilfred. My mouth tasted metallic and my tongue felt thick. I couldn't speak, so I merely nodded. A rustle of fabric told me my mother was sitting down in the chair behind me. I saw my dad's knees in the chair to my right, but I kept my focus on Wilfred, who'd flopped back down in front of me.

Then my mom started to speak and my life was never the same.

Chapter
Twenty-Nine

~

My mom took a deep, shaky breath. "First, we want you to know that we love you very much."

That's rich. They loved me so much they treated me like a prisoner my entire life. Sure. I sighed before I could stop myself, but then flashed my eyes up to Dad, saying, "Sorry, sorry. I just . . . know that part."

He nodded and my mom went on. "I need to tell you about Maxwell and Patricia Davenport."

A flicker of recognition crept up the back of my neck. "Who are they?"

"I need you to listen without interrupting. This isn't going to be easy." Mom took another deep breath and closed her eyes, like she did when she was about to meditate. Impatient, I tried to not to sigh. I also felt a bit of an *oh shit* kind of feeling deep in my bones. I wasn't sure if I wanted to hear what she had to say.

"There was this guy I knew named Maxwell Davenport. His dad was William Davenport, a lawyer in a big firm named Davenport, Chase, and Bannock. You'd think the names would be in alphabetical order, but that meant the Davenport name would be last and Davenports are never, ever last. Davenports win at all costs.

"Maxwell spent his younger years trying to get his father's approval. But nothing he did was right. And sometimes his dad would hit him. To toughen him up. Make him not such a sissy. At fifteen, to his relief, Maxwell got sent to a boarding school in Maine. Finally, he'd be able to do what he wanted, but William had Maxwell's life all mapped out for him. Maxwell was going to be a lawyer. In fact, one day Maxwell was going to sit on the Supreme Court."

Was there a Maxwell Davenport on the Supreme Court? I wasn't sure. I didn't pay attention to that kind stuff. I saved my brain space for other important things like Oscar winners for documentary films. Meadow would know. I used to use her reactions as a barometer for how fucked a situation truly was. My own barometer seemed a bit broken, and right now I felt like I was trying to make it through rapids in a boat with no oars.

Mom went on. "Maxwell went to college at Berkeley. He met an artist there with a heart-shaped face and brown hair named Patricia Nelson. She was everything Maxwell wasn't—impulsive, creative, passionate, free—and he loved her for it. He loved her wildly and irrationally. William didn't like Patricia. He thought she was the wrong kind of wife for a Supreme Court justice. He tried to get Maxwell to break up with her, but he refused. William didn't like that, but he respected the strength it took. Strength was the one thing missing from his son's character, but now he'd found it. This woman had given it to him. Maybe she wasn't so bad.

"Maxwell and Patricia got married. As a gift he bought them a house and a car. When they had their baby girl, William was overjoyed. He wanted to name her Beatrice, after his mother, but instead Maxwell and Patricia named her Maya—after the Roman goddess of spring."

Maya? Did they just say Maya? My heart stopped beating. *Maya Davenport? The girl who kept getting mail at my apartment?* This was too weird. What the fuck was going on? I clutched onto Wilfred's fur, concentrating on the rough texture while commanding my heart to start beating again.

Mom's voice grew stronger as her cadence took on a story-teller quality. "As Maya grew, Maxwell started to see the world through her eyes. He saw what the world could be, the possibilities and horizons his daughter might strive for. He started to hate the cold, corporate world of loopholes and gray morality. He wanted something more.

"So they bought a farm. Maxwell cut back his hours at the law firm and Patricia gave art lessons to underprivileged kids. William was puzzled when he learned they had a garden and were keeping sheep, goats, and chickens. He about had a stroke when he learned they installed solar panels and spun wool. Hippies were bringing up his granddaughter! If this kept up, she'd be dancing naked in the moonlight and casting spells. She'd never be a lawyer at this rate. But Maxwell and Patricia were so happy that they believed William would come around once he saw how happy Maya was."

Mom's voice became choked with tears. She grabbed a tissue and blotted her eyes. Dad moved next to her, putting his arm around her shoulders. "And Maya was happy. She was laughing and clapping and starting to crawl and then walk. Then the Bad Thing happened. When she was thirteen months old Maya almost drowned. Patricia and Maxwell were working on building a catchment for their wastewater. They didn't see Maya fall into the pit where the water was already collecting. But William did. He'd come by to see what crazy new scheme his son had cooked up. He saw Maya fall in and he saved her.

"The next day Child Protective Services came and accused Maxwell and Patricia of negligence and abuse. The judge who heard the case was a friend of William's. They thought things would be fine, but then the judge decided to grant William sole custody of Maya. Patricia and Maxwell were devastated. They argued and pleaded, but it was no use. William took Maya and locked Maxwell and Patricia out."

Fat, silent tears started to fall down my cheeks. The movie in my mind started playing. Maya, crying for her mother and father. Her grandfather frowning down at her as she refused to eat. My heart was breaking.

"Every day for three months they went to William's house. Every day they heard Maya crying for them. Every day they feared William was teaching her to be cold and heartless, that morals have loopholes. That he would *beat* her, like Maxwell. Maxwell and Patricia couldn't let that happen. So they made a plan.

"Maxwell's best friend from boarding school, John, had a little farm in the Adirondacks with a big red barn. He and his wife, Janice, decided to help. They formed a shell company and bought the farm from John's parents. Together they made a plan to keep Maya safe. Then one day, on the nanny's day off, the housekeeper took Maya for a walk in the park. Maxwell and Patricia followed them, and when she wasn't looking, they stole her back."

Chills ran up my arms. *A big red barn.* My eyes cut toward the window where our big red barn loomed in the winter sun. *Stolen. Kidnapped.* I'd been stolen. My parents were kidnappers. Or were they? William had stacked the system against them so that he—my grandfather—could take this child and raise it as his own. *Me.* Was that why he kept writing? Was he trying to steal me back?

"It took them four days to get from California to New York. All the while the police looked for them. Then the FBI started looking too. They changed their names and moved onto the farm. William would never stop looking for Maya. William was a Davenport and Davenports don't lose."

No, he certainly hadn't stopped looking. In fact, he'd found me.

*   *   *

Big tears splashed down into Wilfred's fur. This changed everything. They hadn't been keeping me a prisoner. Not on purpose.

"You were keeping me safe," I said, my voice cracking apart.

"Yes," Dad said, tears running down his own cheeks. "We were." He got off the chair to sit down next to me on the floor. He gently put his arm around my shoulders and I sank into his familiar embrace. "My dad was a horrible man. We couldn't let him have you. I'd seen enough corruption through the old boys' network to know that going back into the courts wasn't going to work. We weren't going to win that way."

"You left everything. Your jobs, your home, your friends," I said. *You became fugitives. You broke the law.*

For me.

"It was worth it," Mom said, kneeling on the other side of me with one hand on my shoulder. Her hand felt warm and gentle.

I'm a horrible daughter. For six years I'd let them suffer. Six wasted years. "Why didn't you tell me all this? I wouldn't have left," I asked.

"We didn't want to burden you with it. We're all fugitives. Your Uncle Chuck and Aunt Bev—"

"You mean John and Janice," I said. *Oh God. Meadow and Sage's whole lives had been changed to protect me.*

"Yes," she said and smiled. "I do. But they love you too. None of us have regretted a single day. Your father and I can't go into town or we might be spotted and arrested, but they can. They were our proxies into the world."

"But when I left, you could have told me." Then a new thought occurred to me, one that left me shaking. "Am I safe out there? Is he the one coming after me?"

"Oh no, sweetie," Mom said, rubbing my back. "Your grandfather died right after you turned eighteen. You're safe."

Well, all the letters I'd received addressed to Maya Davenport from William in Mexico said different. William Davenport was out there, alive and well.

And close enough to knock on my door.

I couldn't tell my parents. Not when they believed the reason for protecting me was gone. Not when they believed I was safe from him. Did Meadow still have the last letter I'd given her? After this was over, I'd be reading the next letter Maya—I—received from William. Once I knew what he wanted from me, I'd figure out what to do about William. On my own.

"Once you turned eighteen and were an adult, we knew you'd be safe. You had legal status. He couldn't make you do anything you didn't want to do," Dad said.

Let's hope. I always suspected Dad had been a lawyer. It was nice to know I'd been right about something, because I'd been horribly wrong about everything else.

"We'd planned to tell you, since it was likely that you'd inherit his estate, but we chickened out. Too scared to open that door back up. What would happen if you tried to inherit? What kind of conditions had William put into his will? Would the FBI finally find us? It was better to keep it buried," Mom said.

I'd almost drowned, had been given to a grandfather who abused me, was kidnapped by my own parents, and was forced to live in seclusion for my entire life. I didn't remember anything except the seclusion part. My head felt like it was going to come off my shoulders. "This is a lot to take in. I'm having a hard time. I don't remember any of this," I said, my fingers worrying Wilfred's fur.

"We know, honey. You were so young. We hoped you'd just forget. We're sorry. We made the best decision we could," Mom said.

"It was the right decision," Dad said. "I don't regret any of it." He took my mom's hand and gently rubbed the back of it with his thumb. "This has been the best life."

My mouth opened. Words sat at the back of my throat trying to come out, but they wouldn't budge. Wilfred gave me a sympathetic whine. I was the worst person in the world. My parents deserved an apology, but it wouldn't come out. Wilfred's tail started to thump on the floor as he looked up at me. I wasn't a bad person to him. I was *his* person. His kid.

"Wilfred wasn't just a pet, was he?"

"No. Wilfred was also protecting you. We trained him to guard you when you went out running through the woods," Dad said. "My father was unpredictable and unstoppable."

Wilfred, my constant companion. Sometimes my only friend. Meadow didn't like to go adventuring in the woods, but Wilfred would always run with me. And unknowingly he'd been my protector. Was there anyone here who hadn't been focused on protecting me?

I was an ungrateful brat.

Then, as Wilfred licked my hand, all the words came tumbling out. "I'm sorry," I said. "I didn't understand. I should've known that you'd have had good reasons for keeping me at home. I should've known you were protecting me."

"Oh, honey," Mom said in that mom-way that means *all is forgiven, don't be silly, we love you, and my heart is breaking.*

The anger I'd been carrying for the last six years dissolved into anguished guilt. I'd wasted so much time being angry. I'd wasted so much time hurting everyone who loved me.

"I'm sorry I'm a disappointment," I sobbed out.

My parents fell on me with hugs and kisses, making soothing noises.

"Sweetheart," Dad said, hugging me so tightly my ribs squeaked. "You're not a disappointment."

"We are so proud of you," Mom said.

"But I'm a mess and in trouble, and I'm sleeping with my married advisor," I said, continuing to sob.

My mom's head popped off my shoulder as she squawked, "You're what?"

Dad reached over with his big hand and pushed her head back onto my shoulder. "Not now, Rosie."

Then he said, "We're your family. When you're down or in trouble you can always come back to your family."

Chapter Thirty

～

Paul Boese once said, "Forgiveness does not change the past, but it does enlarge the future."

As the six of us ate a weepy dinner around my parents' table, my future felt very large. I'd been scared and alone, but was now surrounded by a group of people who'd turned their entire lives upside down to protect me, who loved me.

Because that's what family does for each other.

When I hear about people having epiphanies, I envision lightning crashing, a bright light shining around their head, possibly even a moment of levitation. In reality, it's a click that sounds in the brain, shutting off ambient noise, leaving you in total, awed silence.

Another movie started to play in my mind. Suddenly, I knew what'd happened. I knew that Jonathan was innocent. I knew that Rachel had been killed in vain. And I knew that Blanche was hiding a giant secret.

I excused myself from the table more politely and apologetically than I had in the twenty-four years I'd been alive, before running back over to Meadow's room in Uncle Chuck and Aunt Bev's house. Up in her bedroom, I dumped the entire contents of the purple suitcase onto the green shag rug.

Five heads appeared in the doorway of the bedroom, finding me elbow-deep in papers.

"You okay?" Meadow said.

"I'm fine. I just figured it all out," I said, panting with excitement.

"Can we help?" Mom asked.

I looked around at the forest of papers. I was never going to get through them all tonight without help. Picking up a stack of paper, I shoved it into Mom's hands. "Yes, please."

An hour later, the six of us were leafing through our own piles of papers. I'd told them what to look for. It could've been a story or a journal entry, but there were certain markers to guide them.

"I think I have it," Dad said, handing me three pages, creased at the corners from their long hibernation in the purple suitcase.

My hands weren't trembling when I took the page. A calm of certainty had descended upon me, making me unshakable. Dad gave me the plot summary for a new story—one Greer must've started right before she disappeared. I sat, reading the pages under the eager stares of my family. Each word confirmed my theory.

Greer was alive.

Cynthia Perkins is a wealthy heiress married to the dashing Bennet Dawes. Their marriage was never great, but at least he didn't beat her like her last boyfriend. A year into their tumultuous marriage, Cynthia finds that not only is Bennet cheating on her with her best friend, they're also plotting to kill her so he will inherit her millions.

But Cynthia isn't going to take this lying down. Over the next three months her family helps to set the foundations for a new life in Italy, while planting clues that will implicate Bennet in her murder. When the day comes, Cynthia gleefully takes a plane under her new name and an Italian passport, while Bennet is arrested and convicted for a murder he hadn't gotten around to committing yet.

When I finished reading, I looked up at my family, grinning. Not only was Greer alive, she'd planned the entire thing. Her disappearance. The framing of Jonathan. She'd even gotten a new identity.

It was all there in this story.

The grin dissolved off my face as I looked back down at what I had read. I knew Greer Larkin was alive. I could almost prove it.

But I'd never be able to tell anyone about it.

*   *   *

"You've made the right decision." Meadow and I had volunteered to feed the goats. The sky had grown dark as we'd searched for the key to Greer's disappearance. I resigned myself to my fate of knowing and never being able to tell, but that didn't mean I had to like it.

"I know," I said, "but this would be an amazing ending for my movie. I can't ever tell anyone what I discovered. Jonathan will hunt her down and make her pay. She'll be arrested for fraud."

On top of being resigned, I was sulky. Meadow called it pouting, but that made me feel like a three-year-old. At least if I was sulky, I felt teenaged. An Angora goat nuzzled my hand. I ran my fingers through its soft fleece and down its long, floppy ears. She was pregnant and would probably wait to give birth until the last snowstorm of the season. That seemed to be the way with goats.

I flipped flakes of hay into their feeding trough while Meadow followed me with grain.

"It sucks," she said, "but *you* know what happened. You got your answer, finally."

True. I'd been puzzling through what happened to Greer Larkin for ten years. Now I knew.

It didn't feel as satisfying as I'd anticipated. It didn't feel satisfying at all. It felt hollow.

Greer wrote the truth in her books. Jonathan was the impoverished Eddie, who Oberlin fought her mother to marry in *Swingline*. I imagined the fight between Greer and Blanche being just as heated. I could hear Blanche calling Jonathan "common."

Then there's the chilling way the villain in *The Girl Who Sang a Tune* manipulated his wife, controlling her through her addiction to alcohol and drugs. Rachel said that Greer had been an addict and Jonathan had kept her compliant through pills. Greer was writing out her call for help.

I thought how Ruth MacMillan had been killed by her horrible husband and his awful mistress in *The Book of Deuteronomy*. Did Greer know that was the fate Jonathan had in store for her? Uncle Chuck had pointed out that in the Bible, Deuteronomy was a book of leavings and goodbyes. Was Greer saying goodbye? How had Greer felt deciding to leave Jonathan? Scared? Happy? Nervous? Elated?

The movie in my mind started playing again. Greer found out Jonathan was plotting to kill her. She asked Rachel and Blanche for help in the pages of her novels. They'd recognized the truth in Greer's writing and realized she was in trouble. Rachel and Blanche helped Greer disappear.

Greer Larkin was very, very clever.

She'd gone back to her mother, that was clear. As I'd just learned, no matter what happened before, your family is the one group of people you can always count on. For anything. Her mother came equipped with the money and connections necessary to set up a new life for Greer.

Then there's the trust that Uncle Morty handled for Greer. The only question was whether the trust was being signed over to Blanche or if they'd risked adding Greer's new identity to the paperwork. It's just as well that Uncle Morty had dementia. Greer could stay hidden.

I had my answer, which I couldn't share without endangering Greer. Blanche or Jonathan. One of them had murdered Rachel because she might've had the key to finding Greer. Who knew what they might do to Greer if they found her.

"So, what're you going to do with your movie?" Meadow asked as the goats bleated.

"I guess I'll finish it with a generic 'and we may never know the truth' kind of ending," I said, shrugging. It wasn't going to drive people to see my movie, but maybe that was a good thing.

"Sounds like it'll work. What'll Paul say? Are you going to tell him?"

Oh, lord. What was I going to tell Paul? I was so overwhelmed by the power of reconnecting to my family and the revelation that Greer faked her own death that I'd forgotten Paul would wonder why I'd suddenly given up. I never lied to Paul, but this was one time I couldn't tell him the truth. The need to protect Greer trumped my need to be honest with him. The fewer people who knew she was alive the better.

"I guess I can tell him I need to wrap it up. He wouldn't disagree. I'm running out of time before graduation and I've been threatened. He'll be relieved. He thought this was becoming dangerous," I said. That didn't sound half bad, actually. Especially if I rehearsed it in the mirror before I talked to him.

"Do you love Paul?"

I sighed. "How long have you been waiting to ask that question?" I said, already not liking where this was heading.

"A while. I guess I don't understand it."

I looked up, confused. "What part don't you understand? I love him. Isn't that enough?"

"But he's *married*," she said. "Doesn't that mean anything to you?"

People have all kinds of marriages. At least that's what I told myself. "Paul's a big boy. He's capable of making his own choices when it comes to relationships," I said, more defensive than I intended.

"But his decisions also affect his wife. Don't you owe her anything? As another woman?" she asked, incredulous at my defensiveness. "She loves him, Pear."

I remembered how horrified I'd felt reading about the man who'd been cheating on his wife in *The Girl Who Sang a Tune*. His wife killed herself over a broken heart. Plus, the mistress was a horrible tramp. Was I a horrible tramp? Was Martha's heart breaking? Would it break if she ever found out? Would she end up . . . *killing* herself?

My cheeks burned and my shoulders slumped. I didn't want Martha to end up like that. Throughout our entire relationship I'd been focused only on Paul and me—I hadn't thought about what this could be doing to Martha.

"Am I a horrible person?" I asked Meadow.

"Oh, honey, no. You aren't a horrible person. You're just . . . figuring things out. You've always been there and accepted me," she said as she hugged me. "I just can't figure out why a nice girl like you would, well, do something like this."

"I love him," I whispered, tears welling in my eyes.

"I know you do."

"What am I going to do?"

"I don't know. But I don't think you've got to make a decision right now. We can save that for later."

The goats were bleating with full stomachs as we held onto each other. When we broke apart, a wicked smile painted Meadow's face. "Did I tell you Sage has a girlfriend?"

"No!" I gasped. We'd all thought Sage was going to stay married to his work. Being a doctor was The Most Important Thing to Sage. He'd always maintained he couldn't be a good doctor and a good husband at the same time, so he was going to choose being a doctor.

"Who is she?"

"Her name is Becca and she's a surgeon," Meadow said.

I rolled my eyes. "Of course. That's the only way he'd notice her. He's probably dating her for her skill and not her personality or looks."

Meadow giggled. "I saw a picture of her. She's pretty."

"You have a picture? Where is it?"

"Inside on my phone. I'll show you when we're finished here."

We were nestled in that comfortable space we'd occupied when we were teenagers, giggly and gossipy. A cozy, familiar peace floated in the night air. I planned to enjoy it for as long as it lasted.

Unfortunately, it didn't last long.

Chapter
Thirty-One

I was laughing when I came out of the barn. Meadow and I had been singing, our arms slung around each other like sisters, before I left to check the lock on the pasture gate, leaving her to sweep up the barn. I guess that's why they came to the barn and not to the house. They must've heard us singing.

Lucky, in a way. Lucky I'd already drawn them away from the family.

But very unlucky for me.

I say they, not to obscure their gender, but because there were two of them standing out there, hovering just to the right of the circle of light provided by the yard lamp high in the air.

"Where is she?" growled a voice from the dark. "Where's that lying bitch?"

I almost didn't recognize his voice. It was strained and rough. As he spoke, my body went eerily still, like I'd jammed a lid onto that place inside where panic oozes out. I looked behind me as the sounds of Meadow's song floated out on the night breeze along with the scent of clean hay.

"Where's who?" I asked, my voice a squeak.

He laughed then, high and trilling. It made all the hair on my arms stand straight up. I began to tremble.

Paul was right. He *was* dangerous.

"Where's who?" Jonathan said. He turned to the person next to him, a smaller, slighter figure. "Does she honestly not know?"

The figure stepped closer, and the light shone onto her face. I gasped. Bethany Allen shifted the gun, rolling her wrist as if to work out a kink from the weight of it. She gave me a long considering look that was even colder than Jonathan's laugh. "I'm not sure. We might have to ask again." She cocked the gun. "Where's Greer, June?" Her voice was flat and cool.

Shock numbed my arms and legs. I tried to forget I'd just been celebrating how I'd figured it all out. "I—isn't Greer dead?" I asked, the words stumbling over my thick tongue.

This time Bethany laughed, the tone like tinkling bells, as if she'd just been told the funniest joke. Jonathan joined her and the lid holding down my panic started to wobble.

"Of course she isn't dead, silly thing," Bethany said. "We know you figured it out, and you know where she is. It's why we followed you all the way up here. Your friends live in a cute building."

The blood in my face drained down to my shoes. I'd led them to Meadow. I'd led them to my parents' sanctuary. How could I have been so stupid?

"I don't have anything figured out," I said.

"Don't lie to me," Bethany said. "You were putting it all together at the funeral—the books as a window into Greer's life. When you ran with the suitcase, that told us all we needed to know."

"You know, it was quite fun to follow you on that fan site you're so fond of. Reading all your theories. Pleading our case for Jonathan's innocence. You people. You'll believe anything you read on the internet," Jonathan said.

"*You're* on GreersGone?"

"Of course we are. We have to be in case one of you idiots actually figures out where Greer is," Bethany said. "Thank you for sharing your site name when we met in the bar, by the way. That was very helpful."

"Who are you?"

Bethany gave me a sly wink. "That'd be telling."

My brain scanned through the names on GreersGone. She'd have to be one that posted often, but not *too* often. Then a likely name hit me. "You're QueenB, aren't you."

Bethany's smile broadened. "Clever."

Jonathan said, "Now be a good girl and tell us. Where. Is. Greer? Is she in one of those houses?"

"No! I don't know where she is!" I said, panic now banging against the lid, trying to break free.

"But you do know she's alive. I can see that," Jonathan said.

"She's dead," I said, trying to stick to my new script.

Bethany tsked at me. "You really must become better at lying if you expect to make it in Hollywood, June. She's alive and she's here somewhere." Bethany started looking around the farmyard. "Is that her with you?" she said as Meadow's silhouette crossed the open barn door.

The lid cracked and panic seeped out into my bones. I couldn't let them hurt Meadow. "That's my cousin. She doesn't have anything to do with this," I said. "This is between us."

"I'm going to take a look and then *I'll* decide how involved she is," Jonathan said. "Bethany, love, make sure this one doesn't get any ideas."

His voice caressed her name with an oily purr that brought me up short. Puzzle pieces started clicking together in my brain. Holding my panic at bay, I steadied my voice. "Love, huh. Is this why you kept dodging my calls?"

"Better than listening to one more inane question about Greer Larkin. *What was it like working with a genius? Why was Greer such a tortured soul?* Blech. Pathetic. It was bad enough I had to read about it on the message board. I didn't need to hear about how great she was from some super-fan."

They cackled and every hair on my body stood at attention, but I plowed on. Maybe if I could keep them talking, Meadow would see I was in trouble and sneak away to call the cops. Not ideal for a family who've spent their entire lives hiding from the feds, but this was an emergency.

"How is it possible you've been together for *twenty years?* And *nobody* knew?" I said, "I've been sleeping with a married guy for one, and in the last two months we've almost gotten caught three times."

"More than twenty years, actually. We're very good at keeping secrets, June. You need to be more careful," Bethany said and smirked.

"I don't understand, though. Greer's gone. Why not just . . . go public. You know? Have a real relationship?"

Confusion overshadowed my fear. If they loved each other, why not just move on together? They didn't have to admit that they'd been lovers before. I couldn't believe Bethany had been content to be a secret mistress for more than twenty years. A large part of my relationship with Paul had been focused on Not Getting Caught. I could only imagine the logistical acrobatics a twenty-plus-year relationship entailed. Maybe that's why Bethany had so few clients.

"Not while I'm still the world's number one suspect," Jonathan said, stroking the back of her hair and resting his hand at the nape of her neck. "It wouldn't be fair not to have the wedding we deserve."

Bethany looked at Jonathan like an acolyte looked at their guru. Or a dog at its master. My stomach looped over itself. *Twenty years.* I'd never survive a life of secret rendezvous and hiding under the bed. I couldn't be placed in a box like some kind of toy, ready to perform only when he wanted to play, my whole life on hold while he got everything he wanted. Jonathan was staring at me, grinning.

My breath came in shallow gasps as Jonathan casually stepped closer to me. "Wait here. Greer and I need to have a conversation. Move and Bethany will shoot you. She's becoming quite proficient at killing."

Fear rolled through my limbs, making them feel loose and wobbly. "*You* killed Rachel. I thought it was Jonathan."

"How sexist of you," Bethany said.

"But *why*? If she'd had any evidence, she would've turned it over to the police."

"She did have evidence. Evidence she held onto for twenty years. Greer's writing notes."

Jonathan snorted. "Rachel was never going to stop trying to prove I killed Greer. The only question was, what secrets had Greer revealed before squirreling them away? I'm going to need those papers. They can wait until after I've dealt with Greer, though. Mother always said I have the patience of a saint." Deranged danger rolled off him, pushing me back half a step.

A lump rose in my throat. Rachel hadn't deserved this. She'd been hopeful I'd finally be the person to come through to get justice for Greer. She'd believed in me. However, she'd underestimated how crazy Jonathan actually is.

Jonathan leered as Meadow appeared briefly, a broom in her hand, her back to the door. "I assure you, Rachel had it coming. So let's go say hello to Greer, shall we?" he said, starting to stride toward the barn. "Because now Greer's got it coming."

I jerked in front of him, stopping him from getting to Meadow. "Is what Greer wrote about you true?"

Jonathan turned his attention to me. "What other lies did that bitch say about me?" The words seethed through his teeth. "She and her mother have made my life a living hell. I can't start a new business. Finding a job for someone of my status is out of the question. All I had was my art collection, so I've been selling it to keep afloat. That Pollock is the last piece I have. But now that you've cleverly figured out where Greer is, I can kill her, plant the body somewhere, and get that eighteen million dollars from 'my' account in the Caymans, as I will appear completely innocent."

"So this is all about the money. You *were* stealing from her for all that time!"

Jonathan snorted. "No. She kindly set that aside all on her own—she and her pet accountant. I *never* stole from her. I only took what money I was entitled to. I think after all the shit I've been through, I'm entitled to that money." He shoved me aside and I landed hard on the frozen ground.

"No! You can't. Not Meadow." I couldn't lose Meadow. I couldn't have her be another victim to this crazy quest.

"Then where is she?" he hissed, turning back to me.

"Bethany," I pleaded, "you can't possibly think he's going to share this with you. He's in this only for himself."

"He loves me and as soon as he has enough money to give me the life I deserve, we're going to be married." She spoke with a serene certainty; all the while her gun was trained on my midsection.

Love truly is blind. Even I could see that Jonathan wasn't capable of loving anyone but himself. I shuddered thinking about what he had in store for Bethany. Would he kill her? Or frame her for both Rachel and Greer's murders? If she's lucky, he'll simply leave the country without her.

A light went on upstairs in the Uncle Chuck and Aunt Bev's house behind Jonathan and Bethany. Wilfred started to bark. I fought to think clearly, but adrenaline surged through my body, flooding my logic centers with RUN-FIGHT-RUN-FIGHT messages. Finally, a clear thought made its way through.

Get them away from my family.

"There's a house. A cabin. Out in the woods. That's where she is. I've hidden her there," I said. Hopefully I was better at lying when my brain was threatening to melt down.

Jonathan beamed a triumphant smile at me. "I knew it! I knew you'd figured it out. Clever, clever girl." He pinched my cheek and gave my head a shake like a particularly aggressive aged aunt. "Now," he said, eagerly, "where is she?"

"It's this way," I said, pointing off into the woods.

* * *

My one consolation as I walked along the snowy trail I'd galloped down in my youth was that Meadow was far behind us, safe in the barn. My heart was in my throat and with every beat threatened to jump out. I also really had to pee. Extreme fear does that to me.

I did experience some glimmers of delight hearing Jonathan and Bethany curse as branches slapped them in the face and they stumbled through the ankle-deep snow on a trail lit only by their cell phone lights. Of course, I didn't need light. I could've walked this trail in my sleep.

"It's not far now," I called over my shoulder, trying to sound brave and certain. I didn't have to call loudly. Jonathan had a death grip on my wrist, and his breath was harsh and ragged in my ear. His nails bit into my skin when he stumbled, making me wince.

Bethany cursed the cold as snow slid into her stilettos. "You keep saying that. We've been walking for twenty minutes. How much farther is it? Jonathan, my feet are cold."

"Not far now!" I was trying to sound upbeat, but not too chipper. I couldn't afford to have them grow suspicious. We needed to keep walking.

The farther we walked, the safer my family got. I veered to the right, taking a trail that was practically nonexistent anymore. The pristine snow made the forest look as though we were walking through a snow globe. There were no other footprints—no one had bothered to walk the trails since I'd left home, but it didn't matter. We were on my turf.

I wasn't lying when I said there was an old cabin back in these woods. The last time I'd visited it, the roof had been rotted out in spots, and it had a musty, raccoon-fouled smell. Meadow, Sage, and I used to dare each other to go inside when we were ten years old and fearless. I hadn't been back there for six years—since I'd left. I was hoping there'd be enough of it standing that Jonathan wouldn't immediately figure out this was all a wild goose chase and have Bethany shoot me on the spot.

I needed to keep them talking so they wouldn't notice.

"So, the knife and the threat in my door?" I kept my voice casual, like we were old college friends talking about a hilarious prank.

"Still interviewing me?" Jonathan said.

"I can't help but be curious. It's a scene directly out of Greer's book. But I can't figure out how you beat me from your apartment to my apartment. And then there's the note that ended up in my pocket at the bar. I didn't see you there."

"Bethany," he said. "She worried you were going to figure everything out and ruin our plans. But, as it turns out, your brain worked in our favor, right, Bethany?"

Bethany grunted as her heels sank into a particularly deep pile of thick snow.

"Why from the book, though? Why not something else?"

"I hoped you'd remember what happened to Oberlin at the end of that book. Kidnapped. Beaten. Tortured. I wanted you to be afraid." Bethany's voice was flinty. A shiver of pure fear shot down my spine.

Beaten. Tortured.

Maybe it was time to stop asking questions.

My grand plan, which evolved with every step, was to lead them out into the woods, lose them, and run back to the commune. These woods are thick and dark and a place I know better than anyone else on the planet. Every day I ran into the woods to escape the oppressive confinement of the commune. A confinement I learned only today had been intended to keep me safe. As a result, though, I felt free here. This was my domain. I didn't need to be scared of Jonathan and his psycho love bunny.

Except I was. They were dangerous, desperate, and full of rage at Greer—who wasn't actually waiting for me in these woods. I had no idea where she really might be. When they finally figured out Greer wasn't anywhere around here, they were going to shoot me.

I'm going to die.

I choked back a sob. I'd just gotten my parents back. They'd sacrificed so much for me. They'd changed their names and cut off everyone from their old lives to protect me. In return, I'd treated them horribly and left without a backward glance. I'd finally learned what I'd do in the name of love as I marched through the snowy woods to my inevitable death.

Breathe! You're Pear Blossom Jubilee Masterson! You once fought an Upper Eastside housewife for a leather jacket at Goodwill. You're going to get through this! Just breathe!

We were almost there. I tried to pull my normal plucky confidence up out of my boots and get it back into my chest, but it seemed to stick in my stomach, making me nauseous. My eyes teared up as acid climbed up my throat.

"I'm going to throw up," I said.

"You *will* keep walking," Jonathan hissed.

"I mean it. I'm going to hurl." My throat started constricting, emitting gagging noises.

"Oh my God, Jonathan," Bethany said, panting. "What is happening up there?"

"She says . . ." Jonathan pushed on my arm to keep moving me forward. ". . . She's going to throw up."

"Then let her get on with it so we can keep going."

"No," Jonathan said, but it wasn't up to him anymore. In one heave I spewed out everything Mom and Aunt Bev fed me for dinner. It arced out of me like I was in the middle of an exorcism.

"Jesus Christ." Jonathan dropped my wrist and stepped back.

I was sweaty and shaky, bent over with my hands on my knees. My vision blurred with tears, but I saw Jonathan backing away from me, Bethany's mouth open in horror. She started to gag and Jonathan spun her away from him.

"Don't you *dare*. This is a Tom Ford suit," he said, as Bethany made retching noises.

I wiped my mouth with the back of my hand, dreading the next wave, when an idea hit me—this was my chance to run for it! Jonathan still had his hands on Bethany's shoulders, making sure that whatever came out of her didn't hit him. I started backing away down the trail, praying I didn't crack a branch or slip on some ice. When I was about ten feet away I turned and bolted.

"Hey!" Jonathan yelled behind me. "Get back here!"

I ran faster. The underbrush pulled at my clothes, slowing me down. But just up ahead was a different trail. I'd have to jump a dry creek bed to get there, but I was sure this one was well maintained. It's Dad's favorite walk. I could speed up there.

Those thoughts were eliminated by the crack and whine of a bullet going past my ear. I screamed and plunged ahead, trying to duck as I ran. I heard another crack and felt a hot punch to my left shoulder. It pushed me off balance for a moment. I stumbled forward as I heard another bullet zing over my head. The creek bed was straight in front of me. I dove for it and rolled down the snowy embankment to the bottom.

I pulled myself out of the snow, wincing at the hot pain in my arm, and scrambled to get my feet under me. I ran about ten more yards before I leaped up the creek bed and started running into the dark woods, away from Jonathan, Bethany, and the gun.

Chapter Thirty-Two

～

I have no idea how long I ran. They say adrenaline does funny things to a person's strength and stamina. It could've been ten minutes or thirty.

All I know is that when I finally slowed down I was covered in a frozen mud created by my own sweat and blood, snow, and dirt from various locations around the woods. I'd taken the very long way home, just in case Jonathan and Bethany found my footprints and started tracking me.

I'm proud to say I didn't pee myself.

I did, however, pass out.

The yard was a disco of blue and red emergency lights. As I came around the edge of my house, I saw Mom and Dad, Aunt Bev and Uncle Chuck, and Meadow huddled together. Mom and Aunt Bev were crying. Uncle Chuck had one hand on Dad's shoulder and his other was holding Meadow around her waist.

I stood for a moment taking it all in. My family.

I loved them. And there wasn't anything I wouldn't do to protect them. My heart swelled and a different kind of tear welled up in my eyes. Slowly, I walked closer to them, unsure if I should call out or run and throw my arms around them.

Would they be mad at me? Mom and Dad had always yelled at me for being reckless.

But it was different now. I reminded myself that I understood. They couldn't live without me, and I didn't want to live without them.

My knees were wobbly as I trotted over to them, calling out, "Mom! Dad!"

As they turned toward me, their pinched faces relaxed into relieved smiles.

"Oh my, Pear Blossom," Mom yelled as she closed the distance between us at a run. "That man said he shot you. That you were d—dead." She choked on the last word.

"Mom, it's Jonathan and Bethany. They're the ones—"

"We know. The police caught them already. They were lost up by that old cabin, shivering in three feet of snow, blue as a couple of crayons, and begging to be taken out." Mom's smile dimmed as her brow furrowed into an expression I knew well. "But, Pear, don't you ever do anything like that again. You're just lucky Meadow saw them march you off into the woods!"

She grasped my upper arms in her firm, callused hands, preparing to pull me into a hug. Searing pain shot down one arm. I shrieked and dropped to my knees.

"Pear?" she asked, her worried face close to mine. "What's wrong, honey? Are you hurt?"

I tried to speak, but it felt like my left arm was being jabbed with a red-hot poker. I was gasping, trying to catch my breath. Mom looked me over and when she pulled at my arm it felt like it was being cut open with a knife. I screamed again and she looked more closely.

"Dear God," she said. Then she yelled, "Help! She's been shot. Help us."

Feet were already pounding over. A flashlight glared into my eyes as hands wearing blue rubber gloves gently helped me to lie down. The blue hands took my arm, and the flashlight hovered over where the fiery poker was sticking me. A deep, male voice said, "She's been shot. Through and through."

I peeked over to see how bad it was. Dried blood glued my sweatshirt to my arm. The EMT gently cut the sleeve away to reveal a jagged reddish-brown hole the size of a fifty-cent piece. Blood poured out of the hole and dripped off my arm, melting into the snow and forming a crimson and pink stream flowing through a snowy canyon.

That's when I blacked out.

When I came back into the land of the living, I was on a stretcher and being loaded into an ambulance. My arm was, mercifully, covered and wrapped with gauze, and a soft blue blanket was draped over me. Mom and Dad were holding onto each other.

That's sweet. They looked so good together, even with their worried faces. The whole night sky flashed with the red and blue of the emergency lights, reminding me of fireworks. I felt so much better. My arm barely hurt. That's when it dawned on me I was drugged out of my gourd.

"Hello," I called, putting on an English accent. "I'm fine. Don't worry about me. It's just a bit of a flesh wound."

Meadow let a hysterical laugh escape before clamping a hand over her mouth. My parents exchanged bewildered looks and then looked at the EMTs who stood around me. They didn't seem concerned, but I was a little offended that my one opportunity to use a classic Monty Python line hadn't been appreciated by more people.

Mom came with me in the ambulance while Dad, Aunt Bev, Uncle Chuck, and Meadow followed in their cars. The drugs they'd given me for the pain made me feel like I was floating around in the clouds. Reality was a vague and tenuous concept that came sharply back into focus as soon as the doctor started to examine my arm in the emergency room.

The doctor and nurse numbed my arm and cleaned it thoroughly. It felt weird and uncomfortable. I squirmed on the table and started to cry again.

"No stitches for you," the doctor said. "This needs to drain and heal from the inside out." He looked at my mom. "You'll need to buy plenty of gauze. This'll take a while."

As I was pondering how long "a while" might be in a cosmic sense, a nurse loaded a huge syringe with antibiotics and pumped it into my thigh. It hurt worse than the actual bullet.

I was released that night, much to my surprise and Mom's delight. Thirty minutes later she had me tucked into my old bed, in my old bedroom, in my old house, with strict instructions to go to sleep.

She didn't have to worry. I wouldn't be sneaking out tonight. I was exhausted and asleep within ten minutes. It turns out running for your life through the dark woods and getting shot takes a lot out of you.

It was well into next morning when I finally convinced Mom to give me my phone back. I had about twenty missed calls, with messages. Most of the calls were from reporters. I deleted their messages without listening to them. No way I'd be talking to any reporter.

However, three of those calls were from Paul.

I was astonished to realize that I hadn't thought of Paul once throughout my entire ordeal. When the bullet hit me, when I thought I was about to die, my final wish wasn't to see Paul's face one last time. The thought that jumped into my head as I ran for my life had been regret for all the years I'd wasted being mad at my parents.

My feelings for Paul were now all twisted up in the rules I'd built for our relationship. No sleeping over at his house. Always eat first. Leave no trace behind. Never go to his wife's favorite restaurant. The mistress always comes second. No promises. Ever.

Love wasn't supposed to be like that. Love wasn't having your favorite pair of jeans ruined getting literally dragged out of an art gallery. Love wasn't getting shoved under the table at a restaurant. Love's supposed to be putting your partner first. Love's leaving a change of clothes behind for those nights when you spontaneously sleep over. Love is promises and forever.

I thought about Bethany, forced into the background for over twenty years. Never able to hold his hand in public, share a bed for longer than a few hours, or have a picture of them together on her desk. I wondered how many rules she'd written for their relationship. I had ten and we'd only been together for a year. She must have hundreds of rules that bent her into torturous contortions. And she was still by his side. I pitied her. That's the worst thing to feel for another human. It isn't an emotion that moves you to action—it isn't hate and it isn't love, it's a squishy disappointment, like ice cream that's fallen to the floor.

Was I pitied?

If I loved Paul, shouldn't his have been the face I saw in my head and the name on my lips as I was being death-marched through the woods? He was special, and we had an undeniable chemistry that threatened to make me combust when we were together, but did I love him? I'd thought so, but I didn't want to—couldn't—settle for a man who I could never really have. The one time I'd needed him, begged him to be with me, he didn't come. It turns out, the people who show up when you need them the most are the people you think about. Paul wasn't there. He'd never be there.

My heart broke a little, and I felt my eyes grow hot.

I had to tell him it was over.

I listened to Paul's messages.

"It was on the news that you were shot. They used your name, but no picture. Was that you? I don't know of anyone else named Pear Blossom. Are you okay?"

"Are you there? Are you okay? Call me. I'm worried."

"Call me as soon as you can."

I swallowed hard. My mouth felt sticky and my hands shook as I dialed his number.

"Oh, thank God," he said like an exhaled prayer. "Are you okay? How bad is it?"

"I was shot in the arm. Nothing major was hit. The doctors said I was really lucky." The happy tingle I'd felt at the relief in his voice froze into a block of ice and settled onto my shoulders. This was going to be hard.

"That's the best news, Pear Blossom. When are you coming home? I want to see you to make sure you're okay." He sounded eager and happy.

Fuck. I couldn't do it.

But then I thought about how he was talking to me while hiding from Martha in the bathroom, and it made me feel a little sick. And angry.

"Paul. We need to talk."

"Uh oh."

I plunged on. "Yeah. Well, the thing is, I need more. This, you and me, isn't working for me anymore."

There was a long silence. "June . . . I can't leave Martha right now. She's in a bad place emotionally and—"

"I don't want you to, Paul. This isn't an ultimatum. I'm not asking you to choose. I've already chosen."

I heard his breath stop for a full minute before his air came back in a gust. "I don't understand."

"It's over, Paul," I said gently. "We're over. I need, I *deserve*, more."

"Is this about me not coming over when you called?"

I sighed. "Not exactly. But when I'm terrified and alone and I call the man I love asking for help, I want him to drop everything, rush to my side, and hold me while telling me everything is going to be okay." My voice broke and tears I hadn't known were welling up in my eyes spilled over.

"Pear Blossom. Give me another chance. I'm sorry I wasn't there for you. We can fix this. We can make this work."

God, he was begging.

"I'm so sorry, Paul. But I need to be by myself for a while. This is about me, Paul. Not about you."

"Don't do this now," Paul said, pleading. "Wait. Let's talk about this when you come back to New York. When are you coming home?"

"I'm not sure when I'm coming back to New York," I said carefully. "I'm going to finish my movie here. My arm is going to be in a sling for a couple of weeks. My parents will help me. I need my parents to help me," I said, hoping he'd understand I was also talking about how he would *not* be there to help me.

"I'm sure the police also want to talk to you."

I'd already given them an initial statement at the hospital, but no doubt they'd be back for more. "True. That's another reason to stay here." My phone made a click and a beep. I looked down to see Blanche was calling me. "I have to go. Blanche is trying to call."

"Okay," he said sadly. "I'll talk to you tomorrow."

I clicked over to talk to Blanche without promising I'd call. Or rather, I clicked over to talk to Gerald, who informed me that Ms. Larkin would like to speak with me.

"It's good to hear that you are okay, miss," he said, giving Blanche the phone.

Before I could say thank you, Blanche's husky voice came on the phone. "Is that you, June?"

"Yes, ma'am," I said, obediently, hoping my voice sounded strong and not like I was fighting back a gigantic sob.

"I heard you were shot."

"I was. In the arm."

"I see. What did Jonathan want?" Blanche's voice had a hard edge to it. Her hardness helped push back the mushy grief I felt about ending my relationship with Paul.

"He knows Greer's alive and wanted to know where she was." I was blunt. I wanted to hear Blanche's reaction.

I wasn't disappointed. She sucked in air and went quiet. Then, very carefully, she asked, "What did you tell him?"

"That I had no idea what he was talking about. I've found no evidence that tells me where Greer Larkin might be—dead or alive." It was the truth. What I had was a theory with no real direction to point me to where Greer was today.

Blanche exhaled very slowly. "And what is the status of your movie?"

"I'll finish filming with voice-overs, reenactments, and old news footage. I'll be editing it and turning it in. It's a shame that it's going to remain unsolved."

"Yes, a real shame." Her voice had regained its usual briskness. "Well, if you need anything else from me, let me know. You'll be taking time to recover?"

"Yes, I'll be at my parents' house for at least a month or two," I said.

I didn't know what I was going to do next. Staying here sounded as good as anything for now.

"Good. Take care of yourself. Let me know when you're back in New York."

She hung up before I could say anything else. I curled up into a ball on my bed and fell into restless dreams of the dark woods.

Chapter
Thirty-Three

～

I finished my movie. I had to end it with a stupid "We May Never Know" ending since I couldn't tell anyone what I'd figured out about Greer's disappearance.

I also, hooray for me, graduated! My parents were so proud. They're also delighted that my film would be shown at the Montana Investigative Film Festival, and that I'd had a job offer for a research and production assistant at the Doc House, a documentary studio in Los Angeles.

It was a dream. I was the envy of many of my classmates. The door to Hollywood was open to me.

But I wasn't sure I wanted to step through it.

I felt like I'd failed. I had the answer. I knew that Greer Larkin faked her death and was out there somewhere living a life as someone else. With more digging, I'd probably figure out where she was. There were still more clues in the suitcase of notes Rachel gave me.

But I couldn't. Greer deserved her hard-won rest. She didn't need people poking around for her like my grandfather had relentlessly searched for me. My parents lived life fearfully, looking over their shoulders any time they left the commune. Their only friends had been Aunt Bev and Uncle Chuck. They couldn't afford to let anyone else in. Trusting is a dangerous game when you're hiding.

We're still trying to stay out of the spotlight. The police had been so focused on Bethany and Jonathan trying to kill me, they hadn't suspected anything about my parents, but we still needed to lie low. There's no statute of limitations when it comes to federal kidnapping charges.

Four months later and I'm still living with Mom and Dad. I took a job at a diner in a little town called Phoenicia. It's close to the commune, so Mom or Dad could drive me to work. They didn't want to let me out of their sight, and for once I didn't mind. It's kind of nice to know that I'm expected somewhere by somebody.

I was wiping down the counter, watching one of the lawyers for Jonathan and Bethany on the news proclaiming Greer is alive. A lawyer the morning show hired to lend some sort of credible expertise to this story was disagreeing. "It's impossible for a famous person like Greer Larkin to be alive and well and not have ever been recognized. Just impossible."

I smiled as I shook my head, wondering if Blanche had called in any favors or if that guy genuinely believed what he was saying.

My arm stung as I ran the cloth over the counter. The hole was closing up and the muscles were healing, but I'd have a chunky circular scar right above my left bicep for the rest of my life. Mom stayed by my bed the first week I'd been home just to make sure I didn't wake up scared when I couldn't move my arm. Because that's what moms do. I choked up a bit as I remembered her gentle hands smoothing back my hair as I drifted off to sleep.

The bell over the door *ting-a-ding*ed and I turned away to collect myself as I grabbed a couple of menus.

A lone woman with shiny wheat-blonde hair cut into a choppy soccer mom bob stood inside the door. She looked around and, seeing the diner was empty, picked out the stool at the counter in front of me.

"Welcome. What can I get for you today?" I asked, pushing a bright smile onto my face and handing her a menu.

"I'd like a coffee and a muffin, I think. Which is your favorite?" she asked.

"Definitely cinnamon," I said. "But all of them are good. We make them fresh every morning."

She gave me a conspiratorial grin as she handed back the menus. "I'll take the cinnamon and a coffee."

"Coming up."

In the three minutes it took me to assemble the coffee and muffin, she'd pulled out a book. It was a mystery I hadn't read before by a woman named Paris O'Hurst.

"Is that a good book?" I asked, unable to help myself.

"Pretty good," she said.

"A mystery, right?"

"A procedural thriller," she corrected. "It's about a woman in a bad marriage with a mobster who escaped and made a new life for herself, only to have him find her when her picture is published on an internet bulletin board."

"Sounds intense."

"It is."

I left her alone, but couldn't help sneaking glances back at her. There was something familiar about her. But then she's like a lot of tourists who come through the Adirondacks. An upper-middle-class suburban mom in khaki capris and a blue boat-neck top. She's probably snatching a few quiet minutes away from kids while they hiked with her husband. Or wife. This is the twenty-first century, after all.

She sat there, legs crossed, flipping pages and sipping her coffee. Because I'm too curious for my own good, I kept coming by and filling up the coffee to get better looks at her. She remained unperturbed, reading her book.

I was pulled away by the *ting-a-ding* of another customer, who sat himself in a booth by the window. I greeted him with water, a menu, and a list of specials. It was closer to lunch now, so I told him he had his pick of breakfast or lunch. He grunted and buried himself in the menu.

I heard another *ting-a-ding* and looked up to see the woman leaving the cafe. I turned to see money and her book on the counter. Weird. Was she coming back? But she'd paid. Did she just forget her book? I ran to the door, but she was nowhere on the street. I decided to grab the book and put it behind the counter in case she came back. She seemed nice, and it'd be a shame for her to lose a book she hadn't finished yet.

As I lifted it up, a plain white envelope slid out and thunked onto the floor. I picked it up and almost dropped it again when I saw my name—June—was written on it. I whipped my head around looking to see if there were cameras watching me. Was I being punked?

The gentleman tapped his menu on the table. Some customers think that's a great way to signal they'd made up their minds. I just found it annoying. But I needed my tips, so I scurried back over and took his order as politely as possible before heading back to the counter to take another look at the envelope.

The handwriting was in an elegant script and the envelope was unsealed. I took out a single sheet of paper and began to read.

"Dear June," it started.

My mother tells me I owe you nothing, but I feel like I do owe you something. At the very least you deserve an explanation.

As you've realized, I'm still alive. I escaped from a horrible situation with a horrible man prepared to murder me to get what he wanted. It was made more awful by the fact that one of the people I trusted most was also part of the betrayal.

My intent had been, of course, for him to be framed for my murder. I'd figured out he was using my drug and alcohol addiction to control me. He kept me prisoner in that cage for years, not once caring that I was dying a slow, excruciating death, while he slept with one of the few people I counted as a friend. When I heard them planning to murder me after I married Jonathan, I knew I needed to act. With Mom and Rachel's help, I got sober and I started my plan to frame him.

Unfortunately, when I told him I needed to postpone the wedding, Jonathan snapped. I thought telling him in a restaurant, in front of other people, would keep him from hurting me. I guess I was lucky it was only a slap. Then that night I overheard Jonathan on the phone with Bethany. He was going to get me drunk, take me to a justice of the peace, and get us married. Then he'd kill me, while he'd live happily ever after with my money. I wasn't prepared. Not everything I needed was in place, which is why he wasn't arrested for my murder.

My one regret in all this is Rachel's death. Bethany might have pulled the trigger, but in my heart I see her as another one of Jonathan's victims. Rachel loved me, and I loved her. While I'd moved forward in my life, she remained rooted in the idea that if Jonathan was no longer a threat, I'd be free to return to my life and to her. What she didn't understand was it wasn't just Jonathan I was running from, but also a life of notoriety and infamy.

I'd been famous since I was fourteen years old, thrust into the limelight by a single parent who tried her best. Now I'm a regular person with a regular life.

I appreciate what it took for you to stop looking. I don't know if I'd have had the same willpower or decency. Especially if I'd been hurt, like you were hurt.

I wish you well in your life. I hope that you achieve your dreams.

Thank you ~G.

A bell was clanging behind me. Billy, our chef, was smacking the pick-up bell with his metal spatula.

"Christ, Billy. I'm right here," I said, sticking the note into my apron pocket.

"I called your name, like, four times! What planet were you just visiting?"

"Sorry! I got it!" I picked up the plate of steaming hot food and took it over to the gentleman in the booth.

Back at the counter, I took the note back out of my pocket and read it again. I couldn't believe it. Not only had I been right, she'd been *here*. I'd fed her a muffin and coffee. Her eyes had been brown instead of green, but colored contact lenses would take care of that. Her nose was also a little more pert than I remembered, but I guess if I were hiding from the world,

I'd also consider giving myself a nose job. The shape of her eyes, however, was still cat-like, and her mouth still curved up at the ends when she smiled.

I slipped the letter back into the envelope. Should I destroy it? Was it safe for me to keep something that definitively proved Greer Larkin was still alive? Was it safe for her? My head was a cacophony of thoughts. I tucked the envelope back into the book and promised I'd decide later. I opened the front cover and found, in the same beautiful script as on the envelope, the words "To June" written on the title page.

I gasped and fumbled to open the book to the back cover where the author's photo would be, hoping there was another clue.

Paris O'Hurst is a librarian and full-time cat mom to Rowdy and Pickles. She lives in a cozy little town in Maine where she dreams up her stories during long walks on the rocky beaches. This is her first novel.

There was no picture for Paris O'Hurst.

Acknowledgments

Writing and publishing a book is a mammoth task. During this journey, I've been supported by an extensive team of people who provided guidance, expert information, moral support, and margaritas. Without these people, producing a book, much less a book worth reading, would be impossible. It's equally impossible to thank every individual who helped me bring this book to life, so if you're reading this, THANK YOU.

I am eternally grateful to my agent extraordinaire, Abby Saul of The Lark Group. She saw the potential in this book and pushed me to make it better. Thank you for your guidance and wisdom as well as your enthusiastic love of June.

I owe Dawn Ius a thousand cocktails and several barrels of Red Vines along with my undying gratitude. Thank you for having confidence in me when my own was flagging and shepherding me along the path to publication. Without you this book would be trapped in a desk drawer. You're my secret weapon.

I wish to thank my editor Terri Bischoff and the rest of the team at Crooked Land Books, including Melissa Rechter, Madeline Rathle, Karintha Parker, and Rebecca Nelson. Thank you for your insight and vision of what June could be and your efforts to make her as great as she believes herself.

Linda Brant, thank you for reading my first draft and telling me, "I just read a very nice mystery." You started out as my mentor and you've become a dear friend. Trying out for *The Man Who Came to Dinner* was one of the luckiest decisions I ever made.

Patrick Pederson, thank you for answering all my texts and assuming I had no nefarious plans.

Kimberley Moran, Gretchen Walker, and Annie Oldenberg for being my cheerleaders, critique readers, idea bouncer-off-ers, shoulders to lean on, and lobster roll partners.

Diana Peterfreund, for being just a text message away every moment of this process. You always show up armed with wit, humor, hard-earned knowledge, liberal doses of reality, and bottles of champagne.

Ken and Mary, for having a front porch that's perfect for early morning writing and late afternoon reading.

John and Michelle and Erik and Ellie for being excited for me when I was too tired to remember to do it myself.

A multitude of thanks and appreciation go to all the people who have taken my calls, emails, and texts, answering some of the more absurd questions I've had, and talking me down from several different ledges. They are K.J., Shaun, Cate, Abby, Margaret, Anisa, Kathy, Mabel, Kate, Debra, Mary, Max, and the G-Street Book Club.

I cannot thank my parents enough. No book was off limits to me, and there was no "lights off" policy when I was reading in bed. After I'd read all the Nancy Drew books my school library had to offer, Mom and Dad handed me an Agatha Christie book at the age of nine, and I never looked back.

They also read the first version of this book and, as all parents should, lied and told me it was good.

A special thank you goes to my husband and my kids. You encouraged me to dream, you took care of everything when I was up to my ears in deadlines, and you celebrated my every success with champagne and Indian food. Your love means more than I can say. I am the most fortunate of women.